OUR ALASKAN WINTER

Epicenter Press

6524 NE 181st St., Suite 2, Kenmore, WA 98028

Epicenter Press is a regional press publishing nonfiction books about the arts, history, environment, and diverse cultures and lifestyles of Alaska and the Pacific Northwest. For more information, visit www.EpicenterPress.com

ISBN: 978-1-941890-44-8 (Trade Paperback)

ISBN: 978-1-941890-45-5 (Ebook)

Library of Congress Control Number: 2021938407

To Ruth and Ook-Sook
companions of the white trail

Books by Constance Helmericks

We Live in Alaska, 1944, Epicenter Press 2019
We Live in the Arctic, 1947, Epicenter Press 2021
Our Summer with the Eskimos, 1948, Epicenter Press 2021
Our Alaskan Winter, 1949, Epicenter Press 2021
Flight of the Arctic Tern, 1952, Epicenter Press 2018
Down the Wild River North, 1969, Epicenter Press 2017
Hunting in North America, 1956
Australian Adventure, 1972

Books by Jean Aspen

Arctic Daughter: a Wilderness Journey, 1988, 2015
Arctic Son: Fulfilling the Dream, 1995, 2014
A Child of Air (a novel), 2008
Trusting the River, Epicenter Press 2017

Documentaries by
Jean Aspen and Tom Irons

Arctic Son: Fulfilling the Dream, 2013
Arctic Daughter: A Lifetime of Wilderness, 2018
Rewilding Kernwood, 2019

OUR ALASKAN WINTER

CONSTANCE HELMERICKS
& HARMON HELMERICKS

Epicenter Press

Kenmore

Connie and Bud, spring 1946

Contents

Preface

Three quarters of a century have melted away since my young parents, Connie and Bud Helmericks, embarked on this amazing odyssey. New to Alaska, and with scant equipment or supplies, they paddled down the Yukon River in their homemade canoe in June 1944 to emerge twenty-six months later on Canada's Mackenzie River Delta. *Our Alaskan Winter* concludes Connie's trilogy about this audacious journey. Told from Bud's perspective, it depicts their second winter and third summer wandering the Arctic with nomadic Inuit—Iñupiat families—who helped them to survive. Connie wrote these books by hand with light from a kerosene lantern as she sat cross-legged on the floor of their tent. Beyond the snow-banked canvas, the arctic coast drifted in ceaseless wind and auroras climbed the winter sky.

I'm alone in the Arctic this spring in my seven-by-ten-foot log cabin—our remaining habitable structure. It's late April, and I'm reading my mother's books while saying goodbye to my own lifetime of wandering Alaska's remote Brooks Range. Because of Connie, these mountains have always felt like home. Beyond my tiny haven the river begins to stir, seeping teal-green through tracks left in the snow by little bands of caribou headed north to their calving grounds. For three years my husband, Tom Irons, and I have been dismantling and rewilding everything we built here over the past quarter century. He will join me once the ice goes out and a chartered plane can land on the river bar. Returning our home to wilderness is our act of gratitude, for the Arctic is no longer infinite nor inaccessible—as it seemed to my parents and to my younger self. The plants and animals that inhabit this sparse country are as vulnerable as they are tenacious. The wild

Earth which birthed us depends now upon human mercy. That is the way it works, for everything is connected. We are the living planet—all of us.

I stumble a bit as I read *Our Alaskan Winter*, realizing how dreams can kidnap one into unexpected realms. This abduction is an opportunity to evolve beyond safe boundaries—and yet it is painful. My mother's fourth book of embodying her adventurous dreams whispers also of loneliness and suffering. Connie was a romantic, not a hunter. I doubt her vision of untrammeled nature and wild people prepared her for watching a dog team tear apart a wounded caribou, or being left for weeks in the dead of winter. Living with the Iñupiat was very different from her previous year with my father in the forested mountains. The role she was called to play in these barren lands fell short of her image of "co-explorers." Nevertheless, she measured the rest of her life by this grand peregrination. How many of us have the wisdom or courage to step through a portal when our heart calls us to mystery? Every birth requires a death; to become something new, we risk all.

My mother was delicate of stature; her feet and hands were dainty. She had neither the stamina nor temperament for the constant hunting required of an Iñupiat man, nor was she welcome in that capacity. Conversely, my robust father bloomed like a boy let out from school, thriving under the punishing miles and the constant hunt. I suspect it was the pinnacle of his life—living by his strength and wits, commanding the respect of other wild young men, and running a thousand miles before the dog team across a vast and frozen landscape. For Connie, being left in the tent—without dogs, husband, sleeping bag, or even food at times—must have been a pervasive hardship. She slept in her parka and arose every few hours to fill the sheetmetal stove with willow twigs, which she gathered during the brief twilight of day. While Bud, the hunter, had an inner and outer parka and pants of caribou skin, she had only an outer parka with her old woolen trousers. In a world where survival depended on men with dogs, she held no status and lacked even the Iñupiat woman's skill at sewing hides.

As she did most of her life, Connie turned to writing, composing five bestselling books in eight years under the most difficult conditions. Three manuscripts covering this great trek across the top of Alaska would emerge in her meticulous handwriting over this winter by the frozen Itkillik River and spring out on the polar ice. In writing she steps graciously into the background, as she did in later adventures with my sister and me. I found her signature two-thirds of the way through this book, hidden within a paragraph about making camp on sea ice. "Connie," she writes, "set up her little wooden box of writing materials beside the wall where she sat. As an artist and a naturalist, Connie literally wrote her way through the arctic . . ."

Constance Helmericks was a perfect witness for the Iñupiat at a pivotal moment in their history. Her education in sociology and intimate daily life among them, combined with a generous heart and artistic skill, gave her tools to paint them as individuals with compassion, humor and understanding. In this and her previous book, *We Live in the Arctic*, she gives us a rare glimpse into an ancient culture in collision with the rapidly-changing modern world. Not only was their way of life vanishing, but the Alaskan Iñupiat themselves were melting like the snow under an onslaught of new diseases and new ways of living—a third of their scattered families decimated in the previous year.

Connie was a courageous dreamer and promoter of dreams. Her life would remain precarious because she navigated toward adventure and away from the "deadening" security others craved. My earliest memories are of afternoon naps lulled by the sound of her tapping away on a little typewriter. Even as she sat at the Itkillik River, she was planning their next adventure: seeking an airplane and movie cameras while setting up national lecture tours. Her letters were carried by dog team to Beechey Point, on to Barrow, and then Outside by plane. By the time my parents arrived in Canada in August 1946, these plans were already in motion. She had never met Bud's parents, yet was soon living with them in Colorado: editing, signing contracts, and writing endless letters. The following spring as *We Live in the Arctic* was published, the couple flew back to Alaska in a new Cessna 140 on floats, and Connie began her fifth book, *Flight of the Arctic Tern*. Yet, while Bud was welcomed into the prestigious Explorer's Club on the merits of the book you now hold, Connie was excluded because of her gender. It would take another generation to open doors of equality for my sister and me.

As I listen to the first birds of spring, I am grateful for my two remarkable parents whose combined skills carried them places neither could have attained alone. Without their example, my life would have been very different. My mother inspired me to dream, to take an ethical stand, and to belong to the natural world. It's no surprise that in later years she worked tirelessly to conserve wild areas of our endangered Earth. Because of my father, I learned pragmatism and that ideas could be crafted into form. You have only to think of him building a seaworthy canoe—using a rusty saw, two boards washed up on the arctic coast, and some old canvas—to see how adept he was.

I am thankful to Epicenter Press for republishing six of my mother's classic books and to the University of Alaska's Polar Archives for preserving my parents' slides and documentaries (as well as my own) for a new generation of dreamers. Without the perspective of our evolving place in a greater community of life, we risk losing our roots in a living world and reaping a harvest of separation, loss and grief. Yet within each of us sleeps the seed of remembering: a personal dream of beauty, creativity, and play which beckons beyond straight lines. It is my prayer this last magical spring here in a breathing wilderness, that together humans may awaken as a species and find our way Home.

Jean Aspen, April 2018
www.jeanaspen.com

Bud and Connie Helmericks

Foreword

This is the third and last book in a series describing a trip of two winters and three summers of exploring by homemade canoe above the Arctic Circle of North America.

The first book, *We Live in the Arctic*, tells about the year we lived alone in the arctic Brooks Range of Alaska, on wild meat when our food gave out, seeing no other human beings.

The second book, *Our Summer with the Eskimos*, tells how we crossed the Brooks Range and floated down the thousand- mile-long timberless Colville River to the Arctic Ocean, where we summered with the Eskimos, adopting their food, clothing, and speech.

The present book is the story of the winter spent among those Eskimos, until with the coming of the next summer and the opening of the Arctic Ocean to boat travel once more we finally canoed our way from Alaska to Canada, to resume contact with civilization and ultimately fly out to the United States. It tells of the Eskimo life as lived in a land of no houses, for we lived in our tent converted by winter into an igloo, in the company of two young Eskimos who taught us much about Eskimos and Eskimo ways. And that is why this book is dedicated to

Ruth and Ook-Sook
companions of the white trail

All of these books were written while we were in the arctic as I sat on a floor of caribou skins, by the light of a coal-oil lantern, far from the modern world.

Constance and Harmon Helmericks

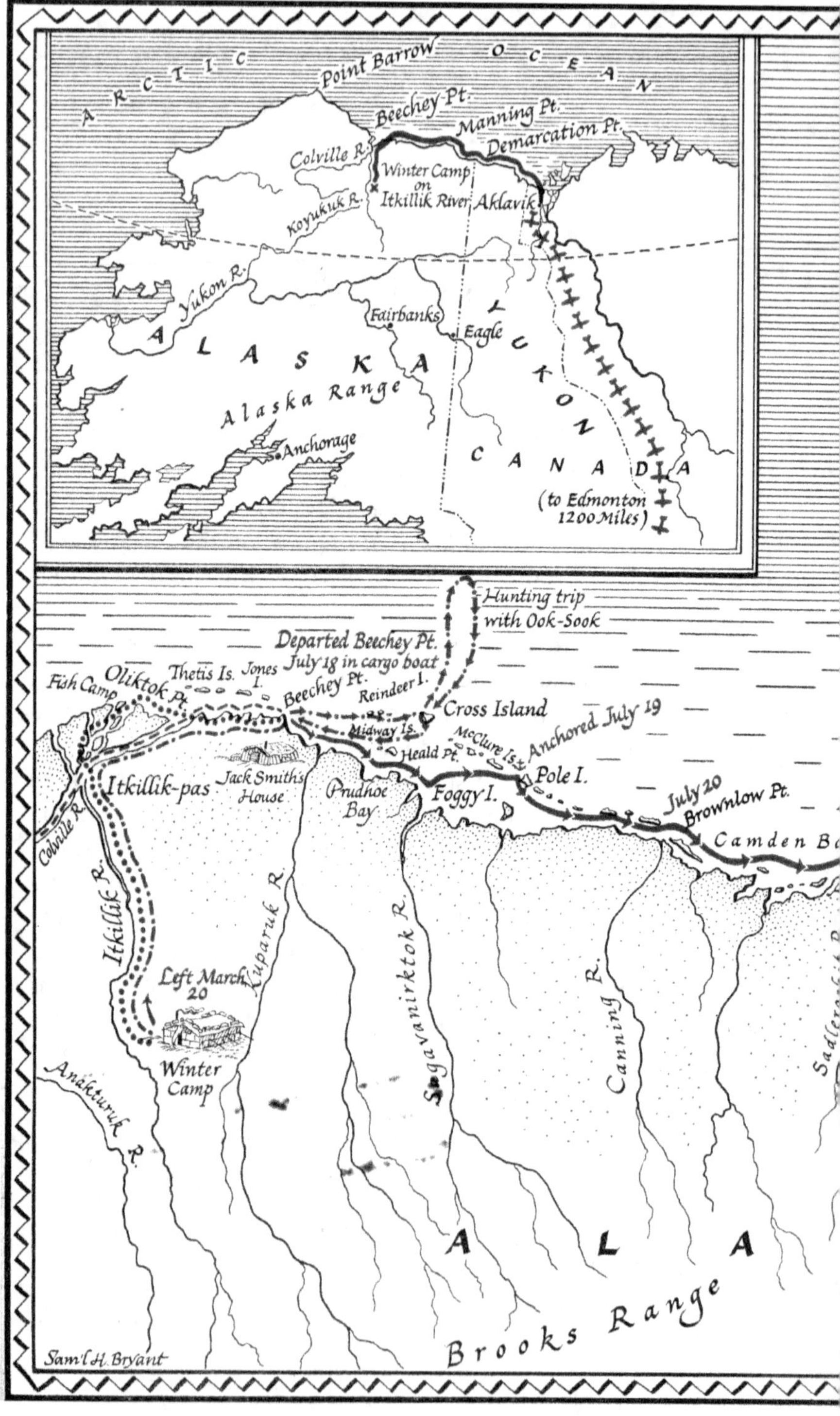
ARCTIC OCEAN
Point Barrow
Beechey Pt.
Manning Pt.
Demarcation Pt.
Colville R.
Winter Camp on Itkillik River
Aklavik
Koyukuk R.
Yukon R.
Fairbanks
Eagle
ALASKA
YUKON
Alaska Range
Anchorage
CANADA
(to Edmonton 1200 Miles)
Hunting trip with Ook-Sook
Departed Beechey Pt. July 18 in cargo boat
Thetis Is.
Jones I.
Oliktok Pt.
Fish Camp
Beechey Pt.
Reindeer I.
Cross Island
Anchored July 19
Midway Is.
McClure Is.
Heald Pt.
Pole I.
Itkillik-pas
Jack Smith's House
Prudhoe Bay
Foggy I.
July 20
Brownlow Pt.
Colville R.
Camden Ba
Itkillik R.
Kuparuk R.
Sagavanirktok R.
Canning R.
Saddleroch
Left March 20
Anaktuuruk R.
Winter Camp
ALA
Brooks Range
Sam'l H. Bryant

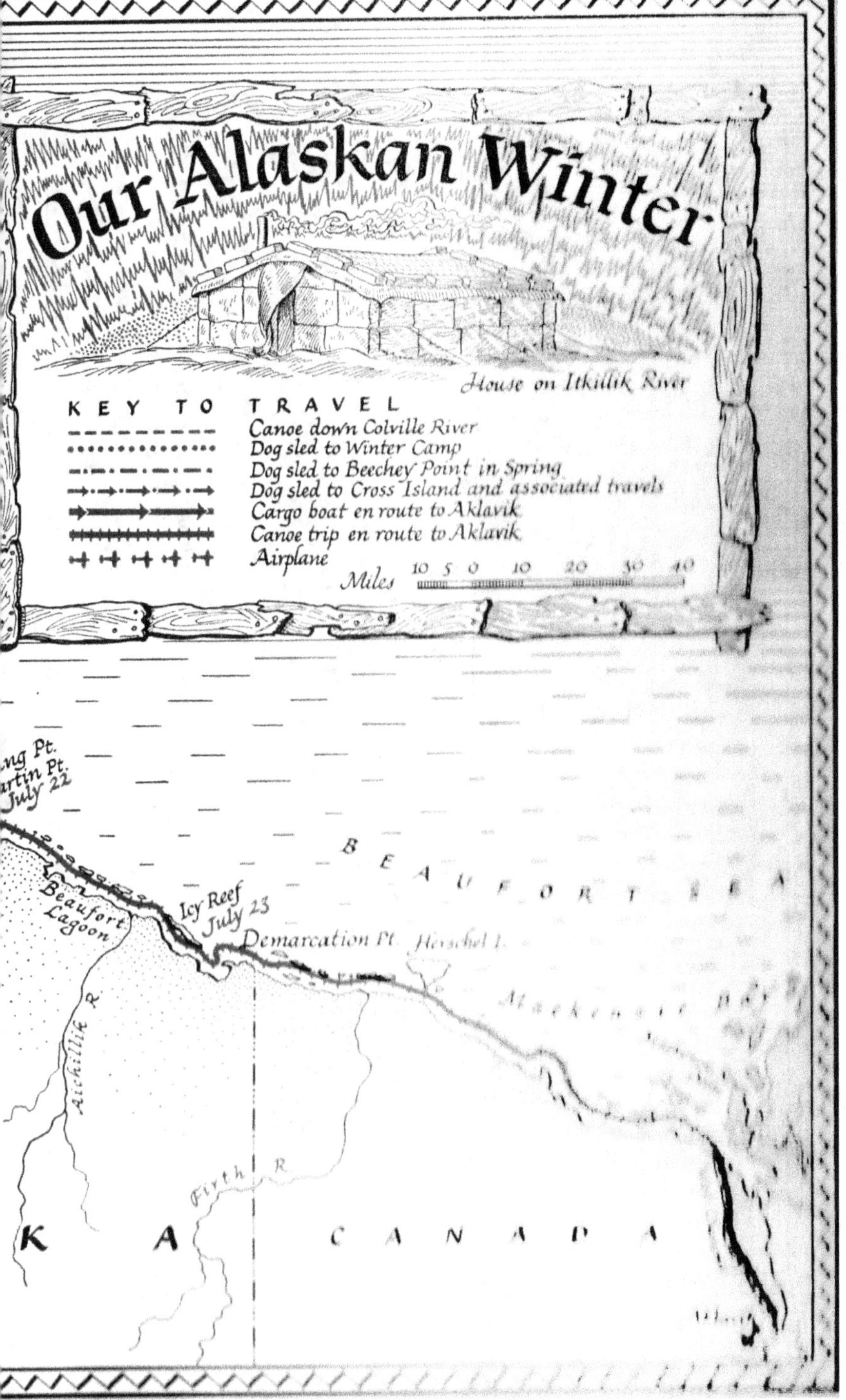

Our Alaskan Winter
House on Itkillik River
KEY TO TRAVEL
Canoe down Colville River
Dog sled to Winter Camp
Dog sled to Beechey Point in Spring
Dog sled to Cross Island and associated travels
Cargo boat en route to Aklavik
Canoe trip en route to Aklavik
Airplane
Miles
10 5 0 10 20 30 40
ng Pt.
rtin Pt.
July 22
Beaufort Lagoon
Icy Reef
July 23
Demarcation Pt.
Herschel I.
BEAUFORT SEA
Mackenzie Bay
Aichillik R.
Firth R.
K A
CANADA

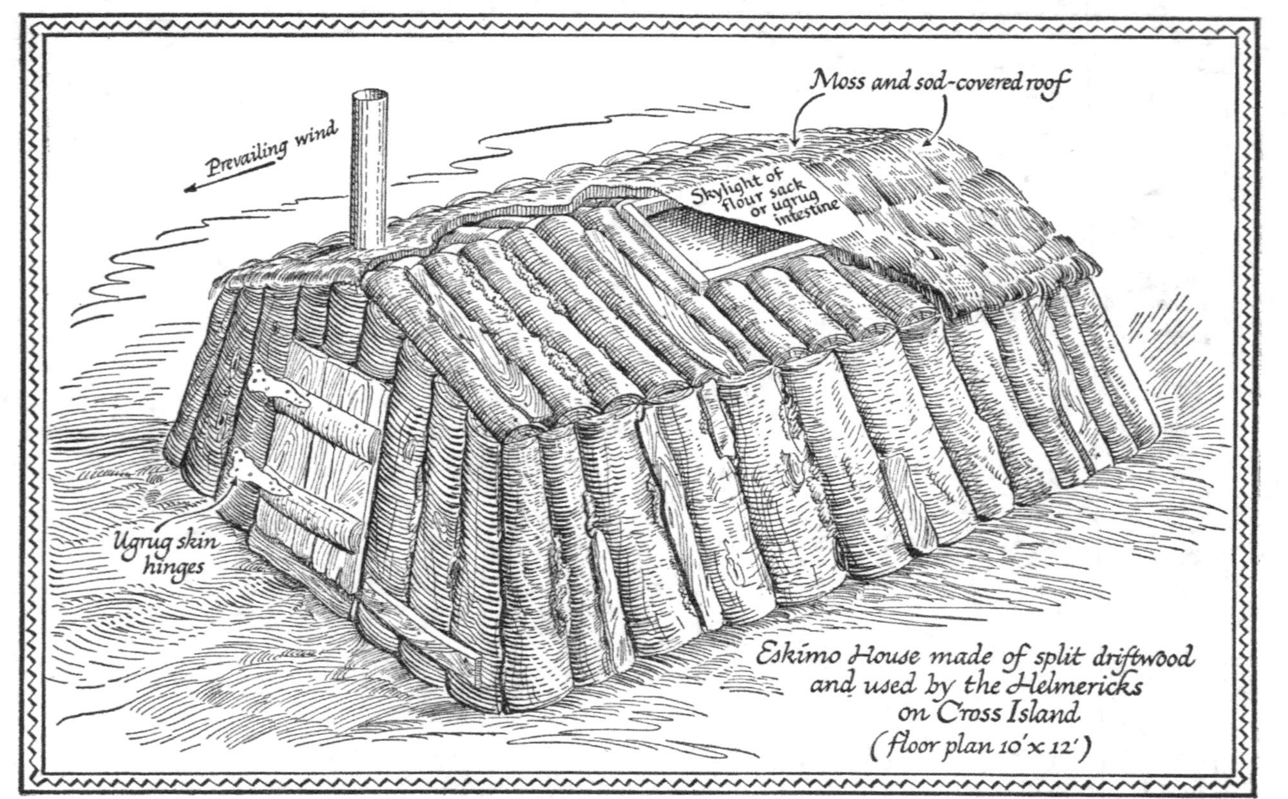

Eskimo House made of split driftwood and used by the Helmericks on Cross Island (floor plan 10' x 12')

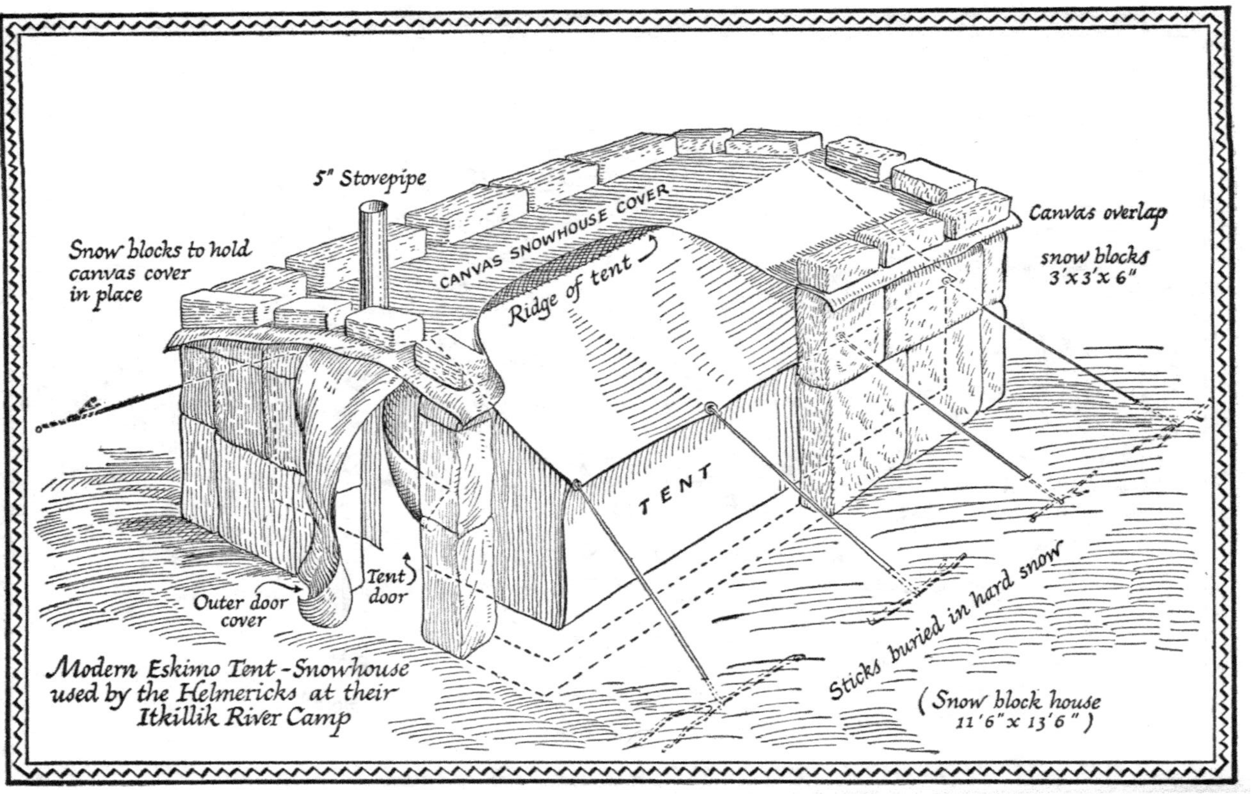

Modern Eskimo Tent-Snowhouse used by the Helmericks at their Itkillik River Camp

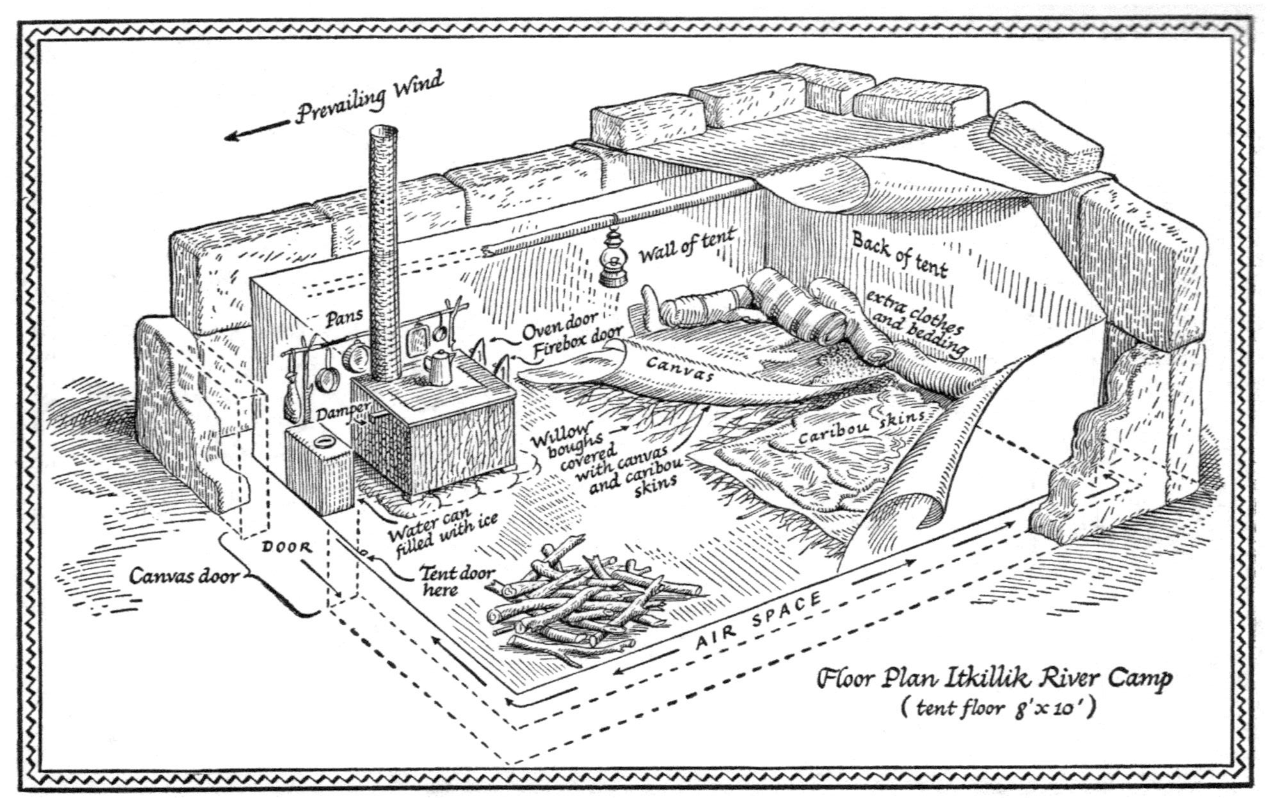

Floor Plan Itkillik River Camp
(tent floor 8' x 10')

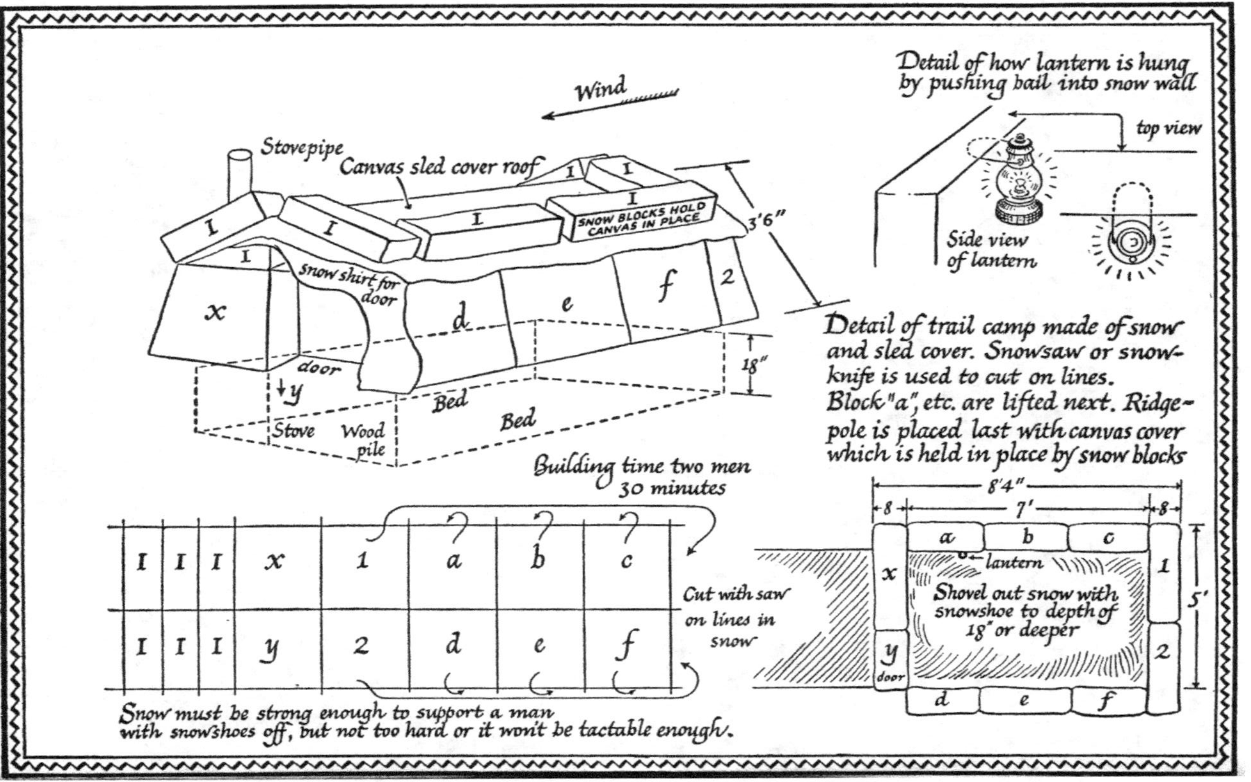

Wind
Stovepipe
Canvas sled cover roof
SNOW BLOCKS HOLD CANVAS IN PLACE
I
I
I
I
I
3'6"
x
d
e
f
2
snow shirt for door
door
y
Stove
Wood pile
Bed
Bed
18"
Detail of how lantern is hung by pushing bail into snow wall
top view
Side view of lantern
Detail of trail camp made of snow and sled cover. Snowsaw or snow-knife is used to cut on lines. Block "a", etc. are lifted next. Ridge-pole is placed last with canvas cover which is held in place by snow blocks
Building time two men 30 minutes
I I I x 1 a b c
I I I y 2 d e f
Cut with saw on lines in snow
Snow must be strong enough to support a man with snowshoes off, but not too hard or it won't be tactable enough.
8'4"
8
7'
8
a b c
lantern
x
Shovel out snow with snowshoe to depth of 18" or deeper
1
5'
y
door
2
d e f

Winter comes to Beechey Point

Ook-Sook hauls firewood to Beechey Point

PART ONE

The Dog Team Trail

Ook-Sook ices the sled runners

Connie and Ruth on the sled

1

The sun had set some weeks ago. It was now November and the arctic night was shutting down. We asked the Eskimos as best we could how many days the sun would be gone, but they said they had never noticed. The wind blew sixty miles an hour or so not infrequently and snow drifted about old Jack Smith's driftwood grave marker standing just outside our window on the prairie. Jack Smith was the last of a succession of white traders who ran the Beechey Point trading post before it was taken over by the Eskimos, and it was Jack's own little house beside the trading post that we had rented from old Abraham, the present trader.

We had spent the summer canoeing down the Colville River to the arctic coast of Alaska. Until we came to the world of the Eskimos along the rim of the continent we had been alone on that thousand-mile-long treeless river. Our canoe, the *Little Willow,* was strictly homemade, and our first task had been to learn the lore of getting food and shelter in a land of no fuel and no landmarks. After some weeks we reached the coast and struck east, working our way among the ice floes—the first we had ever seen—until we reached the trading post here at Beechey Point and set up headquarters in Jack Smith's old house.

A week ago, Ook-sook, Eskimo aborigine, age twenty-three (near our age), came to work for us. He sledded in from up the Colville. His name Ook-sook is a nickname or corruption of Okrogak, which means Oil. His mother had called him that when he was little much as we might call a favorite child Butterball; his English name is Paul. We never mastered his original Eskimo name; it should be pronounced with a kind of explosive belch which it did not seem advisable for us to attempt. So, following popular precedent, we always called him Ook-sook, as the Eskimos called him out of fun.

Connie was ecstatic about getting Ook-sook, and I was much elated myself, inasmuch as Ook-sook is one of Matthew's sons and Matthew's People up the Colville are in high repute as hunters and workers who do not take to themselves the city mannerisms which are so much a part of our times. As Connie put it, "Really wild people are getting hard to find in the world anymore."

Ook-sook was to be paid twenty dollars a month and board for his services with his sled and dog team. He was to convey us out snow-camping to a spot inland where there are some little willows growing which are about five feet tall—the fuel we must go to live by. There we would pass the midwinter months among the caribou herds upon which Ook-sook's people lived. One of the conditions of working for us was that Ook-sook must have plenty of caribou meat. We promised he should have all he was used to. Ook-sook spoke no English but was anxious to learn.

He arrived to work for us after a four-day trip, coughing loudly. We knew hunters living out in forty degree below zero weather frequently cough when they get into a house and breathe the warmer air, but it was merely that he had been visiting George and Nanny Woods and their family and had caught cold there. I thought of Point Barrow. Rumor had reached all of us along the coast that Barrow was in quarantine again with influenza. "The Eskimos are probably laid out there like sticks of wood, awaiting burial," we thought privately, and we began to consider ourselves pretty lucky out our way.

"You want some cough syrup?"

"Yah."

Connie fed the Eskimo hunter some cough syrup off a large spoon, for which Ook-sook opened his mouth obediently and we almost lost the spoon. I had improvised this cough syrup for Connie from whiskey and burned sugar syrup, and it was really quite good.

"Strong!" agreed Ook-sook with an appreciative explosion of wind.

As Connie hustled around to get the tea bucket boiling and some meat upon the table, I could see her stealing covert glances at our hunter perched on a stool in the lantern light, to see what we had got. He was dressed in denim pants freshly laundered for him by the women of his family and he wore a woolen work shirt which, like ours, had come from the Beechey Point Store; his pants were held up by a piece of rope. Besides these clothes which he had on his back, he brought his duffel sack of fur clothing and his bedroll of skins. His rifle, which looked like the Long Rifle we have read about, was of .30-30 caliber, quite an antique. He kept it out of doors in a sealskin case on his sled. It was in a state of considerable decrepitude from having been run over by his sled last winter, to name but one of its mishaps, yet he had killed fourteen caribou with it in the last few days.

Ook-sook's face was deeply tanned, to a handsome copper color, and he looked more "Eskimo" than any Eskimo we had ever seen. His height was about 5 feet 9 inches, he weighed 168 pounds (we weighed him in the warehouse), he was a perfect figure of a man, and he looked like a man; he was proud and honorable to the last degree. That his feelings were easily hurt by any imagined slight we soon learned, but most of the time he was with us he was as happy as a puppy. He was an ideal day-by-day companion to get along with.

Ook-sook had a beautiful snow shirt which we knew at once should photograph brilliantly when the sun came back: it was a lovely orange, scalloped and trimmed, of course, by the dark wolverine fringe on his parka hood and by needlework in several colors on hem and cuffs. The house boots he donned upon coming indoors were made of the leg skins of white Dali sheep. We really hadn't seen anything in primitive Eskimo fashion until we saw Ook-sook's boots. A most friendly, yet independent, casual, careless-appearing young man: Connie was wondering almost frantically if we had enough meat thawed in the house to feed him.

Anyone who has not taken a wild Indian or Eskimo into his house to live has not fully lived. Our first meal with Ook- sook would have been a revelation to persons not used to novelty. Our hunter was not shy, nor did he suffer from self-doubts. He reached and grabbed everything which was placed on the table, smacked his lips, belched mightily, and around his plate were scattered those scraps and bones which were not thrown upon the floor. This was the first time, perhaps, that he had ever sat at a table to eat and he was, in fact, almost totally unfamiliar with even a chair. However, we were glad to see him cheerful and happy; that was the main thing. Without him and his eight strong dogs we might well have a cold time of it; as it was, at best, we never got more than three days' fuel ahead. Far from having him as a house pet, I wanted him to hunt with. Table manners, after all, are not so important. If Ook-sook's feelings were hurt in any way we knew it was likely that he and his eight dogs would go home to his father's tent one hundred miles away without so much as a fare-thee-well.

We put Ook-sook to bed early that evening, not knowing quite what to do with him. He could use the back room we used as storeroom until we left Beechey Point. Inside his sleeping skins he was doubtless warm in this unheated room except that the conditions of enclosure are not the same as merely being out of doors in low temperatures. The difference is that a person confined in such a room for long will suffer from a pervading wetness and dampness due to the condensation of his own breath. The breath, rising as warm steam, adheres to the ceiling and collects there in the form of ice which drips. We had heated this room and dried it out two days before Ook-sook's arrival in an effort to make it livable for him, but since there was not enough fuel to warm this additional room very often, I realized that the time would come soon when Ook-sook, if he was to be our "family," would be obliged to sleep in the same room with us. The discipline of arctic conditions soon makes a person change his point of view on things, so that our first attitudes toward Ook-sook now seem to us amusing.

The following morning Connie fixed baked fish, bread, and tea for breakfast. The pieces of bread Ook-sook had had in a lifetime you could probably count on your fingers. Fish and meat were all he knew. Connie baked the whitefish with their heads on, Eskimo style, as we had rather got into the habit of doing anyway, and we watched our adopted wild man eat out the gills and around the eyes as quickly as a ferret and spit out the bones upon the table. I was unfortunately seized at this time with the evil idea of amusing Ook- sook with a toy airplane propeller which I had carved out and stuck up on a pole in the snowbank outside the door as a kind of revolving weathervane to indicate wind direction and velocity. When I brought this gadget indoors and showed it to Ook-sook at the breakfast table, he blew out his cheeks and into the propeller mightily, right into all the food on the table. That was the end of that breakfast.

"Here, Ook-sook," said I, perceiving that Connie was getting angry at both of us, "you want to blow at it *this* way, see?" But Connie never did see the humor in that game.

Ook-sook then went off right away to get a load of wood. We went out of the house long enough to see him feed his dogs raw frozen fish chopped up with the ax for their breakfast, which they caught on the fly. Then he hitched them up to the sled. The dogs' names were Duk, Autakak, Nel- yokrok, Niksik, Mauga, Parmie, Netsig, and Pot, named for a cooking pot—one word of English which Ook-sook knew. A pup we called Coaly joined us later in the game.

As soon as the dogs had been dragged by the scruff of the neck over the snow and snapped into the harness, they stood shivering with anticipation and became all business at once. They had been curled up sleeping in the snow but a few minutes before. Icy circles where they had lain showed that the snow had melted under them and indicated, although we did not know much about sled dogs then, that Ook-sook's dogs were not well furred. Ook-sook drove them in pairs with the lead dog out in front after a fashion which is common in western Alaska, and his sled was made of planks planed out of driftwood. He had no dog whip to control the dogs; we never saw a whip used among our Eskimos, for the use of it does not seem to be a culture trait of this area; in fact, if a whip is ever used in Alaska for driving dogs, it is probably an importation by the white man. Ook-sook's dogs looked thin and underfed when they came to us, for they had been fed entirely on the poorest and leanest parts of the caribou which had been discarded by the humans.

The dogs had no seal blubber or rice or corn meal to supply the fats and carbohydrates which are necessary to enrich a lean meat fare, with dogs as well as with humans—a corollary which is more important in arctic life than any other dietary principle which we can mention. The dogs' feet were sore and bled into the snow, which made us pity them. We did not want to be responsible for employing a dog team such as that, and immediately began to try to think how to improve the dogs and their driver. We summed it up this way: "Ook-sook's not cruel to his dogs. He's not kind or cruel, either one, because he just doesn't know anything different."

But how did Ook-sook by the sole command of his voice start out that team and keep it going all day? These were dogs which as strangers we wouldn't be able to approach without having a leg taken off! Their traces were so free that all of the dogs could turn around and run back to the sled and jump on for a ride, if they had thought of it. Sometimes they did get perverse ideas. For instance, Ook-sook had just got the team started off on this particular day and had himself jumped onto the back of the sled, holding onto its high back, when all the team suddenly lay down and rolled in the harness. Ook-sook leaped off, kicked the dogs with his soft deerskin boots (a pastime perhaps harder on the driver than on his furry dogs) until somehow, he got that mess of unintelligible harness untangled and the dogs all hauled to their feet again. Plumed tails waving in the air, the team of mismatched and various-sized dogs lunged forward. As one dog, they suddenly smelled the blubber cache of Abraham, the Beechey Point trader, which was piled in the yard, and starved as they were for fats they lost their minds. In total disregard of the sled behind them, they all made for the blubber. We looked just in time to see Ook-sook leap from his sled in a wild dash, grab the leader by his harness, and drag him bodily away from the blubber pile at right angles, then catch the sled again on a mad careen, just as it looked as if it would upset: then all at once everything was in control and the orderly procession of lively dogs headed in a straight line out across the white landscape as though there were nothing to it. Presently the small moving figures were bobbing over the uneven sea ice beyond, bound for the island reefs to get wood. The last to be seen was that wild orange snow shirt. Ook-sook never deigned a backward glance.

Ook-sook's table manners, when he began to understand after a few days that he had been assigned his own cup, tin plate, fork, and spoon, began to improve, or perhaps we just got used to him. For instance, we all learned to crack caribou leg bones commonly at table to get the good marrow out. Ook-sook showed us that. But table manners soon became a very secondary matter when compared to the task of keeping the wild hunter amused during those hours out of the twenty-four when he was indoors with us. He did not know what to do with himself. I started him on what I thought might be a great career in carving ivory in the evenings when Connie and I turned to study table, but he was no inborn genius: he just broke up ivory. I had obtained the raw ivory at Barrow. But Ook-sook just wasn't the ivory-carving type. For a time, he was amused by the pictures of animals he found in our old dictionary. The first animal he asked me the name of in English was "aardvark," and the second one his eye chanced to glance across was "ibex," all of which was rather embarrassing for me to explain, inasmuch as I am myself not familiar with aardvarks and ibexes.

"Heavens," Connie said, "teach him some animals he knows around here. Don't waste his time. Teach him something he can use. Not one person in a million would know he was speaking English if he tried to talk about aardvarks."

It was a lamentable fact that our dictionary came out before the First World War and was sort of handed down to Connie and me, inasmuch as right now dictionaries were not easily obtainable. Ook-sook asked us the names of the most out-of-date old devices shown in our dictionary pictures—telephones the like of which Connie and I have never even seen, outmoded laboratory apparatus, and some of the first experimental aircraft, which looked like flying chicken coops, not to mention the high-wheeled bicycle, the correct name for which I never did know, and which would not seem important, generally speaking, to Eskimos of the modern generation.

Keeping Ook-sook was also going to run us into some work. Every drop of water we used had to be melted from ice or snow, and the increase in the use of water came largely in cooking the great washtub of dog feed which monopolized the complete top of the Beechey Point iron stove for several hours each evening. Warming up the dog food took hours of time before the food so much as reached zero, let alone a thawing temperature; after it started to cook the odor which filled the house was terrific from the innumerable filthy brewings which had before now simmered in that utensil. Connie told me that we were now burning as much wood in a day to boil the feed for Ook-sook's dogs as we had formerly burned in a week. Almost daily Ook-sook and the dogs had to go out and haul more wood.

It appeared soon that we would need somebody to converse with Ook-sook in his own language day by day or we could not hold him with us for long; moreover, we needed someone to help us take care of him, to cook and to sew, inasmuch as he did not take well to these chores which hunters of pride are not accustomed to doing. Also, if Ook-sook and

I was to spend a major portion of the year hunting and exploring together, would not Connie need a companion for herself?

Yes, she would, Connie said. There was a person she had long had in mind: red-cheeked little Ruth of Oliktok, and Ruth happened to be Ook-sook's first cousin Ruth and Ook- sook had played together since they were children, and for that reason old Alice, Ruth's mother, would be the more apt to let Ruth come to join our family, knowing that she would be with her cousin.

Abraham warned me, in one of his rare moments of frankness, about Connie's choice. Ruth came from the most troublesome family of ne'er-do-wells on the entire coast; she was a nice girl, but her family were trouble-makers. But there you were—you couldn't tell Connie that; she liked Ruth and sent Ook-sook to fetch her.

On Thanksgiving eve with a load of whitefish from the Colville, Ook-sook and Ruth blew in. The temperature when they arrived was fifty-five degrees below zero and the wind, which was rapidly increasing in velocity, was probably thirty miles an hour.

THE TYPICAL ARCTIC PICTURE OF popular imagination had become a reality, with the snow driving at a terrific rate as day after day passed. While the sky was actually clear above, the whirling snow clouds drove along on the ground, obliterating everything. Drifts became hard as iron, scoured and burnished; deerskin boots left no track. The brown earth was blown completely bare in places. Drifts collect before and in the lee of any obstruction which breaks the surface of the level prairie, so that the Beechey Point buildings were piled high with snow. Dark objects floated in a world of white where land, sea, and sky were one. Lying curled up like doughnuts on the snowdrifts beside the house, our dogs looked as if they were suspended in space.

As soon as this last gale abated we intended to leave. It was no dream. For the past two months we had tried to scrape up enough driftwood to keep the house warm. Kerosene for the primus stove was rationed to a total of fifteen gallons for our year inasmuch as the Eskimos had to have their share for trapping. "I'm not sure how I am going to like it," was Connie's reply to the impending question of how she would like Eskimo life in a tent by winter. She had been cold in a well-built house when scrimping on fuel and the idea of a snow house left her with visions of real cold.

Our plan was to travel from Beechey Point along the coast westward to the Colville, then inland to Matthew's camp, and from there strike overland in a southerly direction until we hit willow patches growing on the upper Itkillik River. The entire journey was to be made during the darkest part of the year, while the temperature seldom rose above thirty degrees below zero and often hit fifty below. We could carry but little food for our long trip with four people, considering the amount which the dogs would have to haul on the sled for their own rations which they would eat along the way; camp equipment soon filled the small remainder of the sled's load capacity. For camping our primus stove gave about as much heat as a blowtorch. A new little sheet-iron stove which burned wood was going along on the sled for use when we reached our permanent camp, but we did not expect to find so much as a stick to burn on the way. The necessities of life were few—namely, an 8' X 10' ordinary canvas wall tent, a 12' X 14' extra tarpaulin, a little sheet-iron camp stove, the down sleeping bag Connie and I owned, and Ruth's and Ook-sook's bedding, our tin plates and cooking pots and water can, our rifles and a little spare clothing—then whatever sacks of biscuits and tea we could haul in left-over space. Five gallons of kerosene went with the primus stove and lantern. Scarce as the bare essentials seem, they made a load of six hundred pounds before we knew it.

The eight slender dogs made a brave effort to pull the sled with us all sitting on it, but it was too much. Ook-sook couldn't tell me at that time, but it is generally considered that no person is fit for arctic life and work unless he can walk or run beside the sled, and people are not expected to ride. The best we could do for that hundred and fifty miles was for one to ride at a time while the rest would have to walk. Thus, out over the sea ice we started one day, skirting the shore, with Ook-sook running ahead to encourage the dogs, while the rest of us started running beside or behind the sled. Because of the dog-feed situation and also to gain the benefits of human shelter it seemed best to make a circuit of all the inhabited Eskimo camps along our way, and this in turn provided us with the opportunity of doing some of the most interesting visiting in the world—visiting in their winter homes the Eskimos whom we had known by summer.

You can imagine us now, dressed all in Eskimo clothing, riding and running alternately by the side of the sled at a dogtrot, accomplishing in all perhaps twenty-five miles in one day, moving along the hard-crusted snow of the frozen Arctic Ocean, cutting across capes and bays, the temperature holding around forty degrees below zero, which is considered good traveling weather here, and finally up the delta of the Colville River and so inland, seeing the country now in its winter dress.

At the end of each day's travel we find some new dwelling where we are taken in: biscuits, tea, great platters of boiled fish are set before us on the floor, and everybody eats with his knife and fingers. The smiling women soften and rub our boots, which we take off as soon as we enter, and they attend our every need while we recline on couches of furs—well, so to speak.

Connie's Ruth, a little grinning idol, makes herself extremely pleasant; there is no need to tell her anything in packing a sled.

The sled bumped and squeaked along over the hard drifts, and perspiration streamed down my face at forty-five below zero, for I wasn't used to this steady running; my fur clothes, especially footwear, became quickly soaked. Connie rode more than the rest of us because she was the softest of us all. Ruth jumped off and, on the load, often holding on behind by the handlebars in a standing position where the driver rides, while Ook-sook just continued running ahead. Four hours and a low snowbank ahead of us suddenly erupted people and our dogs broke into a run. Onto the sled all of us piled then, while it shot from side to side, glancing off the hard drifts and thumping down on top of others. We pulled up in grand style and here was Richard's camp.

Richard's People were all living in a drift and sod house probably 20 feet square indoors with a 6i/£-foot ceiling; Abraham had built it at one time. It was lighted by a glass skylight set in the roof and warmed by a big fine sheet-iron camp stove. It was built of drift covered by sods, now completely hidden under snow blocks. The wind had drifted loose snow over it until only the stovepipe and very edge of the flat roof showed above.

We shook hands with everybody who came out to meet us. Eskimos always remove the glove for shaking hands, no matter how cold the weather; this ritual always holds. Inside the house a table was already laid upon the floor for us and the tea bucket boiled. A gasoline camp lantern lit up the neat house, kept by Richard's precise and very proper older daughters. You get used to the light a kerosene lantern gives during the winter until presently you can see like a cat: it seems a lot of light, until the sun rises again.

Friendly hands helped us beat the frost from our furs, which must not be allowed to melt on them. Our mittens were hung on a line above the stove so that they might be warm and dry when we left. Richard's wife Emma, who spoke some English, asked us to sit down. We sat on the floor. Richard himself, though he looked much like a white man, seldom deigned to speak a word of English. After a little lunch of tea and fresh bread, Ruth and Ook-sook having paved the way to social ease for all of us by their chattering, we continued on our way towards the next camp, where we would spend the night.

Our shelter this first night was a large tent, 12' X 14 which contained about a dozen people when we entered it; this we did via a snow alcove equipped with wooden pegs in its walls for the hanging of one's outer parka. Here we got our first chance to see what tent life in the winter is like. The tent had been pitched and then a snow house had been built around the tent, leaving a six-inch air space between tent and snow wall. This is important: tent and snow wall must not touch. The snow house was made of blocks three feet square and six inches thick; they had been sawed out with a wood saw and neatly fitted together to make a house. This is not the kind of snow that the southerner knows, but snow beaten hard by the winds. Driftwood logs were laid across the snow walls to form rafters and more snow blocks were laid over the top, and the whole structure chinked with soft powdery snow and made nearly airtight, the tent being thus walled in from the winds and buried from sight. A similar structure, only smaller, had been built adjoining the front, with a snow hall leading into it. The doors between the outer house and the inner house in the tent were hung with old canvas curtains, and the outside door closed by means of a hanging caribou skin.

Inside the tent there was the familiar floor made of gasoline box boards in the front half, or what we would call the living room, while the back half was covered with caribou skins, fur side down because the hairs shed. The back half was the family's sleeping loft. Rolled-up caribou bedding provided backrests along the tent walls. A gasoline lantern lighted this house brilliantly for sewing and social life, while a large sheet-iron stove heated the tent to a very high temperature. Behind the stove on the floor sat a box used for a cupboard.

We have said in *Our Summer with the Eskimos* that the house of our friends George and Nanny Woods, at whatever spot it may be found, is a prosperous and industrious one for this society. As community religious exercises are much a part of this household, George and Nanny, as we said before, are social leaders of some importance. Besides their own immediate family of seven members, they are usually to be found boarding numbers of other people who may be overnight guests, indigents, or the like. We were greeted with a show of enthusiasm by our friends, as George asked in English: "Where do you plan to stay tonight? Are you going to make a camp here?" at which Nanny at once said quietly and decisively, "You will stay with us."

George, a well-to-do man and consequently much imposed upon by others less fortunate, at this time had his fish nets tended for him by others in return for a part of the catch. He burned an expensive gasoline pressure lamp all winter, being the only one except Abraham and Richard to have such a luxury. We had expected to have supper with the family that night but were more than amazed to join in the eating of four meals before the bedtime hour rolled around.

It was in George's tent that we were introduced to raw frozen fish—famous food of the North, and one of which any reader of arctic literature hears many stories.

Raw frozen fish and raw frozen meat, called *quak* by the Eskimos, are liked by every native and almost any white man who has lived in the arctic for any time. I never did find an Eskimo who didn't like *quak,* although I found many who dislike ice cream, some who eat no sugar, and many more who like no salt on meat or fish. *Quak* is a staple part of daily diet in Eskimo life and dogs and humans alike usually have it for at least one meal during the day; for one thing, it saves on fuel. There seem to be no parasitic diseases associated with arctic fish and meat which would endanger people eating them raw.

I don't remember just exactly when it was that I ate my first raw frozen fish with the Eskimos, but it was new to Connie when we visited the Woods camp on our winter journey. She would not try it while we were living in our house and had other things to eat, although Ook-sook and I frequently started off a cooked meal with some *quak.*

Connie was obliged to come to it on the trail and soon became as fond of it as I already was.

Brought in from the forty-below-zero weather outside, the fish were dumped by one of the children upon the Woods family board before us. They had been frozen solid just as taken out of the water weeks ago. Steam arose from the fish and they sprouted hoarfrost as soon as they met the warm air inside. Allowed to warm a few moments by the stove before the human beings tackled them, the individual fish rapidly froze together wherever they were in contact with another fish.

The raw frozen whitefish we were going to eat were about fifteen inches long on the average and weighed a little over a pound each. The general procedure was to hold the frozen fish up by the tail with the nose against the table board on the floor, and with your knife cut a thin strip from the back from tail to head. This cut just through the skin, taking off all the back fins. The next cut was down the belly of the fish. The head was next cut off and the tail nearly cut off, being left attached on one side by the skin. You could now take hold of the tail, the skin being very resilient, and skin one side of the fish. You then used your knife to strip the skin from the other side, and the fish was peeled. The result was a skinned fish, minus head, tail, and fins. To eat the fish, you cut thin slices from it much as you would whittle a piece of soft wood. The women used their *uluruks,* the men usually a common jackknife. Ook-sook just went down his fish like a person eating an ear of corn— the typewriter method. He even ate the head and eyes; the skeleton and entrails remained in his hand when he had finished.

Fish or meat frozen at this temperature is brittle and will break if it is dropped, or if it is pounded or chopped it may splinter; in general, it is handled much like an armful of wood. Its ease of handling in these temperatures is in fact one of the great conveniences of arctic life. One great advantage of handling the frozen foods is that they do not have to be wrapped up in anything, since, not being sticky, they pick up no dirt.

Quak seems to be an extremely digestible food for human beings. It is the cooking which makes meats tough and fibrous. In their raw frozen condition, we find that chemically and nutritionally we are dealing with an entirely different product from what we are used to in cooked meats! Each climate has its local products which through the course of centuries have come to be the best there, and so the arctic produces its *quak*. *Quak* is another Eskimo word for which we have no good English equivalent. We have found among the Eskimos that *quak* not only makes a strong, red-blooded people, but that it is the food you eat when you have been having stomach trouble from eating white man's concentrates in a land of no vegetables. In other words, *quak* is a medicine and a salad. It is my opinion that it cannot be too highly endorsed for the arctic environment.

What does raw frozen fish taste like? It is nut flavored and scarcely tastes like fish at all. Because the fish are oily, they can be cut and chewed like soft ice cream in this frozen condition; a fat fish is by far the best to eat, and can be recognized, after a little experience, by its depth of body. A narrow fish is in poor condition. A man will eat about two fish of this size for one meal in the arctic. The small bones are sliced fine and even these may be consumed because they are not more noticeable than are the bones in pressure- canned salmon. As mentioned before, a person living here must eat fresh foods, and it is highly preferable, in order to gain the greatest benefit from these foods, that some of them should be eaten raw as an insurance for good health; scurvy comes quickly when fresh foods fail, be it in the arctic, on board a ship, in an army camp, or in any city on earth. But the inhabitant of the arctic, from long tradition, is especially conscious of this.

2

At George's and Nanny's home we all slept together laid out on the floor in rows, each in his own bedding. To people used to separate bedrooms and private baths it may sound strange that so many people could sleep in such a small space with any privacy at all. Yet after you have spread your sleeping bag you have a sort of small room all to yourself. Your parka supplies a little tent to undress in, and it becomes easy with practice to slide down into your bag and finish undressing there. Your clothes are put under your head along with your parka for a pillow. Thus, everything is enormously simplified. As the bedding and other fur apparel are bulky, the lines overhead fairly droop with the party's combined stockings, belts, and mittens, and during the period while everyone is undressing at once and arranging his bed it is crowded to say the least. During the night there is usually a good deal of belching and wind from this host of people who make no efforts to constrain themselves at any time anyway; they are a riotous crew. Yet after three nights of it you get used to sleeping publicly with a dozen other people lying close beside, and there seems nothing strange in it. You are thankful for a shelter. I won't recommend it for anyone except the Eskimos, but it does well for them and fits into the pattern of life they must lead to survive in their environment.

The morning came some ten hours later; Eskimos sleep long nights during the winter as there is no hurry, and nothing else in particular to do. The wonderful sleep one enjoys in this life is only comparable to the appetite with which he enjoys his food after a vigorous day on the trail. The first sight that greeted my eyes when I opened them again was of Nanny serving coffee from the stove to all the household, who were still lying in their beds. There is not the humblest Eskimo today who does not have his coffee served to him in bed each morning by his wife, so long as coffee is available. It was a good thing Connie had started to eat fish *quak* as that's all that was offered for breakfast with the coffee, to start us out on the trail.

As we came out of the Woodses' snow house the faint dawn on the horizon illuminated the endless miles of white arctic about us. All this could be ours to enjoy. The happy Eskimo faces in their tall fringed hoods, the smell of wood smoke on the clear morning air at forty below zero, the furry dogs raising their muzzles in an eerie wail, unknown trails before us—this was living! Our happiness with our fur clothing, in being dressed just like the Eskimos, was complete at last. Overhead in the northern zenith the aurora borealis was putting on a brilliant display in green lights, wavering, moving, changing, never the same. It was not a dream; this fantastic life was real!

That day's journey was a long one. For twenty-five miles Connie, Ruth, and I kept jumping on and off the sled at the dictates of our bodily temperatures and endurance, except that our endurance was not lasting, and we grew progressively more sweated out and chilled down as the day wore on. Every time Connie or I jumped off the sled to run, the dogs, feeling how light the load was, seemed to double their speed. A few strides at this gallop would freeze the runner's nose from rapid breathing. He would have to run half blind with his hand over his nose, and ultimately fall onto the sled again; later, the skin came off the end of the nose as it does with a very bad sunburn. Our Eskimo companions suffered no frosting of their faces, curiously enough; I was deeply scarred into the flesh of both cheeks, which after a few days of repeated exposure and deeper frosting in the wound developed into nasty running sores. These healed eventually, and Connie and I learned to prevent frostbite before it happened. The tendency towards frostbite comes only when one is forced to travel faster than his natural pace, and I think Ook-sook set the pace too fast for us at first on the smooth sea ice. Armies in the arctic will suffer dangerously with frostbite if regimentation is enforced in out-of-doors maneuvers.

Frostbite is the result of ignorance or carelessness. It can be prevented by merely removing the mitten from one hand and warming the face for a moment with the palm, as a rule. A note to remember is that one does *not* rub snow upon the afflicted area—a malicious superstition.

At times the dogs fairly flew over the smooth bay ice. As for Ook-sook, he ran ahead of the leader all day without pause, a dashing orange figure in the pose I best remember him, a handsome fellow in his natural setting with frost wreathing the hood of his earnest vigilant face, crying "Go ahead Duk!" to his leader, and so down the miles. "Mush" is what they say to a dog team in Canada; it comes from the French explorers of long ago who first brought into the country the term *en marche,* from which "mush" is corrupted. Say "Mush" to the dogs on the north coast of Alaska and they would merely look around and expect something to eat.

"Go ahead" is the cry here, and one which every Eskimo as well as dog understands, even where no other English is spoken.

Once at Oliktok's ice cellar Ook-sook paused in mid-flight to light the primus stove, since it was necessary to melt snow in a pot and apply water to the runners of the sled for a new ice sheathing. He had taken off the iron shoeing which is used on sleds only during spring and fall in the warmer temperatures and his runners were now of wood. Wooden or ivory runners are about the only thing possible for forty and fifty below, since iron runners then stick to the ice with a friction comparable to that generated in dragging them over sand.

To fuel a primus stove like ours we used alcohol. I had to heat the alcohol by holding matches under it before it would burn. Once the little burner had started, we soon had water melted from snow. Putting a sheath of ice on the runners was accomplished by my holding the sled in balance on one runner while Ook-sook dipped a piece of caribou fur into the ice water and quickly ran it along the lifted runner; it left a thin coating much as a sponge would do, and this instantly froze as he applied it. A few swipes over each runner at fifty below zero and the sled pulled fairly easily. The ice was applied in this way each morning at camp just before loading the sled, and then again at noon during travel. Oftentimes Ook-sook carried his water ready-melted with him from the morning's camp, to save lighting the primus stove. His Eskimo vacuum bottle for this was a glass coffee jar which fitted into a pouch of caribou fur that tied with a drawstring: if the water was poured warm into the jar, it would not freeze for several hours.

Past Oliktok we left the land and cut out across the sea once more. Far ahead, a tiny black dot moved against a horizon of white. Ruth, standing up in the driver's place on the back of our sled, saw it first. From words in English written on a paper by her mother, she had memorized her first sentence: "Dog team is coming!" Connie, sitting on top of the load of the jogging sled, thrilled to Ruth's pointing hand.

As our party watched it, the black object far out on the ocean elongated into a line, only to shrink to a dot as the dogs once more swung straight towards us. Sometimes it disappeared momentarily behind ice ridges. Then suddenly it emerged large in the near perspective and we could hear its runners bump and squeak and the dogs pant. As the approaching teams saw each other, each sled leaped forward to irresistible encounter. Shouting and bodily dragging our team off the throats of the other team, and casting out the ice anchor, to hold each sled at a safe distance, we all stepped forward to shake hands.

Who were the strange Eskimos grinning but Ada's little girls, Jennie and Maria, and a boy whom Connie and I had always regarded, in the summertime, as one of the "little boys" who played around Beechey Point. Ada was a poor widow who lived to the eastward. The children were on their way to board awhile at George's tent, from which we had just come this morning. We all had many miles yet to go from the halfway mark, and although it was "noon" now, it would be long after dark when we got to our destination. I myself alone would have doubted my abilities to find it. Yet Jennie and Maria had such blooming cheeks as I thought I had never seen before and from their hoods rimmed with frost their smiles were gloriously reassuring.

It was black night when up an incline and into a small settlement of snow and ice houses our tired dogs pulled us to the fish camp situated at one of the mouths of the Colville.

Down a steep snow tunnel, we hobbled, pushed aside a Barren Grounds grizzly hide hanging untanned over the doorway, and entered the winter home of Cyrus and Alice, Ruth's mother and father.

For flooring in this house there was nothing but sticks and the bare earth. Why didn't these people have caribou hides, which are free for the getting? The skylight in the roof was of stitched panels of the intestine of the *ugrug;* some of the Eskimos save their flour sacks for their skylights, which give a better lighting effect, but the *ugrug* intestine wears longer and some old-fashioned people still prefer it. The sodden walls of the sod and stick *baribari*—a word used more commonly to describe the houses of the Aleuts than of these people—oozed dampness and slime. Frost showed all over the inside, even on the roof. Illumination from the enfeebled kerosene lantern swinging on its thong from the igloo's roof was supplemented by several little trays around the sides of the room burning wicks of cloth in fish oil.

Miserable, filthy waifs, Ruth's little brother and sister, Thomas and Hattie, crouched in the dark comers of this ill- made cavern, clad in tom breeches of sorts and a general conglomeration of rags, scratching their lice. The older children of this family, without exception, were the loveliest children on this coast—friendly, attractive personalities, all of them. They all got out and left home as soon as they were able to; they were go-getters.

"Perhaps the poor old fellow is helpless to get ahead," I thought of Ruth's father as I talked with him; he seemed a kindly, gentle soul. As for Alice, the suspicious-appearing old mother, I liked her less the more I saw of her. Both mother and father had had schooling at Barrow. Cyrus told us he once worked for the Canadian Arctic Expedition for fifteen dollars a day, with "rice and all kinds of *tuniktut*" (white man's food) to eat, too. How long had he worked? Three days. Then he went home. This was a quarter of a century ago.

Because the family was so poorly equipped with fur clothing and bedding, we imagined the old man to be a poor hunter or one who had had bad luck. I know now that the caliber of any Eskimo family can be told by the kind of clothing they wear and the abundance of meat and fish in their pots.

Ruth's wage of five dollars a month from us was immediately taken over by her family before it was earned. Here domestic labor is counted as nothing, and according to Abraham, the girl would have been eager to work for us just for her food and a place to stay. We saw at once that since Ruth herself would never get the wage, we could only make it up to her by personal gifts—things which Connie would somehow spare from our own equipment. The mother's list which I made out for her upon the store from Ruth's first wage was as follows: small amounts of tobacco and coffee, one gallon of kerosene for the lantern at $1.05

the gallon, some matches, needles for sewing, a half-pound of tea, and five pounds of sugar to put in it. That was all, and Ruth's first wage of the coming month was gone. Rather to our amazement, we realized that out of this money, which we supposed, even in this small amount, would be a godsend to the family, no *food* had been bought. It seemed to us that we had not helped the family improve a whit from what they were.

As this list of items seemed to satisfy them, I signed for it, and Cyrus or Johnny would sled the two days' travel to the store at once to claim the credit and bring back the pitiful items. We left a pound of tea from our own provisions as well as a tin of tobacco in exchange for our lodging: we had come well stocked with each. Our fare was baked fish while we stayed there, and we furnished some loaves of bread for everybody which was eaten so eagerly that time was not taken to so much as thaw it in the chilled house. The mother informed us that the tots liked our bread so much that they wanted to come along and live with Connie. I think Connie would have taken them, at that, except that I put a stop to it. The sharp old eye of their mother boded trouble, and we should not dare to take the responsibility, even if the home we could offer them might be better than the one they left. Cyrus and Alice had had ten children altogether, and of these but six lived. Connie was happy to get Ruth out of there. What a future for a young girl, Connie thought, crouched in darkness in an igloo where one could not even stand erect, and a slave to the mother who ordered her about!

Flaming banners of northern lights, veiling the stars, undulated across the clear sky as we traveled onward about our visiting in the very midst of the arctic night. Ook-sook again ran ahead, while Connie and Ruth rode, and I drove. The dawn stole softly over the white low Colville delta, while little wisps of steam arose from the trotting dogs. The freshly iced runners slid over the snow and on and on the trail stretched. Several sleds had passed this way, yet it wasn't a trail either because the tracks wandered about over the broad river, scarcely leaving any continuous indentation in the hard-packed snow.

The next stop was the home of Ruth's younger married sister, Carrie, age seventeen. Built of sticks and sod, and snow-covered in the usual manner, it looked nonetheless like a palace inside, owing to the difference in the living habits and outlook of the inhabitants compared with what we had just left. Using the same materials, this 8'

X 10' home, with a 6-foot roof sloping to 4 feet at the walls, was tight, clean, neat, and the coziest little nest of a young married couple you ever saw anywhere. No couple are cozier, I think, in their Park Avenue flat than Little Jacob and his Carrie.

The house spoke not of money but of careful work and planning. Everything inside was in such perfect arrangement that we were almost taken aback. The house was built atop a little knoll so that in entering the snow alley, one went *up* rather than *down.* This is in keeping with a prime principle in building arctic dwellings: that heat goes up, and if the entrance is above the room, the household heat continually manages to escape, but if the entrance is at a slightly lower level than the room the heat can be conserved. Ruth's and Carrie's parents allowed their heat to escape by having the entrance to their igloo come in from above.

The driftwood walls inside this igloo were lined with sides of cardboard boxes which had apparently been obtained by asking at the trading post at Beechey Point. There was no frost on these walls, while the box sides threw back the reflected heat of one of the cleverest little tin can stoves we have yet seen anywhere. Built of two discarded five-gallon gasoline cans shoved together in a way that Connie and I have used ourselves in the arctic quite comfortably on occasion, this shiny little heater worked perfectly. It had a fitted pipe and roaring draft; it was set up erect on empty milk cans for legs. The stove had a fitted door with a wire latch and although it could not be expected to last indefinitely, not being made of very good material, it served better than Cyrus's own old burned-out stove, over which those people were moaning when we first saw them the previous summer and were still moaning now. Any camper can improvise this kind of stove and be warm with it.

All that is needed is an old gas can or oil can and a pocket- knife. Of course, for a really fancy job regular tools are preferred. To attach the stovepipe, you draw a circle the size of the stovepipe on one side near the closed end, and starting at the center of the circle, cut to the rim with the small blade of your knife, much as you would cut a pie, only making eight or ten pieces. Then you bend the pieces up so as to form a collar for the stovepipe to fit over. The door is made in the front or side by marking out the size and shape you want and then cutting it out with the pocketknife. If you have no hinges you can bend the top of the door up to form a small lip, and by making a corresponding lip on the piece of tin you have just cut out you have a hanging door; the draft comes in at the bottom. Such a stove has an advantage in that it is very lightweight to carry around. In any case, it is much to be preferred to the open campfire for cooking efficiency in any land, and it will heat your dwelling adequately even in the arctic, if you have a small tight dwelling. The stovepipe can be made of tin cans or any suitable pieces of tin or pipe.

Since this type of stove has no oven, the young couple we are describing ate everything boiled that they didn't eat as *quak*, except for a kind of biscuits or pancakes they could fry in the skillet; these are often, I suppose, referred to in books on camping as "bannock."

Four of these pancakes, golden brown, happened to be warming in a pan as we crawled into the house. Wiggling onto a caribou rug and reaching into the cupboard which sat by the wall on the floor, Ruth prepared tea for the four of us as familiarly as though she had been to this little house many times. We each got a pancake and ate it docilely and with much gratitude. Carrie's husband was present, and he said little. He didn't speak any English. Carrie was absent on her trap line and we waited with interest to meet her, the keeper of this doll's house, wondering if she would be as nice as Ruth.

Finally, she came. Of taller stature than squat little Ruth, with a tall white wolf hood fringing her blooming cheeks, she was a wild sort of beauty, half a child and half a woman. She was heavy with pregnancy. Contentment shone from this unusual face in a way which quickened the dullest observer, as she took a frozen red fox from her pack and tossed it to thaw in back of the stove on the woodpile.

The eyes of Little Jacob, a bit older, not a handsome man himself, and rather like the average grocer or bank clerk or someone of the sort in our own society, followed his gentle wife. He had a small trimmed black mustache and his eyes were veiled to others; he was no extrovert like Ook-sook. Later that evening as he lay smoking on his elbows in their bed and all seven of us were preparing for sleep, I saw them looking into each other's eyes. Carrie was one of those women who are born to be protected and adored—and she was. Alice had told us about Carrie, come to think of it—her daughter who had always said she would do no work that she did not wish to do. Her husband had built this house for her with his own hands and installed her in it. He had even baked those pancakes we had eaten.

Few of the Eskimos we know have slant eyes, button noses, or the "Oriental" cast of countenance. Carrie has a very fair skin; her shiny black hair, coarse as a horse's mane, looks native in texture, but the way it falls to her shoulders thickly in an untrained natural long bob is anything but typical Eskimo. Poor Ruth's hair now is flat and skimpy, with a pigtail tied in a string down the back. Ruth's eyes are two genial almonds. But Carrie's eyes, wide, swimming, open, are "American" eyes. Several of the other children in this family have this same kind of eyes. Carrie has slender arms and long delicate hands. The figures of most Eskimo women and of the men also are beyond reproach for their type and build; they are a strongly built people without being fat. Very, very rarely does one see a fat person among the Eskimos—so out the window with another superstition we have held about them Of course big fluffy parkas make all of us who wear them look fat, but the parka makes for illusion. The Eskimos do not admire fat people. Connie learned from Ruth presently that the women dread getting fat and that all of the people have some pride about keeping in good condition. Much of their uniformity of figure in this way I believe is accounted for by their meat diet, which tends to build a strong rather than a fat flabby people.

Just four nights later, to our immense amusement, Ook- sook patted his belly upon finishing supper with us after running all day on the trail, grinned and plainly said: "Diet."

"What?" we said, not believing our ears, asking him to repeat it.

"Ook-sook diet," he explained lucidly. Connie and I just gaped. "Now where did he pick that up?"

The temperature was somewhere around fifty below zero in the darkness of early morning when we left Little Jacob's house to travel onward. By two that afternoon, after seven hours of steady travel, we could have been seen icing the runners as we stopped to make tea at the Itkillik-pas; the corn bread I chopped with the ax broke and chipped like coal, and when we tried to eat it, it froze to our tongue and lips. The tea was scalding and tasted smoky and the corn bread which we dunked into our cups in an attempt to thaw it out so that it could be bitten came up coated with ice from its own cold. So much for eating out of doors in such temperatures. We never achieved pictures of Eskimos eating raw frozen fish or meat out of doors in winter because they don't eat out of doors.

From here our party began cutting overland across the loops of the

Colville River where the sled broke through in the softer drifts of the inland prairie.

Soon we came upon the tracks of a sled which Ook-sook said belonged to his brother Leffingwell. Leffingwell, named after the explorer, but presumably no relative, is an example of the Eskimo children who have been named after explorers or people whom the Eskimos have liked. Leffingwell had gone to Barrow months past to trade skins and buy supplies; we had all rather worried because he had not got back, so that the sight of his sled track on the prairie was great news. Presently we found a cache of things he had brought, intended for Beechey Point. Connie and I hoped for our mail, and rummaged through the cache, but were disappointed. Later we learned the reason for Leffingwell's long stay: he had been in the government hospital at Barrow with pneumonia. Our own disappointment about our mail was grievous when we realized, by signs and otherwise, that the carefree Leffingwell had never thought to stop at the post office at Barrow and bring the mail back with him.

Darkness came, and we were still miles from our destination. The dogs smelled something in the snow; Ook-sook shot forward and beat them to it. He picked it up joyfully—a piece of whale blubber, which had tumbled off the sled preceding us a few hours before. Yes, the Barrow people had killed whale after all, late in the fall! Later we learned the details and that they had secured three whales in all. This news was several months old in coming to us.

The familiar banks of the Colville loomed in the darkness. The tired dogs would stop whenever the sled hit some slight incline of a drift and I would have to shake the sled to start them again, for when the sled stopped with its 600-pound load, it would quickly freeze down to the spot.

Connie, riding on the sled, had refrigerated quite stiff. The girls were never properly dressed. Connie needed fur pants or some kind of long fur leggings over her trousers, besides her parka for a long trip. But Nanny never got around to providing these that year, while Ruth, a lady of fashion, would never have considered wearing them if she had had them.

In the pitch darkness of snow and shadows and starlight we at last smelled smoke. The dogs knew the end of the trail was near and the last half mile was covered at a great rate. Suddenly the darkness erupted people all about us, dogs barked uproariously, the smell of smoke and habitation was intense now, and friendly hands grabbed the towline to help the dogs make the last grade up a bank to the house.

The house which stood on that bank resembled a glass greenhouse. It was lighted up by a lantern which shone through the glass windows! This was the alleyway leading into the house, which was made of panes of clear lake ice or river ice cut at the right thickness for glass early last fall—a real work of native Eskimo art! The tribe of some fifteen souls, Matthew's People, that happy family, led us en masse into a large dwelling covered with snow blocks which we recognized as a driftwood igloo. The driftwood had been hauled from the ocean. Matthew's People inhabit it by winter and, so we understand, periodically move the house around piece by piece, up and down the river during the different years, according to where the whitefish are running the thickest.

Exhausted, frostbitten, wreathed in ice, absolutely famished for food, our party staggered into the warm dwelling. We found ourselves so tired we could hardly get out of our parkas; the old lady, Ook-sook's mother, pulled Connie out of hers. Ook-sook and his brothers unhitched our dogs and tied them to toggles with the forty resident dogs, each dog tied just far enough away so that he could not fight with his neighbor. The dogs lay down waiting anxiously for their meat which must be cooked indoors.

Inside we saw that the plank floor of the room was lined with fragrant willow branches and with the bedding, hides, and duffel sacks of the hunting clan who were beaming at us. The interior was mellowly lit with three generous fish-oil trays; these lamps do not smoke and are very pleasant. Vigorous women, Ook-sook's sisters, who knew us well, hastened to thrust more sticks into the roaring large stove and to set food before us; they had long heavy braids of black hair and their bedewed foreheads were quite as shiny as when we had seen them before in the heat of summer: apparently, they were always this way.

The usual table top without legs was spread upon the floor for us. There was *akotuk* or Eskimo ice cream, made in this country beyond the timber with mashed caribou tallow and dried meat; there was scalding tea with canned milk and sugar; and baked whitefish to start with. First, I think I shall pause to further elaborate upon the charms of the whitefish, so that this creature may get really its proper due. I quote from Ernest Thompson Seton for support, who said many years ago:

It is difficult to convey to the outside the charm of the word, "whitefish." Any northerner will tell you that it is the only fish that is perfect human food, the only food that man or dog never wearies of, the only lake food that conveys no disorder no matter how long or freely it is used.

It is so delicious and nourishing that there is no fish in the world that can even come second to it. It is far superior in all food qualities to the finest Salmon or Trout. They [are] radiantly white, celestial in color; their backs a dull frosted silver, with here and there a small electric lamp behind the scales to make its jewels sparkle. The lamps alternated with opals increased on the side; the bellies were of a blazing mother-of-pearl. It would be hard to imagine a less imaginative name than "white" fish for such a shining, burning opalescence. Indian names are usually descriptive, but their name for this is simply "the Fish." All others are mere dilutes and cheap imitations. The Indian who has his scaffold hung with Whitefish when winter comes, is accounted rich.

"And what," says the pessimist, "is the fly in all this precious ointment?" Alas! It is no game fish; it will not take bait, spoon, or fly, and its finest properties vanish in a few hours after capture.

The Whitefish served in the marble palaces of other lands is as mere dishwater to champagne when compared to the three times purified and ten times intensified dazzling silver COREGONUS as it is landed on the bleak shores of those far-away lakes.[1]

Mr. Seton did not go into the various kinds of whitefish there are, but we shall go one step further in saying that the farther north you go, the sweeter are the flavors of fish, in our experience. It was the whitefish of the waters of Great Slave Lake nearly a thousand miles south of here that the famous naturalist was speaking of in those former days! The whitefish which Ook-sook's family caught in the Colville River were

---

1   Ernest Thompson Seton, *The Arctic Prairies*, pp. 183-184. Charles Scribner's Sons, New York, 1917.

different again from our little fourteen-inch whitefish of the Arctic Ocean in being thick-sided, heavy, and weighing up to fifteen pounds each. As Mr. Seton has intimated, no people of southerly civilization know what real fish flavors are, because the fish of southern waters do not have them, and secondly, the people of civilization do not get fish fresh as a rule. Fresh fish do not have that strong "fishy" flavor disliked by those who say they do not like fish; fish are sweet, in their original state, and have no perceptible odor.

Fish caught under ice in winter are better than summer fish! They get fatter and better as winter progresses. Again, the summer sportsman and his friends eat fish at their poorest! The fact that the fish are lean and often even wormy in summer, at the time when underwater vegetation seems most abundant may be due to their breeding cycle— for fish spawn in summer.

Our eyes bugged out when we saw a huge roasting pan filled with hunks of this baked whitefish; alas, it was served salt less and cold. In another pan we spied a great roast of caribou which set our mouths watering. "Roasted rare," we thought. It was in a roasting pan, all right, but it was not from the oven it was brought. It was brought from out of doors, to be placed before us! There it sat in the beautiful roaster, completely raw! A bucket filled with cubes of raw frozen whale blubber was set beside it. Such was dinner, and we ate it, since we were starved enough to do so. *Mucktuk,* or black whale skin, with a little blubber attached, is considered one of the delicacies of the North. The only hot thing we got for our meal was the tea, and on thinking it over we realized this had been more or less true every place we visited. If fish and meat were boiled expressly for us while we waited, in each case it was allowed to cool before it was eaten. Eskimos do not like hot food. The more primitive and unchanged the Eskimos you are visiting the more true this holds. Cold food that is rich and fatty, such as the Eskimos eat a good deal of, probably warms the body as quickly as hot food when one is in the vigorous health of arctic outdoor living; it has staying powers and its warmth becomes one's own. Cooked food is eaten cold so that it can be taken in the fingers, for there are few dishes and spoons and forks. A bag of peanuts brought from the Barrow Native Store was passed around at the completion of this meal.

Of all the foods we ate and of which we were skeptical, the only one that really puzzled us was a horrible-looking kind of mush like mixture.

"What is it?" Connie asked me, rather doubtfully.

"It may be some mixture of fat and brains," I told her, to make a guess.

At this point Ook-sook's sister Bessie came to our assistance. "Role-owe," she said, and several people repeated, "Role- owe."

"Role-owe," I said. "Role-owe, what?"

Obligingly Bessie went out and brought in the box. It was Rolled Oats. It had been boiled for hours like beans until you couldn't tell what it was by consistency. But I suppose we should have been able to tell what it was by taste.

I have no wish to change anyone's food habits; I only want to point out that what is good food to one person may seem an unbearable hardship to another, and usually the more ignorant the person, the more biased his viewpoint towards the strange, especially when his imagination starts to work. If people, ask us how we could stand to live on the food of the Eskimos and how we could give up foods of our own civilization I can only say that the world is too interesting a place to roam in to be limited by the range of com and cattle. If other people wish to lead their lives confined by their appetites and limited by their stomachs, that is their own affair, but for us we cannot see it. Adaptability is its own greatest reward—for the fact is that we came to enjoy the strange foods and the strange life more than we would ever have thought possible.

While I passed around a package of cigarettes to each smoker in the family, one of Ook-sook's brothers struck up a chant on a stringed guitar made of dried braided caribou back tendons stretched over an oil can; the group chanted rhythmic Eskimo songs without self-consciousness to entertain the visitors and probably because they were happy. Someone produced a pack of cards and the young men and I played on a caribou skin blanket. The game was of Eskimo invention, called *parnuk*; everyone on the coast knew it, and I had picked it up. As the next day was to be Sunday, I knew we would have to remain over. The Eskimos are so adverse to traveling or hunting or doing any work on that day, due to missionary influence, that there was nothing else to do but just take it easy, be entertained, and relax.

I happen to recall that Ruth's feet hurt her because she had put too small soles on her boots. There is a serious danger of freezing the feet in such weather if boots or fur stockings are in the least bit tight. Connie suggested to Ruth that now she could sew on some new soles and enlarge her boots during our stay, but Ruth said flatly, "No sewing. It is Sunday." There was no more to be said on that. So, we sat and chanted the second day, played cards, had services, and ate many meals.

Sunday evening a little girl with very pretty hands began to explore Ook-sook's mother's scalp as a sort of indoors occupation, while we watched covertly, wondering. With a quick motion the little girl caught something. She put it on the bottom of a white enamel cup the nodding old lady held in her lap, and the old lady took some satisfaction in mashing whatever it was against the hard surface with her ancient thumbnail. Ruth explained to Connie in their moments of confidence weeks later that all Eskimos have lice. It took some time for the truth to come out in full. Nowhere had we seen people scratching where we visited; even little Hattie and Thomas had not scratched much while the white people were present; such remarkable restraint! You see the Eskimos are rather ashamed of their lice nowadays, but they consider them inevitable, like mosquitoes in summer, and they have no way to get rid of them. Yes, one by one Ruth named over the people we had lived and boarded and bedded with, and they all were inhabited by the undesirable crawling creatures. There are few Eskimos in the world who do not have body lice or are potentially a host to them because Eskimos are great travelers and visitors and the lice go right along with them from family to family, from Greenland to Siberia, from Baffin Land to Ellesmere, carried in the robes of the caribou, from which, up to present times, they have never been successfully eliminated. Freezing kills the lice periodically, and periodically the teachers and nurses at Barrow delouse the children, and this helps. But as long as the Eskimos visit with each other and travel about, new lice are brought along or picked up to replenish the number of the ancient human pests, which have lived with these humans since times immemorial. Ruth and Ook-sook and Connie and I were able to delouse our family by using precious wood alcohol brought to prime the primus stove, and after that we lived fairly isolated from visitors for much of the winter.

Nanny Woods and friends

Some of the Woods family

3

I had been asleep several hours when I awoke with a start. Loud commands in Eskimo, or rather roars, filled the dark house. I couldn't decide what the uproar was about. Could it be that this was the alarm for us all to get up? But I didn't think so, from observing Eskimos thus far. Then I heard a pattering over the roof above our heads and dogs beating a retreat. It was just that the dogs had been up on the roof trying to steal the meat from the top of the house. This is an easy matter for any dog that happens to break loose because the roof and the ground are all on a level of drifted snow. Therefore, old Matthew had just told the dogs to beat it.

The next I knew the fish oil lamps, augmented by our kerosene lantern, were burning brightly and the smell of coffee filled the house. It was Monday morning and the Sabbath was gone. Some shivering little eight-year-old girls helped to hitch up our two dog teams. A mother dog which had recently whelped was wrapped in a "dog parka" of caribou to protect her belly from the cold as she was put into the harness. The going from here on inland was softer sledding, so we had hired one of Ook-sook's brothers to go along with us with his own sled to share our load and help make the camps—Koloyuk, the singer. He wanted five dollars a day. I asked, "How many days to get there?"

"Three days."

"All right," I said, "I'll give you fifteen dollars for the trip if you will get us there. You will get fifteen dollars at the end of the trip no matter how many days it takes." Kolo-yuk agreed to this.

All day we traveled over typical prairie land with grass showing above the snow everywhere. That night we camped beside a big frozen lake where a few willows grew. Wolves howled, and our dogs answered; we ate boiled whitefish and slept within our tent.

In interior arctic Alaska we found that the wind rarely blows. Thus, you can camp for a day or two in a single tent without discomfort if a few sticks for fuel are present, although there is some hazard connected with this, as will appear later. The soft snow makes erecting a snow house difficult if not impossible in some areas.

As we were breaking camp the next morning, a lone raven circled low overhead. A few ravens spend the winter here as do some falcons. The cold in itself is not the determining factor in the distribution of most wild creatures, but their range is controlled perhaps entirely by their food supply.

After three full days' travel from Matthew's camp we arrived at our destination as promised. This was about ten acres of little willows growing about five feet tall. They grew in a loop of the Itkillik River sheltered by some high bluffs on one side. In the heart of the caribou grounds, in a spot probably altogether inaccessible by summer, we pitched our camp. Ook-sook chose the campsite for I knew he understood this land better than I; he was qualified to do so from all his life's experiences. His judgment did not fail.

This camp we pitched with care. First of all, trash and snow were cleared off down to the ground and the tent was pitched, the stove set up in its accustomed place inside, and we moved in. The girls were tired; we all were, for that matter. Tomorrow we would make the snow house and complete winter camp. I will describe the snow house in some detail for it is the easiest, simplest, and warmest structure that I know of in the winter arctic.

Because it was not possible to get snow suitable for blocks nearby we had to haul our blocks by sled with the dogs a distance of half a mile from where fortunately there was a hard-packed drift in the open river bottom. The snow walls were constructed all around the tent out of three-foot blocks sawed out of the drift with our saw; the blocks were six inches thick and cut off the surface of the drift in its hardest parts. After carefully transporting them on our sled to the willow patch we built two layers of them around the tent, leaving a six-inch space between tent and snow walls. The front and back walls we built up to the height of the ridgepole of the tent and shaved them down with a snow knife so that they sloped gently from the ridgepole to the somewhat lower snow walls. After chinking all the cracks carefully with soft snow and cutting a doorway, we then threw the extra canvas 12' X 14' tarpaulin over the top. Our structure now looked square. There was a place fitted up with a tin safety for the stovepipe. When we had this cover in place we put snow blocks a foot high on top of the walls to hold the canvas cover down all around the sides. A blow on top with our mittens settled them firmly in place so that they froze solid. After standing a day or two the snow walls froze together like iron in all their parts, especially as some escaping heat from the interior glazed them and turned them into ice. No gale the rest of the winter would be likely to blow these walls down and the tent was protected from the outside elements. Over the doorway we hung a canvas curtain and the camp was complete. The curtain was long enough so that we could latch ourselves inside when settled by securing it with a stick of wood. Such a camp may not require a snow alleyway for its entrance if it is built in a sheltered spot. Along the coast you must have a snow alleyway, and preferably one with a turn in it, to escape the wind. On the coast the canvas roof is also replaced by a complete snow roof supported by beams.

Koloyuk remained with us one extra day after he had helped us pitch our camp on the upper Itkillik, erecting his own small bachelor's tent and tin can stove, and boiling his own meat alone by preference nearby, from whence we could hear him happily singing and chanting the hours away. Then he hitched up his dogs and left one morning, when it seemed to him the right time to do so.

With winter camp made, Connie and Ruth settled down to making a cozy home of it and they succeeded very well. Ook-sook and I had to get to hunting caribou right away.

FOOD TO THE INLAND ARCTIC hunter means only one thing. Caribou would be our only food except for a little flour and the food concentrates we had brought here. Caribou: the very word has a charm all its own. Caribou are probably among the least understood of our game animals, although there is little mystery about them. The word "caribou" has always spelled mystery to the white man because the caribou's home is beyond the white man's usual reach. The sudden appearance and disappearance of caribou in the southern parts of their range have given rise to exaggerated estimates of the number of caribou there are.

In school I had learned that in the arctic there were six months of daylight and six months of darkness. Although there are many grown people who still believe this myth, the ones who have seen the arctic through its seasons know differently. It was now the darkest part of the year, mid- December, and we were going caribou hunting. In fact, we had to find caribou for food within the margin of a very few days. To an arctic hunter who knows caribou, this is like going to the meat market, and there is little of the heroic about it. It will be a matter of days, perhaps, but he is certain of his meat.

Whenever you talk of the arctic the question of equipment comes up. Our "equipment" was simpler than that most deer hunters carry for a week end in a thickly settled land. A battered sheet-iron stove (not the one we left in camp for the girls, but Ook-sook's own camping stove), a badly torn sled cover of canvas 7' X 9' (our trail tent), two common .30-30 rifles, one being in such a state of decrepitude that no civilized person would dream of using it, two common stewpots— the one for tea and the other for boiling meat, and they never had to be washed—tin plates, cups, spoons, sleeping bags, Ook-sook's own kerosene trail lantern, our pocketknives and matches. I kept my matches in a waterproof container; Ook-sook kept his matches inside his sealskin rifle case in a little pocket which had been made by hollowing out the gunstock until only a framework was left. As an Eskimo's clothing has no pockets, this nest was handy for Ook-sook to carry small possessions in, as sometimes extra shells for his rifle.

Our food was a pinch of tea in a jar, a sack of frozen biscuits already baked for us by Ruth (who had learned quickly from Connie), perhaps a pound of sugar, and a little salt in another jar—luxury for me, you might say, because I am fond of salt on my meat when I can get it. Our Eskimo clothing, dog team, and sled were the only equipment that the usual deer hunter in civilized lands doesn't need. We each had snowshoes along with us on the sled, which we needed to use part time, and of course I had my binoculars.

We started out with Ook-sook walking ahead over the prairie and picking the trail, while I tramped behind, driving the dogs and keeping the sled moving. It is quite a trick to run on snowshoes if the dogs start to run, without tripping and pitching headlong into the snow, but you learn. You also quickly learn how to jump onto the sled even with the clumsy snowshoes and catch a ride whenever the dogs speed up on hitting hard snow. Most of the time, however, you are pushing the sled to help it along, or you may drag sled and all the eight or nine dogs together across the prairie.

Ook-sook's dogs loved him, strange as it seemed to me, considering what he expected them daily to undergo. They got so they would obey me somewhat but there was never a question of whom they called boss.

The day was one of those calm inland arctic winter days when distance vanishes; we were in a world of dreamy white. The cliffs of the Colville River seemed close enough to come to soon—but we knew they were twenty miles away, those conspicuous landmarks beneath whose familiar scallops we had wound last summer through this prairie in a Canoe.

A flock of willow ptarmigan rocketed away as we crashed through a willow patch, only to vanish. White melted into white, leaving only the dark tail feathers to flash an assurance that the ghostly birds were real. The dogs put on a burst of speed at the sight of the game. Foolish dogs—they always thought they could catch it.

As we left the serpentine river bed of the Itkillik and climbed onto a ridge, or "hogback" as Westerners call it, caribou tracks wound across the sides of an elongated hill in a maze of trails. To an observer the pattern was reminiscent of a feed lot on a big range where thousands of cattle trampled. Wherever we went there were caribou tracks always before the eye, and we were never absent from them! There had been thousands of animals here a week ago. But today there were none, and there might not be any for the rest of the winter. The herds, while large, roam in an area of country that is still larger, and they are lost in it. The caribou which had scattered in summer had joined together in bands now, and such a band had simply fed by here, leaving their signs, and were gone. We would have to travel to find another band or, if lucky, we might find a few straggling groups from the main band.

The dogs knew what we were after. They had hunted these animals with their master all of their lives; at every main caribou highway, the leader would attempt to turn and follow. This kept me busy shouting gee, haw, and whoa—the terms which north Alaska Eskimos used to drive their dogs. The Eskimos learned to drive dogs in this way from the white men, for although these people have always had dogs they never used them in big teams until the white man introduced the idea and at the same time introduced the rifle to feed the dogs.

We had covered fifteen miles and darkness was gathering when from the end of a ridge I made out fourteen dark spots. As someone has since said jokingly, of my abilities to find caribou on the prairie: "He just counts their legs and divides by four." The spots seemed to float in space, but I knew that actually the caribou were lying down, since their position remained fixed. They were a good four or five miles away.

Ook-sook agreed with me that the spots were caribou. A big silver moon appeared which made it easier to travel because it cast definite shadows, while the reflected and diffused light of the sun below the horizon lit up a scene of blue and silver and rose, delicate beyond belief. As the moonlight grew stronger so also grew the sense of reality. That rock- topped ridge had definite shape now, due to shadows. No longer was it only a spot floating in space. The distant Colville cliffs took on a clear remoteness, while a silvery-lined shadow followed the palpitating form of each of our dogs in harness. Once more distance was readable to the human eye.

In an hour we were near the caribou. There had been a lake here once but now only a border of arctic willows some six feet high marked its outlines. Behind this convenient fringe we secured the dogs by tipping over the sled. We had made sure long before now that the wind was not in the caribou's favor as we chose the direction of our approach. Poets who have written about the arctic from their London garret and novelists who have depicted it from home and fireside always speak of it as silent. The silence of the arctic is a familiar phase. Well, I suppose it was silent tonight.

I could plainly hear Ook-sook walking a mile away, as he made his stalk and I made mine. The least sound will carry for miles on a still day in the low temperatures, which, added to the deer's natural sensitiveness, acts as ample protection to warn them of approaching enemies upon the prairies of winter. While we were yet a mile away from them, the sleeping caribou got up and began moving away. Ook-sook had known they would hear us but had hoped they might circle us to get our scent, and thus give one of us a chance for a shot.

But there was no use chasing caribou now. We would have to wait for the weather to change. We would have to wait for a wind when they couldn't hear us approach. A blizzard is fine caribou hunting weather for the Eskimo! Almost all of our kills have been made in the midst of what a person in civilization would call a ferocious raging blizzard.

Beside the fringe of willows, we might as well make camp. A snow house such as the Alaska Eskimos use when traveling was new to me and I watched the proceedings carefully. Ook-sook selected a piece of snow that held him up when he walked over it. Next, he cut it into some rectangle some five by nine feet long, using a piece of broken crosscut saw he had brought along. Sawing the block squarely in two the long way, he then cut it into equal thirds crosswise as we might cut a rectangular cake. The respective blocks he stood up on their ends to form a wall around the pit exposed from taking them out. Since the drift was a foot deep and the blocks three feet high, when we were finished we had a snow- house four feet high. Snow blocks were cut for the ends and put in place. Last, the old sled cover was stretched over the top of the walls, making a roof for our house which was satisfactory enough for our temporary camp and a great deal safer than an ordinary camper's tent, unprotected by any snow walls, would be. Snow blocks placed on top of the canvas to hold it down soon froze securely there as the structure solidified. A piece of sacking served for a tiny door. Willow brush made a mat for our sleeping bags since we yet had no "bed skins" by which to insulate our poor flooring. Of course, some extra caribou skins always should go along with the northern camper wherever he goes, but we didn't have them yet. The little gas-can stove inside heated up the place quickly when we had crawled inside with our few sticks, and we soon had tea and biscuits. The heat from the stove did not melt the snow walls because the snow blocks were porous and the heat within was equalized by the intensity of the cold outside.

The biggest problem in this life is feeding the dogs. It took probably two hours in all to boil the dog bucket on the tiny stove within our tiny snow house. How did we get enough wood to do it? Well, I suppose the fact that we actually did shows how much fuel can be found upon the prairie. Sometimes when we could not get enough fuel where we camped, we boiled the dogs' food and our own with the primus stove; sometimes, when very hard up, we would be obliged to feed our dogs and ourselves only *quak*. But it is considered much more important to give the dogs their one warm meal in the evening than all other considerations, for the hunter's own strength in this land depends on the mobility of his dogs and their stamina.

"Tomorrow's another day," I told Ook-sook, as, having discarded our fur parkas, our fur pants, our several sets of underthings and all, we settled down inside our sleeping bags within the tiny snow house. Ook-sook's old kerosene trail lantern hung on the snow wall into which its handle had been stuck. I stuck two matches into the wall beside it and blew it out.

A BREAKFAST OF TEA AND biscuits leaves much to be desired from the standpoint of a hunter. Perhaps this was why we started hunting the next morning while it was yet only moonlight. We had very little more feed for the dogs; their slim breakfast of frozen fish from the Colville was in fact the last food we had.

A haze obscured objects at four or five hundred yards. We had traveled half a mile when out of the haze dim shapes appeared, coming towards us. Beloved caribou: Ook-sook and I both knew it simultaneously. Down into the snow we flopped, having grabbed our rifles in their cases from the sled. Our white snow shirts which we used at times in our prairie hunting merged into our surroundings. As the caribou came on at a quick gait straight for us, we saw that they were four old bulls. At seventy yards we opened fire and all four fell within a few feet of each other. When we examined them, one proved to be a reindeer with a Barrow tag in its ear. The only way either of us could tell it from a caribou was by its identification tag, since it had gone wild and joined the wild caribou.

Why had these deer been so easily secured this morning? Had they heard us and thought we were caribou? I think they were just traveling our way and bumped into us, for if a hunter stays in the caribou grounds, caribou are almost certain to come right to him sooner or later.

Ook-sook skinned two and I skinned two. I was certainly glad to have the help of another skinner this year, for Connie was no skinner in our hunts, only an assistant at best; skinning at forty or fifty below zero, which must be done barehanded, is no lark. It is best to have plenty of practice at skinning in the warmer temperatures before one tries this. "Well," I thought, "I guess I'll have Ook-sook skin everything I can from now on and live a life of luxury."

I noted he poured the blood into the center of his skins and when it froze solid he cut the skin in a circle. Saving the blood for the dogs and handling it in bulk in this way was convenient except for the fact that it ruined all the skins for human use. Why save heavy old bull skins? For tent floor and bedding, I tried to explain. Ook-sook thought me crazy, but he didn't know how to say so. I managed to save my two skins and one of his to take back to camp for the girls, on the understanding that Ruth would thaw and scrape and fix them—which I subsequently learned she was not too willing to do. But she had to do it to live with us.

We had seen people shivering because they had no bedding and flooring in their tents, yet to Ook-sook—and he was no exception to Eskimo psychology—a caribou skin was extra bother on his sled unless he needed it himself.

After eating and resting in a snow camp, we would leave for home the next day. In the field Ook-sook and I fell into the habit of eating the tongues, brains, and fatty delicacies first, since we were always too hungry to resist them; here we ate all four of the caribou heads. Had I not eaten a good many caribou before this time, it is possible that I would have had the usual civilized person's squeamishness about a strange food, but it so happened that Connie and I had learned to eat the heads of caribou and moose during periods in which you might say that we were "starving," in the sense that we had nothing else to eat. Therefore, it was no surprise to me to find head meat a favorite among the Eskimos, and to learn that since heads are bulky to carry the heads are often eaten first in the field. Cleaning the heads up satisfactorily is easy in the clean snow, where they may be chopped up for the kettle and cooked in sections.

Next day we loaded all four carcasses on the sled and prepared to start back to our main camp. It looked like too much of a load to me, but I figured Ook-sook should know how much his dogs could pull. After several attempts, he had to give up. He might not know the names of sugar, tea, or bread in English, but Ook-sook did know how to use the Lord's name in vain, I'm afraid. Mule skinners and dog drivers have that trait in common, but at least a mule isn't always looking for some scented pole that lies a little off the trail and a mule skinner doesn't have half as many mules to get untangled as a dog driver has dogs.

We were obliged to dump half the load. The trail was broken towards home and because Ook-sook could get more pull out of the dogs than I could, I walked ahead. We had left traps beside the extra meat; a return trip would have to be made for it. The reflected light of day faded once more, leaving the illumination to the great globe of the moon and the countless freshly polished stars. From afar came the sullen boom of a frozen lake as the lowering temperature wedged open some crack. I was warm, and I carried my mittens in my bare hand at intervals and loosened the rope which I had tied around my furry waist for a belt or threw back my hood until it barely covered my ears, which is the arctic person's way of cooling his overheated blood and preventing the sweating into his furs which is one of the dangers and annoyances he must avoid.

The air was calm and the scene a study in white moonlight. From afar back of me the words, "Go ahead, Duk," drifted up and I could plainly hear the heavy sled creak and the dogs pant, although they were a half mile away. Ook- sook's snowshoes made a terrific din when I paused for a moment in my own stride, although he was but a spot in the distance.

Fifteen hours' travel today since that breakfast of fatty caribou heads. How could a man feel tired upon such a day? Aside from a fox trail crossing the old caribou trails we were the only signs of life in a polar world.

Then—there it was, the thing all travelers dream of, the end of the trail. A plume of smoke spiraled up a quarter of a mile distant from the cliffs of the Itkillik, straight up from the snow house where Connie and Ruth resided, while wisps of steam could be seen trailing from the white walls themselves.

It is a pleasant feeling to return home from a successful hunt, bringing in the meat. You are tired and hungry as an arctic wolf must be—and a warm camp and food and friends await you. We weren't disappointed either. Soon there would be Eskimo card games and laughter in our house again. Ruth, who had gone outside the house many times each day to stand listening for our coming, had heard our approach in the stillness and told Connie an hour ago. The girls in their pretty Eskimo dresses walked out on the trail a few yards and met the hunters with enthusiasm. Inside, the teapot waited, boiling.

Little Jacob's home on the Colville

Overnight camp on the tundra

4

As soon as Ook-sook had made a trip back to get the other two caribou which were left on the prairie and he and the dogs had rested at camp for a day, he and I took off for Beechey Point to haul rations from the store. It would be a round trip of some three hundred miles for a few things, and we would be gone over Christmas and the New Year, yet it was necessary to go. I would be back for Connie's birthday in early January. Connie and Ruth had plenty of dead willows standing about for fuel, and the pile of caribou meat we had brought would supply them. Many people would consider leaving two women to keep camp alone while they made a three-hundred-mile trip for food a dangerous thing to do. This may be true or not, depending on how you look at it. Surely no one thought so here. Connie is one of those hunters who are as completely at home in the arctic as is any white man you can name on the average, and her only complaint, if any, would have been that life for her right now was more quiet than usual.

I shall not trouble the reader in going over every bump in the trail on that same long trip with Ook-sook and me in all its details. Suffice it to say that Ook-sook and I were subsequently absent from our main camp for as long as two weeks at a time on our various wanderings that winter, and that I ran beside the dogs easily a thousand miles during this time, and Ook-sook doubtless more than that.

Midwinter is the happiest season of the year for the arctic dweller because there is plenty of daylight for travel from house to house and the people take advantage of it to go visiting, inasmuch as this is a time of vacation from work. The trapping season has been open a month and the trappers now have money to spend for the luxuries of life, mainly tobacco and tea. The fish runs have ended, and most people have big caches of whitefish. This is the time to wear your best furs and to put your best foot forward. The delicacies in food which the more provident have saved are brought out. The unfortunate or less provident take advantage of hospitality to enjoy themselves by visiting their neighbors.

Two nights out upon our journey we reached Matthew's camp on the Colville. The house seemed deserted as we drew up. Our dogs had put on their best show of speed as we approached their old home. Ook-sook's aged mother, the matriarch, came out to greet us. "Are you cold?" she asked me in Eskimo.

"No," I replied in the same language and began to have a new feeling: I was actually learning some Eskimo. The old mother smiled broadly, beckoning us inside. I was about to enter the "glass" storm porch when I saw a figure that resembled a walking bundle of sticks.

"Matthew, willows," Ook-sook explained; he was learning some English. It is the duty of the children and old people to gather fagots.

As I have often said, fuel for the day is all that is generally gathered, and old Matthew was coming home with it; he was nearly hidden beneath his burden which he had gathered from a thicket a quarter of a mile away and had tied into a bundle slung over his back.

Ook-sook and I were soon sitting beside the stove within enjoying a lunch of *akotuk,* tea, boiled caribou, biscuits, strips of raw dried old bull back fat from last summer, and the large delicious baked cold whitefish which are so typical of Matthew's household. Some whitefish which had been cured in a poke were new to me. They had been first dried in the sun of summer on racks and then were put into a sealskin poke where they had cooked by fermentation in oil. They tasted a little better to me than even the smoked salmon of which I was so fond southward on the Yukon. The open hospitality that I met among the Eskimos never fails to impress me even when I think of it now. These people believe in eating while you have food, a philosophy which serves them well as a hunting and fishing people, and one that fast becomes agreeable to anybody who remains in this land or himself is a hunter.

Most of the young people had gone to Richard's house, we learned, to celebrate Christmas, leaving only the old folks at home or those who couldn't go. The old people were preparing to start snaring ptarmigan and old Matthew showed me how to make the snares of braided caribou sinew.

We played cards until nearly midnight; then Matthew, honorable old man, cut the shavings for morning. This is done by holding a stick in your left hand. You brace one end against your chest and, with the knife held much as a draw knife is held, with your right hand you shave the stick. The result should be a sizable bunch of curled blossoms of the texture of excelsior which are your tinder for the lighting of the stove beside your head tomorrow morning. The Eskimos are very fast at cutting these shavings. I achieved a fair proficiency at it under their tutelage.

In the dim light next morning we were sledding down the Colville; Matthew was going as far as the Itkillik-pas to pick up a sled load of willow fagots there, so I rode upon his empty sled. We had left a lot of our trail equipment at Matthew's house because from here on we would be visiting each night; our sled was much lighter. Dropping old Matthew at the Itkillik junction we sped onward down the hard-packed snow towards the windy coast.

We had hoped to stay at Little Jacob's but when we arrived there no one was home. Jacob and Carrie had gone with their sled the 240 miles to Barrow so that Carrie might have her baby in the government hospital. Night had come; there was no wood at Jacob's house. Because the Eskimo does not have the fear associated with lack of fuel that the sparsely dressed resident of the timber regions knows, he does not always leave fuel ready at his residence for his return or for the benefit of the next traveler, as we do. After discussion, we decided to head for the fish camp eight miles below in the delta. We had intended to make this in two days' travel rather than in one day, but rather than camp alone in a fuelless house we continued on.

It was seven o'clock in the morning when we had started, and it was five in the evening now. Ook-sook ran ahead of the dogs to encourage them. By six it was very dark, and we lighted our lantern. I can still see Ook-sook's fur-clad figure running ahead while the lantern bobbed and jumped like a drunken firefly. I was dog-tired. Just being exposed to a continuous cold temperature of forty degrees or more below zero all day will make you hungry and sleepy without running. Low temperatures quickly tell on one's endurance as well as on his wind, for breathing is hard in the heavy atmosphere. It is in the low temperatures that the effects of smoking most quickly show up on a person in the arctic, according to the explorers Peary and Stefansson, to name but two. They would not bother with smokers in their expeditions. I believe that it was because he was one of the few young men on our coast who did not smoke that our Ook-sook was the most tireless cold-weather runner of all the young men. I alternately ran and rode upon the sled and Ook-sook ran all the time. At nine o'clock at night, after fourteen hours of steady running in these temperatures, Ook-sook saw a lantern glowing ahead over a vastness of level white; warm food and rest lay where that tiny flame burned.

With that special dash all Eskimo sled dogs save up for their entrance into the next camp, our tired old pooches overtook Ook-sook and he jumped on the sled and we rode up to Lynd's camp in style. Mr. Lynd had just been chopping a few sticks. Here with his totally blind wife Mart, his two children and adopted little Hazel, he lived. He had only one dog and a little sled. The old fellow caught fish here in the delta during the early part of the winter before the ice got too thick to manage the nets. His wood had to be hauled to this barren spot from miles across the bay and he even made trips to Beechey Point on foot at times. I had always admired the old fellow, for he did better with what he had than many men half his age. Because his wife was blind, he had to do all the sewing for the children, which is properly women's work.

We were served fish *quak* and I gave Lynd a package of cigarettes which made his face light up in a radiant smile. They were out of everything, so we left all our tea with them. It wasn't much, for we were out of everything ourselves.

Roast whitefish for breakfast sent us off to a good start towards the more prosperous camp of Richard down the line. The now familiar Colville delta and flat arctic coast to the eastward drifted by slowly, our dogs trotting away in a world of white like so many ants on a string. Daylight came and faded. After a while I began to play that old game an arctic sled traveler plays in midwinter. It goes something like this. You begin to wonder if you aren't in sight of your destination, although your better judgment tells you aren't.

"Now could that dark spot ahead be a house? No, it's just a mud bank."

It turns out to be a piece of dirt no larger than a pancake. Steadfastly your eyes search into the white void, for you recall you have often seen your destination pop out of it. Often a dark spot becomes the chimney of a house.

How does one keep from getting lost? Timing one's trip with his watch and clocking the mileage is the main thing in this kind of navigation; you also learn how to strike a course by the lay of the drifts. For instance, you may be cutting straight across all the drifts at right angles, and you must keep this angle the same. You learn to tell old drifts from new and to know from which direction the wind has been blowing of late, and if the wind veers, you must quickly observe it. I had a pocket compass, but with Ook-sook did not have to use it in this familiar territory.

At last, there it was—a dark spot that became Richard's house with refuse scattered around it and perhaps fifty dogs chained to a cast anchor and all barking at once. In the dusk I shook hands with all the many people from old to young, and once inside I no doubt shook hands with some all over again.

There is no holiday in all the year, except the Fourth of July, which has such importance to the Eskimos as Christmas— although they do not rightly understand the meaning of either. After a quick lunch for an appetizer, games were in order, I saw. My long legs and big feet were a never- ending source of amusement to the people; the Eskimos have feet many sizes smaller than we normally have. We played Eskimo cards and a game similar to Pin the Tail on the Donkey except that our aim was for a target on the wall and we merely shut our eyes instead of being blindfolded. The player spun around three times and then pointed his finger at the mark, walked up, and touched his spot. Probably this game was the Eskimo adaptation of a game learned by someone in the schoolhouse at Barrow. The remarkable thing was that the Eskimos in adapting this game never cheated that I could observe. Although everyone was perfectly free to peek a little, apparently no one thought of such a thing. What, then, would be the fun in playing such a game? Swede wrestling and Indian wrestling were popular among the boys and men. Ruth's mother, old Alice, was the champion team runner among the women!

The Eskimos are very good at cat's cradles, or those string games you used to play as a kid, and I understand explorers of early days report this kind of game as being original with them and not imported. To me it is a tinge of the Oriental again in their character. The number of intricate patterns they can make with strings on their fingers is wonderful; each pattern has its special name which is known to all, such as the Sun, Mountains, Sheep, Young Girls, and so on.

After midnight, when the eating and games were over, we all spread our bedding upon the floor. There were forty people, including babies and small children, sleeping upon a floor of some sixteen by twenty feet; the children were well under control, too, and seemed little bother to the grownups. I picked a spot under the skylight for my bed. This was a mistake, for when the fire was started the next morning the moisture that had condensed upon the skylight in the form of frost during the night, from this host of people, melted and dripped down upon me. Hence, I was the first up. The clink of coffee cups and the stirring with the spoon which belonged to the sugar jar introduced the usual ritual of an Eskimo household starting its day.

In mining camps and in the army, I had always been able to hold my own at table both in speed of consumption and in quantity, but with the Eskimos I fell far behind at meals. A girl weighing only half what I did could out eat me. I believe the reason for this to be that an Eskimo has jaws that are two or three times as powerful as any European's. I have often watched the women put the crimps in a pair of *ugrug* soles for water boots with apparent ease. Crimping of *ugrug* soles is the only "chewing of skins" they do with their teeth, incidentally. But we couldn't even dent that tough hide. One morning the key was lost from our sealed coffee can. How would we get at the contents? Ook-sook, for whom I had brought the coffee, broke the solder seal and stripped the tin rim off with his teeth. Anyone who has done this with pliers knows it takes quite a little power. To cut a quarter inch line with his teeth is a simple task for an Eskimo and is often done. Therefore, the Eskimos could quickly consume tough boiled meat and frozen fish which I had to chew for some time to manage. When it came to eating the cooked foods, they were twice as fast with their fingers as I was with mine, and they were even faster at spooning the beans!

One of the most untenable parts of Eskimo family life for Connie and me when we visited places was the reaching for and grabbing of food from a common pan. This might be all right if the people would merely select one chunk of meat or one biscuit and let it go at that, but they have to poke around and feel and handle all the food placed in front of them, oftentimes breaking off or cutting off a section and then throwing the rest back into the common lot for the next person to paw over. One cannot allow himself to be squeamish or he would starve to death in the midst of such company. Far from chewing their food well, the gobbling Eskimos cut it from the bone, swallow it in chunks, and the digestive juices apparently do the rest. Their sound digestion does not seem to be a result of careful chewing with their much-applauded strong jaws, if one can observe them in practice day by day but may just be one of the general results derived from their very excellent diet of pure animal proteins.

After the meal is over, a rag or piece of towel, indescribably filthy, is passed around upon which everybody wipes the grease off his hands. Marvelous conveyance for spreading disease is the whole system of eating and living which primitives have; once disease gets a start among them, all quickly succumb. Fortunately, our friends out Beechey Point way, due to their isolation, were free of disease at the time we visited there, else we would not have dared live among them as we did.

While the crowd was taking up last night's merriment where they had left off, Ook-sook and I harnessed our mixed dogs and left; Richard had invited us to return next day for Christmas, as he said there would be dancing and much fun. I thought we had better get on after our supplies so as to get back to the Itkillik camp.

A sharp breeze from the east had sprung up and spanked us in the face. It was nearly fifty below zero. We rode along in the sled now bundled up with our cheeks mostly hidden, snug and warm inside our caribou skins; the going was easy, and the dogs knew the way by heart. Many teams from the party were going into Beechey Point to buy things for Christmas. We had started out first, but every dog team passed us by except one very decrepit team. There would be a race with each team trying to hold the lead, but soon the faster team would pull ahead, leaving us behind. As the light in Abraham's window at Beechey Point appeared upon the horizon, a team pulled up abreast of us, but this one could not pass us. The reason was that the other fellow had only three pups and one dog. When we got to the trading post the others were already inside drinking coffee. The pup team arrived right behind us.

The use of money in this part of the world is almost negligible. A fox skin is the source of wealth and the dollar is the only money that people recognize. Prices at the store run in cents on small items, but the trader has to figure up the bill for most people. There had been few foxes caught so far. Some trappers had only one, some two, and the proceeds must be shared with a whole family. A white fox sold for twenty-one dollars this year, if grade A, and this was later reduced to eighteen dollars with a drop in the Outside market. The Christmas food lists ran: tobacco, two boxes; cigarettes, four packs; tea, one pound; coffee, four pounds; milk, five cans; flour, fifty pounds; matches, one box. There would usually be a five-gallon can of kerosene and this ran the bill up to twenty dollars or approximately the price of one good white fox. Red foxes paid only twelve dollars.

Ook-sook wanted to go to the dance that evening while I stayed to put up our food list. Abraham and I were consequently the only ones left at Beechey Point that night, for Ook-sook escorted Thelma and Dora, Abraham's family, off to Richard's place. I do not know why Abraham did not go to the dance. Possibly he wasn't wanted, or perhaps there had been some of the little feelings which arise between different families of Eskimos just as with us. Usually in other years the Christmas party had been held in Abraham's house. Perhaps he just had one of his moods and did not feel much like an Eskimo on this night.

The northern lights were brilliant, and the house popped as the fifty-below-zero temperature outside made its stealthy advances against it. Ook-sook and the girls didn't get home until morning. Dora got sick from eating too much polar bear meat and *akotuk,* and a good time was had by all. The polar bear had been killed alongshore just a day ago between Richard's place and Beechey Point. Christmas Eve I slept upon a brown bear hide in my sleeping bag on Abraham's kitchen floor.

Christmas Day Abraham and I got the old freezer out and made ice cream and had a big Christmas dinner of our own choice, consisting of boiled caribou, noodles and gravy, rye tack, fresh frozen peas, and the vanilla ice cream with canned pineapple rings. I gave Dora and Abraham our phonograph at the house for a delayed wedding present.

Christmas passed, and no Santa Claus had come. Perhaps he was busy in the south, for he certainly missed me. I made a new 7' X 9' wall tent on Abraham's sewing machine. The calm weather broke, and a real storm sailed at us out of the east, sending powdered sugar snow smoking over land and sea. But because we were going to travel west, this was fine. We loaded our sled in the lee side of the big house and said our good-byes.

"See you next March," and we were gone into the storm. Fifty yards behind us the trading post disappeared into the flying snow.

I HAD LIVED IN ALASKA nearly five years now, and this was the worst blizzard I had seen. Yet here we were traveling in it, not because we had to but because it made travel so much easier. Our sled was heavily loaded and the wind coming quarterly behind us shoved us along. A strong, wind will usually blow around three days, although some "blizzards" have been known to last a week.

Accordingly, we knew we would have a tail wind with us all the way to Matthew's house. At Matthew's house inland, it should begin to slacken out; if not, we would wait there until it did. We took our course by the snowdrifts on the sea ice and covered the distance to Richard's place with a loaded sled in half the time it had taken us coming with no wind.

At Richard's we stopped only for tea. The Christmas party was breaking up. George Woods's camp was only a couple of miles farther on and as his group was ready to travel homeward we all went together. Outside, some of the little kids were throwing chips of wood and empty milk cans into the storm to see them borne swiftly away. Our dogs almost outdid themselves trying to catch an empty oatmeal box. In this manner we reached the Woods camp.

At George's comfortable camp we had supper and spent the night. Anyone who doubts that a tent can make a comfortable home in the arctic should visit George's home. Inside it on a night like this the roar of the storm could barely be heard. After we went to bed the fire was allowed to go out. With no fire all night the temperature may not have fallen below the freezing point by morn. When I remembered the frozen water buckets of my childhood on the farm in Illinois with a temperature of merely zero I realized these snow camps are better constructed to hold heat than a good many of our modern homes are in the United States!

Now Nanny worked hard to patch my boots and finish some extra clothes for us while I was here. Nanny can sew fur clothing with the best. Many a day when Connie and I have been warm at fifty below zero we have been thankful for the pains our Eskimo mother took in making our clothing. Despite all efforts at hurry, it was nearly noon next day before Ook-sook and I were able to escape the seamstress now that she had got hold of me and had found time for the work. The storm hadn't lessened when we left.

A few feet from the ground the air was filled with powdered snow driving like thick smoke. I found a piece of black paper sticking out of a packing box on our sled and decided to let our dogs have their chance at catching it. When crumpled up a little it resembled a black rabbit in both appearance and speed. The dogs saw it at once as I released it into the wind, and we were off. For five or six miles our poor old dogs chased that paper while Ook-sook and I hung on. At times the paper would catch against a sharp snag, but it always managed to get loose just as the dogs were upon it. Finally, we hit the smoother ice near the Colville delta and the wind whipped the paper away.

Darkness came. On through it we went, while at last even the lead dog was lost from sight in the flying snow and darkness. In a couple of hours, we tried lighting the lantern, but the wind always blew it out after it was lit. By holding it under his parka Ook-sook could keep the lantern going for a few minutes, but it didn't do us any good that way.

Again, we followed the contours of the drifts. Occasionally we stuck a knife down into the snow to find out whether we were on land or on sea ice. Again, we came out nearly at our destination, for in a moment Ook-sook picked up a sled track and at the same time we saw the snow house: we were back at Mr. Lynd's.

Ook-sook's three brothers and three sisters were here also on their way home from the party. Again, we talked nearly all night. It was 5 a.m. next morning when we finally went to bed.

Leffingwell had fixed a small canvas house upon his sled and inside this his two sisters rode the next day. The cut banks of the Colville River fairly smoked as the fierce wind whipped finely powdered snow over them. The other dog teams pulled away from us and we were left alone. Suddenly from out the blur ahead a black shape materialized. Sled?

Man? Dog? It was a dog. There he huddled, alongside the old sled track. Our dogs saw him and pitched upon him. We broke up the fight or rather murder and saw that it was one of Leffingwell's dogs which had broken loose.

This brings up the question which is often asked as to what happens to a loose dog. There are three ends he may meet here: either he will find his way to someone's camp or someone may find him, or he will starve to death. The idea of his making his living by hunting by himself in the wilderness is utterly erroneous. The idea of his mating with a wolf or running with a wolf pack is just one of those tales. There are white men who have tales which claim to prove otherwise, but such cases must be extremely rare. The Eskimos tell us that any dog which meets up with a wolf is a goner, for wolves dearly love to kill dogs; they say even the biggest and strongest dog is easily killed by a wolf and the wolf may eat him. The story of a dog reverting to the wild state doesn't work on the plains of the arctic.

The stranded dog seemed tremendously glad to see us and trotted along behind us all the way to Jacob's house. Here we all camped for the night. Jacob was still gone. Someone got up on top of the roof and dug up the heads of two summer-killed caribou. Improvidently, we had brought no meat with us; as for me, I had too full a load to bother with that, since meat is very bulky. I have said I like to eat caribou head meat when it is fresh and prepared in a clean manner, but naturally I supposed that the spoiled last summer's heads more than half a year old were for the dogs to eat, especially when, with hairy lips and long ears, and with all their teeth and the eyes left in them, they were dumped into our dog bucket and boiled, for lack of other utensil. But I had made a mistake. Well, I hated to be the first to cry hold, but I did hold back a bit and ate the first piece rather slowly. Ook-sook, who was always so careful of my comforts and proud of the man for whom he worked, went out and got me the single frozen fish which was on our sled. The feast of last summer's spoiled caribou heads was eaten by the Eskimos following right upon a holiday feast of a week's duration; all of them had some white man's grub standing right outside on the sleds, but they were hungry for "meat."

On New Year's Eve we approached Matthew's house as the wind dropped. Everyone had again arrived ahead of us, but not far. Tea, fish, and the usual run-of-the-mill trail lunch were served. After supper some of the hunters about my age, Matthew's sons, told me Santa Claus was coming. "Perhaps he hits here on his return trip," I began to think. Sure enough, presents began to drop through the ventilator from the roof. A pair of caribou fawn skin shooting gloves, with a special trigger finger, a pair of caribou mittens, a fancy tobacco pouch—and for me, a caribou bed skin, stretched long and partially tanned! All the presents had little tags tied to them. On mine I read, "Bud. Christmas."

All of the Eskimos have a head start on learning to read and write because you see they all know their A B C's. They have taught each other the alphabet out this way in their spare time, although most of them have never been to school. And using our alphabet they write letters to each other in the Eskimo language. There are many new words in the Eskimo language today that never before existed. The Eskimos have a word for lipstick, radio, Negro, appendicitis.

Ook-sook and I brought back a hundred pounds of sugar and a hundred pounds of flour to Connie and Ruth on the Itkillik, besides twenty cans of milk and some miscellaneous foods of great delight. Then we were off to hunt caribou again.

5

When we talk of people living by hunting and fishing we generally do not realize what it means. Simply, it means that such people must hunt or fish nearly every day of the year. And it means that to plan a trip anyplace they must be able to exist as they go. This implies a whole realm of complications which are among the chief reasons why the exploration of white men in this part of the world has so far been very limited, either by land or by air.

Both Ook-sook and I had to have meat three times a day, and so did Connie and Ruth. Worse still, our dogs had to be fed. The caribou we killed were completely gone. During our absence to Beechey Point, Koloyuk had come by and stayed with the girls three days visiting, as he was setting out some traps in the vicinity, and when he left he took most of their remaining meat for his dogs, with the general understanding that it was his brother's meat anyway because Ook-sook had killed a part of it, and he would pay us back sometime. Could we say anything if we wanted to? Had not I myself been a continuous boarder at Koloyuk's home during trips with Matthew on the Colville? Had not half the Eskimo coast provided for our dogs wherever we visited?

Now one of the projects I had had in mind for this winter was a sled trip inland to explore the upper Kuparuk River, which is completely inaccessible by summer and which Connie and I believe no white person—or possibly any person—has yet seen. This river is one of the several Eskimo rivers whose probable courses are just dotted in on our present maps. Connie and I had developed a personal interest in the Ku- paruk after having built a house at its mouth and having hunted caribou forty miles up it with our canoe in the summertime. By dog sled, Ook-sook and I should find the upper Kuparuk accessible if we could manage a two weeks' trip. Now Ook-sook and I hoped to trap a few foxes—an inducement for him in exploring—and thus we agreed that perhaps the unknown river might be a good fox area.

I understand that both the Navy and the Coast and Geodetic Survey have been working at aerial photography in north Alaska for some time, but this is a job which takes years because such photography is actually practiced only during summer on a few days in the year. Furthermore, for many purposes it can never supply the same information as would be gained right there on the ground where no man has yet stood.

But our main problem in this exploration was the transport of food for dog and man. Whatever explorations were achieved incidentally, it would be one long hunting trip, as indeed our lives were all that year, just to keep alive. All we took with us when we started was our usual sack of biscuits, which would last us about three days, our cooking kettles, and our pinch of tea. In traveling by dog sled a hundred or more miles from your base of supplies—in our case, Connie and Ruth, who made us cookies—you have to travel through in a hurry.

Up over the several-hundred-foot bluffs of the Itkillik's bend we climbed in the moonlight, while Connie and Ruth waved good-by from the valley. Once we were on top, the great prairie stretched away on all sides.

Daylight came and with it the sight that a caribou hunter likes to see. The ground was pawed up by caribou. The dogs loved the scent and for some miles we traveled at a good clip. There was a crust on the snow that let us down so that we kept tripping on our snowshoes; when we reached the "yards" farther out on the prairie which had been trampled by the herds, the trail was a dream. How many animals had been by here? A thousand? Five thousand? One couldn't guess, for of course one caribou can make a lot of tracks. Still, we covered over twenty miles and did not leave the broad trail. The deer were traveling southeast, and we were traveling east. Often the trails would be beaten into the bare ground, showing that hundreds certainly had walked single file in such a place.

At dark we made a little snow house and crawled in. Our primus stove quickly made tea while the lantern revealed caribou tracks even imprinted into the snow blocks which had gone into our house walls. As the blue flower of the primus stove flame died and we settled into our bags in darkness, the caribou tracks in the snow went round in my head.

After several hours' travel next day, I saw a band of them. Since I was quite a little taller than Ook-sook, I sometimes saw animals before they came into his vision. Soon the animals materialized into band after band. There were from twenty to one hundred in each group and some twenty groups were in sight. Scattered about between the main groups were singles or stragglers of three and four. They all grazed contentedly on the plain before us just a mile away. The sight made one think of the buffalo herds of the West.

Passing the binoculars back and forth between us, we studied them, stopping beside the sled. The glasses showed up three more dim main herds in the distance, similar to the one before us. Altogether there were probably four thousand caribou in sight. The binoculars had also revealed the frost- bound Kuparuk River as though in a vision beyond. We could trace its course by the willows and cut banks. There was no use in chasing caribou today, for darkness would overtake us before we could reach any of them by stalking.

I have often observed that animals have really very poor eyesight. With the country before us fairly black with the conspicuous caribou our dogs couldn't see a thing and the caribou couldn't see us, although we were dressed in dark furs with our dark sled and all in sharp view against the sky line.

To get to where we were going to camp we had to pass right through the grazing caribou. There was a slight cross wind, so that the animals could not smell or hear us. The dogs trotted along, never suspecting a thing, until we were about eight hundred yards away. The country was flat with no cover of any kind to hide us or the caribou. At eight hundred yards the dogs first noticed something, and not being restrained they broke into a voiceless run. Ook-sook and I jumped on the sled to take advantage of the ride. While we covered two hundred yards the caribou fed away peacefully. Then suddenly they gave a start as one animal, and all stood looking our way. At this our team set up a howl and away we went. Still not sure of what it was all about, the caribou stopped short to look again. A few of the bolder even ran some steps toward us in hopes that we were approaching caribou. At last, smelling us, away they went as fleet as the wind.

About here someone will say, "Why didn't you shoot if you were out of meat and wanted a caribou?" Yes, I could probably have hit one, two, three, or four with the benefit of my telescope. I likewise would have left perhaps the identical number of cripples for wolves to kill. By such a tactic I might have killed one or more outright if I had fired away several times, but how many cripples would have escaped with the band to die? I have killed caribou at double this range, but it was always a lone animal with no herd nearby. Thus, I could concentrate my fire on it. If I had shot a lone animal near the edge of the mass of deer it would have been quickly lost in the herd unless killed instantly, and instant kills are rare at three hundred yards with the temperature near fifty below zero. The caribou that receives a flesh wound in these temperatures will find his insulating fur blasted off an area that soon becomes wet with blood, and then freezing follows. It would be cruel to the reader to describe the inevitable end.

Ook-sook never reached for his rifle; he knew the animals were too far for a certain kill. This was not out of ideas of charity but because he was an ammunition hoarder in a country where bullets are scarce, even if they were my bullets. Courteous, considerate, Ook-sook was in some ways the finest man I have ever hunted with. He was born a hunter. He had never known any other life, so it bothered him little. I had become used to sailing close to the wind and it bothered me not at all to see the last bite disappear. The dogs got an old caribou windpipe and a stomach divided among them.

The bright moonlight flooded miles and miles of rolling prairie as our camp smoke climbed towards heaven. Steam rose from each dog as he lay curled up in the snow. I believe the temperature on this night was more than sixty below zero or ninety and more degrees below freezing, for I checked this later and found it had been sixty on the sea-coast, and the coast is always ten degrees warmer in really cold weather than is the prairie inland.

Creek! Creek! Pop! Caribou were passing in the moon-light and I guess their joints needed oiling. For extremely fleet animals they always sound in the stillness as though they were on their last legs.

The binoculars showed that these tiny sounds of their joints came to us from about a mile away.

At around sixty below in the heavy stillness the warm bodies of the caribou gave off clouds of steam; as they ran they obscured themselves in a smoke screen. Often a trail of steam marked an animal's flight in a way which was analogous to the tail of a speeding comet. The air is almost always very still during extremely low temperatures; no "blizzard" is possible then due to the fact that if a wind arose the temperature would rise because of the friction caused by air movement. Cold air is also very drying because it is unable to hold much moisture; when it is chilled to this extent the moisture is squeezed out of it. When people begin to talk about the difference in "wet" cold and "dry" cold at fifty below zero, you can keep tongue in cheek. It's all the same.

Every band of caribou that we saw fled as they were alarmed by the original band put into flight. They would run a mile and resume feeding. It was a mystery to me how they could detect the sound of our walking when there were so many caribou walking about near them, making more noise than we. The patterns of the steam trails they left on the arctic prairie resembled the feathery trails airplanes leave at high altitudes, or on cold days at lower altitudes.

A caribou's life is one of listening and watching for danger. His inevitable end is to be eaten by wolf, man, or whatever catches him, and he only puts off this end by careful vigilance at all times. The age of an individual caribou probably rarely exceeds five or eight years. When a band of caribou are fleeing, the oldest animals bring up the rear, with the yearlings and fawns far out in front. Next come young cows, young bulls, the old cows, and far in the rear lag the old bulls. This has led some observers to believe that the oldest bulls or bucks lag behind in order to guard the others. I'm afraid that is another of the stories for children. The fact is, the old bulls are not able to run fast; they have to carry a heavy rack of useless horns plus, at certain seasons, the accumulating layers of fat that come with age. Burdened down by horns, and in the fall with as much as thirty pounds of surplus back fat, the old bull is the first caught by the wolf.

In the nature stories the wolf "slashes the animal's jugular," or "takes a death grip upon its throat." I am afraid that the wolf generally grabs the part of the caribou that he can reach first—namely the fat hams or flanks. In the ensuing struggle the caribou is often disemboweled. The wolf drags the unfortunate victim down and starts eating from there, often before it is dead. Many times, there will be no marks near the throat or the hamstrings either. Of the fifty-odd wolf-killed caribou I have examined I have never found any except old animals.

Since a caribou's hide tears as easily as does the hide of a domestic sheep when killer dogs pitch upon its flanks, the caribou succumbs to the wolf, once it is caught, without being able to put up much of a fight. If the caribou had sense enough to band together for sound mass defense, they could trample their aggressors to death by mere weight of numbers. But their nature is such that they break into panic and flee, leaving the stragglers to the fate which will be the end of all of them in time. Like a sheep or like a rabbit, a caribou is a gentle animal; he has no fight in him.

OOK-SOOK STUDIED SEVERAL HERDS OF caribou and together we decided upon one band. There were seven animals in it.

The seven little black specks were advancing towards us in the lead of an ever-widening wedge of steam; we walked to meet them as they came. When they were a mile away from us we lay down in the snow. This is cold business if you aren't properly dressed—impossible business for a man dressed in army or navy arctic clothing of today. But we had on our double caribou parkas, and the snow at sixty below was as dry as powder. We each dug a little hollow in it and crawled in to wait through the long hours that might be.

The wait indeed proved long. When the animals had come to within three hundred yards of us they all began to feed. Here I might have tried for a shot had it not been for extremely low temperature. This brings up another point which I have found pertinent in my life in the arctic. A rifle may shoot just as hard at sixty below zero as at warmer temperatures, but it certainly is not as accurate. I had tested this out under controlled conditions before in the Brooks Range, using standard targets at fixed distances outside our log cabin at the various temperatures during the arctic winter, so that I had a sound basis of comparison.

I found that a .22 rifle loses so much of its accuracy as to be nearly useless at thirty or forty below zero. The deviation from the norm in accuracy is less with the higher calibers but is nonetheless something to consider. Ook-sook had noticed in his hunting experiences that it was hard for him to hit an animal squarely in the lower temperatures and he explained it by saying that his gun wasn't very strong when it got cold, although, he added, mine might be. As mine was a .30-30 carbine, the same I had made the tests with, it wasn't too strong to start with, I knew, and I would do very well with it today to hit a four-foot circle at three hundred yards. The effect of cold on accuracy probably does not apply to the guns on fighter planes which fly at very low temperatures in the high altitudes, because a short burst of a few shots doubtless warms them up quickly. But a few shots may be all that the primitive arctic hunter possesses for a whole year's hunting and his gun is not, couldn't be, an automatic, for dog sled use. The tests I made on targets were of course made with guns which had been kept out of doors and were chilled for hours at these temperatures, which is a set of circumstances exactly like what the hunter contends with on the winter trail.

As we waited, our animals fed behind a slight ridge. Meanwhile Ook-sook got a cold foot and decided to stand up. Although his clothing, much better than mine for that matter, was perfectly adequate, a cramped position which tended to shut off circulation quickly made him vigilant to the dangers of freezing. The caribou must have heard Ook-sook move, for when we next saw them they were retracing their old trail a half mile away, laying down their smoke screen behind flying heels.

The game was up so far as that band of animals was concerned. But there had walked up nearby another group of three cows. Lean and poor a few months ago, the cows in January and February were in as good condition as the bulls.

Now a caribou has a real curiosity that often goes hand in hand with poor vision. Usually in his experience dark objects have turned out to be other caribou. Yet it could be a wolf. I doubt if the threat of a man ever enters their reasoning, for caribou do not connect rifle shots with danger. Often, they will merely go on feeding at a rifle's report. These three caribou had seen many of their companions all about them just a few minutes before; apparently, they decided we were caribou, for they came on at a trot. At less than two hundred yards they stopped short to look us over. Then, rearing high upon their hind legs, they whirled to circle us. It was time to get ready to shoot. So far, we had stood up so as to more closely resemble caribou in our caribou skin parkas, but now we dropped down into the snow. Offhand shooting is for western movies, for trick shows, or for shotgun fans, but the big game hunter or rifleman who uses a rifle quickly learns to use the steady prone position whenever possible. It is fun to shoot at targets offhand or even standing on your head, but no true sportsman wishes to inflict needless suffering on his game by random shooting. Thus, he always uses the best means he knows to make a killing or disabling shot. Certainly, too, we would consider the trouble we might have chasing a caribou with a broken leg for miles over the prairie at sixty below zero. Need one say more?

At the first shots the three caribou crumpled up and we were happy men. As the short twilight day faded entirely, the arctic moon bathed the land with its enchanting spell. We had hunted hard all day. Our dogs were hungry, and we hadn't eaten since yesterday. Great luxury—I had Ook- sook to help skin.

THE CHANNEL OF THE KUPARUK River is gravel lined all the way except right at the delta, and the water is as clear as any explorer dreams. From its origin in the tiny creeks that rise from the very summits of the Brooks Range to its end in the Arctic Ocean it possesses the enchantment of remoteness from man. There are no spruce or birch trees here, no matter how far you traverse it. There is no drift which would indicate that timber is at its head. We presume that perhaps all of the ten unexplored rivers which drain the north coast of Alaska lie in the prairie lands where only the willow and cottonwood hold sway. But of course, we don't really know. Eskimo friends tell me that porcupine, otter, and mink have been taken on the upper Sagavanirktok. And I suppose it is this sort of thing which kept Connie and me happy in our thoughts of the arctic, and which is why we must always stay a little longer.

On our big map a lake was dotted in at the head of the Kuparuk River which would be, according to calculation, about six miles across.

The Eskimos believe there is no lake there and that the white man's map is mistaken. They did admit that there were plenty of willows for firewood. That had settled me. With part of our meat on our sled and part left behind, guarded by traps—to be picked up for return rations—Ook-sook and I were on our way to the mysterious "lake," following the course of the river which was also dotted in as being probable of existence. We carried two caribou with us as we went onward.

In summer the Kuparuk River hurries over riffles and swirls quietly among flower-covered prairie banks. You had to imagine all this while seeing it now solid in its iron mask. Some summer I would like to visit that happy land! The arctic grayling snap at flies—that I know, because grayling and a kind of salmon trout have been netted by the Eskimos at the mouth of this river—and I suppose they snap at mosquitoes and anything that resembles their fish food, or just spend the lazy days fanning themselves with their fairylike fins. Doubtless the grayling penetrate the side streams to their very source as soon as the ice goes in June. But when winter comes they wisely hurry back into the deep pools they share with the ugly *tictalirk,* as the Eskimos call the ling, a great squirming fish on the bottom that resembles a cross between an eel and a catfish. The *tictalirk* grows some three feet long and is prized for his liver, not his looks. But Connie and I had not become acquainted with him at this time.

When winter settles over the flowering prairie and the melting snows of the mighty Brooks Range no longer supply water, the water level drops until it is only a murmur and the cold of white winter soon grips the land as tight as a drum. A river like the Kuparuk becomes an inconspicuous nonentity during its long sleep, supplying a dog-sled trail. Most people assume the arctic prairie to be frozen solid in winter but as a matter of fact there are lakes which do not freeze to the bottom and there is plenty of deep water to keep the rivers flowing! If the land were frozen solid all over there would be no water to flow. As it is, a traveler on frozen arctic rivers in winter always has to watch out that he doesn't get his feet wet in possible overflow spots beneath the snow! Another danger even in the coldest temperatures the arctic knows is thin ice in certain places on rivers.

Sledding up the Kuparuk, we could plainly see the mountains a hundred miles away, and along the course of river ahead of us there rose pillars of steam like forest fires burning— the overflow areas.

The overflows would spread out and build up an icy plateau until by spring the river would be raised in places far above its natural bed by successive freezings.

We passed two overflow places where the water had flooded. The river ice had spread over the lowlands like a rising tide which had frozen into a mirror by the time we came along. We liked these places, for at this point of the freezing and overflow cycle the sled traveled easily over the slick ice. In one place there was a hole four feet across where the river was flowing. I looked down into some ten feet of water and saw several grayling swimming lazily about.

Near dark that evening we came upon the carcass of an old bull caribou that had been killed by a wolf. We took the remains along for dog feed. As there was no snow suitable for building a snow house, we had to make out with just the tent. Camp was pitched in a willow thicket along the river course; we threw our snow house cover over the little tent like an extra blanket. For fuel we selected, as was our custom, only the driest standing dead willows, which would pop off easily at the base when you pulled them. In these northern lands the process of rot is very slow. Willows which have died years ago have lost all their small branches so that only the large limbs and stumps remain; these break off easily by hand even though perhaps four inches thick. You don't chop them, properly speaking, but instead you break them by the blow of the ax or you may even hold up the ax and strike the wood against it! It sounds queer to hit the ax with the wood, but it works. The dead brittle sticks burn easily with much heat but are soon gone. It was this method of getting fuel that Connie and Ruth practiced each day at the Itkillik camp.

As soon as our tent was up, and a pile of dry wood gathered we took off our snowshoes, on which we had worked, and carried in our camp gear. First the bed skins went in—two caribou skins that were spread upon the snow with the hair side down. There is no danger of a bed skin becoming wet at below zero temperatures unless you are careless and spill liquids on it. After the bed skins came the bedding and spare clothing. This was thrown in the back of the tent to form a backrest and seat. The grub box with our cooking pot and miscellaneous gear was placed near the stove with the wood- pile. The ten-gallon tub in which we cooked the dog feed was packed full of granular snow and placed upon the wood- pile so that the snow might begin to warm up a little while we cooked our own supper.

You can't cook supper until you have some water to cook it in. Food on the dog team trail is always boiled because you cannot easily carry a stove with an oven. Water is either melted ice or snow. In order to save time and work, you don't melt just any kind of snow either. There are many different kinds of snow, and each has its purpose. There is generally granular snow near the ground under the soft snow on top. You can rake away the soft snow with your pan and pack it full of the granular kind—when this melts on the stove you have half a pan or more of water; but if you use the soft fluffy type of snow it takes long to melt, and you have only a very little water in your pan when you get through. Snow is an excellent blotter. Care must be taken to keep it shaken down in the pan, furthermore; otherwise you may burn the pan up. I have often noted how carefully an Eskimo selects the proper snow to use for water. An Eskimo is as particular about the kinds of snow he uses for a house, for water, to pitch his camp upon, or to cut a trap block from as is an expert golfer to choose the proper club.

After making shavings and starting the fire in the little stove, we found the small tent soon warm. I generally did the cooking, so after taking off my outside fur clothes and hanging my boots up to dry the frost from them, I would set the first supper out. We only ate twice a day—breakfast and supper. But at supper we ate twice, or maybe it is better to say we had a two-course meal with an hour's lapse between courses.

The first course was caribou *quak* and tea. Raw frozen caribou meat is only less excellent than raw frozen fish. As I have said before, any kind of *quak* is to a northerner his fresh fruits, his salads, and his vitamin pills all in one. By the time we had finished a pound or two of *quak* and some hot tea, the other pot—the meat pot—would have come to a boil. It was now placed upon the back of the stove and the dog bucket put on beside. The lantern shed its cheery glow and Ook-sook sat skinning a red fox yielded by one of his traps while we waited for our second course to cook.

There is no trouble in setting traps in the arctic. But it calls for a special technique which the Eskimos have cleverly worked out.

You select a stick the size of a broom handle and a foot long. You may have to carry such a stick a long way on your dog sled if there are no sticks around. Scratch a trench in the snow down to the ground or down a foot if the snow is deep and hard. Thrust the stick through your trap chain ring to its center. Place the stick and part of the chain in the hole; now tramp snow over it until the surface looks the way it did before. If you have done this properly, you have a trap toggle that is buried under hard-frozen snow and as secure from being dragged away as though the trap were ringed to a stake driven into the ground. Of course, it is not possible to drive a stake into frozen ground here. But within an hour after setting the trap no fox could pull the toggle up, nor could man either I might add, for you have to chop the snow away when you come to take the trap up. It has been seen in this connection in the building of snow houses that compressed soft snow in low temperatures freezes solid as soon as it sets in any form.

The trap next is set by cutting a hole in the snow to accommodate it. The trap fits into its little snow pocket, which is two or more inches deep, depending on the size of the trap. Its open jaws should lie about one quarter of an inch below the surface. Now the trapper cuts a snow block from drifts which he selects as being not too hard or too granular, shaves the block thin with his knife, and slides it over the hole so as not to knock any snow down upon the trap's jaws to cause clogging or trouble. The trap now rests in an airtight, sealed case, safe from the storms. With your knife you last shave the block down on top until it is a scant quarter of an inch thick over the trap's hidden jaws. The location of the trap is always such that you can find it, yet it must be in the open so that the wind will blow away any loose snow that happens to fall. When the fox steps on the thin snow shield that is over the jaws of the trap—being attracted here by bait, also buried so that the ravens can't get it—he breaks through and is caught by the foot. Quickly the fox freezes to death when held in this vise; most are found frozen by the trapper. A good place to set these traps is on river islands or on top of open mounds and ridges.

Carefully tonight Ook-sook was skinning his fox through the mouth, working the skin off until at last the fox crawled out of its own skin. It was a queer sight to see the transformation so quickly take place; an absurd naked ghost of a fox seemed to come shivering from its warm red parka. Ook-sook held up the fox carcass as if he thought it might get away. Then, picking up his knife, he carefully cut off its head.

"Ook-sook eat fox?" I asked him.

"No," he explained, with a rather foolish smile. "Fox go, I no cut off his head. I see fox house today, me. Lots of new parka, fox house. He—get away. Go get new parka."

It was some fifty below outside and there was silence for a moment while Ook-sook rolled up the fox skin into a little bundle. Then, as a sort of afterthought, he added: "*Alápa*, fox!" meaning it would be an awfully cold fox if it were to get away without its parka.

What Ook-sook was trying to tell me was that the Eskimo trappers always cut the head off a fox carcass which they have relieved of its skin in the belief that if they do not do so the fox might not really be dead. It might continue to roam the prairie as a sort of ghost fox! Just today Ook-sook had seen the shed fur of foxes in a fox den under a bank where we sledded; it reminded him of the fact well known to Eskimos that a ghost fox had been here, having escaped from some trapper and gone to a den to put on ghostly robes to clothe himself again. The Eskimos had no intention of permitting ghost foxes of their catch to roam loose. Subsequently Connie and I realized that every single Eskimo on the coast, the people with whom we had dined and lived and slept—even George Woods and Abraham the trader, who talked to us so sensibly about numbers of things in the world—followed this old superstition or custom of cutting the heads off all the fox carcasses which are in their possession, just to be on the safe side! After Ook-sook told me seriously about this matter in which he heartily believed, he and I always cut the heads off.

And so, we sat in camp and skinned a fox now and then and ate *quak* and tea and cookies and boiled meat. We had come to delight in the raw frozen bone marrow from the caribou lower leg bones— favorite food of most famous arctic explorers, incidentally; they do not usually dwell on it too much in their narratives because the public does not understand easily. Arctic diets are different. You may again live well on a diet of fish and fudge.

Of course, it follows that the people who live by hunting become acquainted with their source of food supply as few others do. Ook-sook could tell you to the pound how much fat any given caribou had on it for as far as he could see it. I soon learned the trick also; fat and fitness told with caribou by the size, but especially by the width of the antlers in the right seasons. I had always imagined that animals fattened up in the summer to prepare for a winter of lean. I held this view, which is common to the average sportsman, until I came north where the winter comprises most of the year. Here I learned that fat with caribou depends upon the breeding habits. (Pasturage in the shallow snows of the arctic is ample at all times.) But it so happens that the two sexes are at their best eating for man at exactly opposite times of the year. During late summer before rutting the old bulls put on immense layers of tallow which can literally be stripped from their backsides; it was this which Matthew's people had saved by the many dozens of pounds, to be dried and eaten raw in later months, such as at Christmas time. Just after rutting, however, the fattest male herbivores in the wild have become walking skeletons held together by shrunken hide; they are even pitiful to see and sometimes almost worthless to eat. This is the time at which most of our deer in the United States are killed because the horns for trophies are at their best just after rutting, and trophies are more important than food to the civilized man! (A surcease from hunting during the rutting season also offers protection for the increase of numbers of deer.) Just after fall rutting and with the shedding of his antlers, no matter how excellent are the feed conditions, every male herbivore will be in the very worst condition that he will ever be in at any time of the year! This is a point we should keep in mind when formulating our game laws if we are interested in game as food, not just as sport. In the arctic where food is of prime importance and the reason for our hunting, we find that nobody shoots bull caribou after rutting season if he can get anything else. But by the turn of the year the bulls are in reasonably good shape again and they continue gradually to get better up to the time of the next rutting season the following fall. With caribou, both sexes have antlers, but they lose them at different times of the year—the cows in July, the bulls in September or October, depending upon the latitude or upon the time summer draws to an end. The cows are in good shape and as fat as they will ever be all winter until they have their fawns the following spring. Neither the cold winter nor feed conditions influence greatly the condition of the fat of these animals. In no case does a slab of back fat collect upon the cows or upon the young bulls that can compare with the fat carried in late summer by the old bulls. The cows always carry most of their fat in the interstices of the meat and internally because that is simply the way they are made. By March both cows and bulls are about equally fat according to their own ways, but by spring when the cows calve they have reached the very lowest part of their fat cycle, at just the time the bulls are beginning to grow very good again. Calves or fawns are never fat enough to make much difference.

If we study this cycle, we see that the fat of caribou has little relation to the seasons but relates to the sex and age and the fortune of each individual animal. A caribou is a northern animal and winter bothers him much less than it does a California publicity man. The relationship of fat with moose and with mountain sheep is similar in principle. In different localities the animals will rut earlier in the fall, and in the extremely deep snow of more southerly Alaska or on long migrations the caribou will all be extremely emaciated in midwinter— and unfortunately it is at this point on their southerly migrations that most white people have formed their conceptions of what caribou meat is like I But the caribou one finds the farthest north in their home on the prairies are fat and fine if killed correctly.

At this point someone may ask, "Why is it important that animals be fat to eat anyway?" And to this I can only say that lean animals may even be so tasteless as to make it hard to swallow their meat, because it is the fat which gives our meat its flavor. If there is too much fat, you can always cut some of it out—or use it, as we would do in the arctic, for baking and other things—but if meat is all lean it cannot be swallowed after a few days, and in this case the person on an all meat diet would of course become very ill. When meat alone is eaten the person will eat more fat than he would in ordinary civilized life because the digestive system must have some kind of fat in the diet along with the lean in order to utilize either.

Our caribou had been quite fat for midwinter. After supper Ook-sook went out to feed the dogs while I made the beds. Soon there came the sound of howling, and then the sound of gulping as some dogs bolted their food and the impatient howls and whines as the other hungry ones waited their turn.

Shortly, Ook-sook returned. In our sleeping bags once again, we blew out the light. As if it were a signal all eight of our dogs pointed their muzzles to the arctic sky and gave vent to a lonesome wail. They were full now, and it was their turn to sing, as the wolf sings after his kill. As if from another signal they all stopped. There was silence for a moment, and then clear and strong came the weird howl of a caribou wolf from across the plains. He sang his song and Ook-sook stirred in his skin bed and said in Eskimo:

"Wolf eat, too."

Bud and Ook-Sook return to the Itkillik

6

A light wind fanned my parka hood trim as I walked easily along the mirrored overflow Kuparuk River ice carrying my snowshoes beneath my arm. I had got into the habit of leaving Ook-sook to attend to the breaking of camp in the morning so as to get a head start; the obstreperous dogs with their barking and howling were a frequent impediment to hunting, and I was the hunter. Sometimes I would walk ahead of the sled all day and would not see Ook-sook until we camped at night; we usually kept track of each other on the horizon. My soft caribou boots were as light as house slippers on my feet. We had hauled most of our last caribou kill back to Connie and Ruth; then, after setting out our traps in a Hundred-mile circuit, we were again gone, and again our larder was empty.

Far up Kuparuk River there were to be seen today many tracks of caribou all about. A ridge a hundred feet high ran parallel to the river for a few miles. I accordingly climbed it to follow along where I could better use the binoculars.

On top I sat down and got the glasses out to study the landscape. A pair of binoculars must be held steady and used with care; I spent a half hour carefully studying the willow thickets upriver and the surrounding hills which had begun to rise. In one thicket there was a dark-colored falcon perched upon a tall willow snag. On the opposite side of the river a mile below him and nearer me sat a snowy owl atop a little mound. In several directions bands of caribou were grazing.

After a few more miles I again found a convenient seat and studied the landscape. This time I saw four black objects slowly moving through the willows of the Kuparuk river bed. Great guns They were moose!

One glance revealed it. Of course, I was very familiar with moose and their habits in the coniferous forests to the south, but who would have dreamed of finding them here, two hundred miles north of the most northern tree? Nothing like this concerning the northern range of moose is to be found in any of the literature I have read on this subject.

All four of the big black fellows were bulls which had dropped their antlers in midwinter. Often an inexperienced hunter will take one glance at game and tear after it. This practice may work at times, but in this open prairie such an effort rewards one with only a good appetite. Accordingly, I sat and watched my old friends the moose for another half hour, doing some thinking and trying to determine where they were going and what they were doing. I had decided to kill one of them if I could: for one reason because I wanted to see a specimen, and for another, because I wanted to photograph it. Ook-sook had never tasted moose!

They were feeding slowly right down the river towards me, passing from one patch of little willows to another and moving at the rate of perhaps a mile an hour. The willows slowed them up to browse but they made good speed in the open places between the half acres that separated the willow patches. Moose are not grazers and they ate no grass. Their only food was the bark and buds of these willows, and by seeing them eat an observer could realize clearly that moose on this continent will go as far north as the willows go—which means they will go right up to the edge of the Arctic Ocean in some places.

Alas, I could see Ook-sook coming already, some six miles behind. But perhaps I would have time to wait for the moose to get to me. For me to go to them was of course out of the question because they would hear me.

The wind was in my favor as I descended the ridge. In a moment the meandering giants were lost to my vision, for when I left the ridge I could no longer look down upon them. But I had their course all planned out for them and thought I knew where they would pass if they continued coming as they were. I walked up the river bed until I figured the moose would pass me only twenty yards away.

Plans are only plans, yet they are essential. Ook-sook made better speed over the frozen river than I had counted on. The first moose had just appeared opposite and was starting to cross the open space to the next willow thicket where I lay waiting. "He is going to come right up to me," I thought, "and I can get his picture before I shoot." I had run all day on the trail these last few days with the camera hung around my neck beneath my parka next to my body, for the sun was coming back.

Then the moose stopped. I could see his big ears go forward. I heard then what he heard—the unmistakable thump of a sled, and close, too. In a moment the moose would high-tail it and be gone. I looked around and saw the sled only a quarter of a mile away, and when I looked back to my moose he was four hundred yards away and I didn't care to try a shot at that range.

But the moose had plans of his own, which he evidently was bent upon carrying out. From the opposite end of the thicket burst the other three moose in full flight, laying down a smoke screen behind them in the cold. But where was the young bull I had been watching? To my right his great dark form loomed. He had followed a small stream bed and was endeavoring to get around the approaching dog team, never realizing that I was there. He would have succeeded, too, for he was well hidden from them. I had become so used to the smaller caribou that I thought he was within two hundred yards of me, while he was really much farther away as he paused, listening, and I shot. Snow flew away below my mark and the moose gave a jump. Again, he stood listening, not knowing the danger in which he stood. I corrected my error and tried again. The bull sagged and fell at the impact of the bullet.

The dogs set up their usual loud clamor when they heard the shot. They were used to this and knew what it meant. Ook-sook, who had been riding on the sled, jumped off to run around to the opposite side of the thicket in case the game tried to get away. Thus, the dogs and sled came up to me all looking expectantly to see game.

The moose had fallen back into the little creek bed and I could see him trying to get up. I snapped another shot at his thrashing head but missed. When I was halfway to him he regained his feet and started running. My first shot struck him, but he kept on; the next crumpled him. When Ook- sook and I got to him he was trying to get up again. A close shot through the atlas joint which connects neck and head then killed him instantly. I was surprised to find a small horn knocked into the snow. It was an old last year's horn and the bull dropped it just as his body fell to the ground.

The paced distance was 336 steps to where he first fell. I don't like to shoot at any big game animal at such a range, especially with a .30-30; while this is an admirable gun, it was never made for ranges beyond a hundred yards and was never designed to kill moose in the first place. It is true that probably more moose are killed with it in the remote areas of the North than are killed with all other rifles combined, but this is because the hunters who use this gun understand hunting and were brought up, as were the cowboys of our West, with a .30-30. I much prefer other rifles such as the .30-06, but since I got the only gun I could get hold of when I went north, I was like the Eskimo who wrote Abraham for some tobacco:

"If you have no smoke, then I take chew."

Of course, the telescope sight I had mounted on my little carbine greatly aided me in estimating ranges in such open country. When I saw snow fly three feet low at my first shot I fired the next time four feet over the moose's back in aiming. Furthermore, a bullet that will not pass through an animal at a hundred yards may quite easily do so at three hundred or even six hundred yards. The explanation is simple. The bullet doesn't often mushroom at a long range but will pass on through like a full-jacketed bullet. This was true here, for although I was using the latest design of controlled expanding ammunition, two of the three shots that hit from a great distance had passed clear through the moose. Incidentally, the smaller gun such as the .30-30 is the one suggested by most arctic experts for convenience in far arctic hunting, when all is said and done, since a person rarely meets with larger animals than the caribou.

Ook-sook was not enthusiastic about the moose. He would have much preferred caribou for food. After skinning and quartering the moose we loaded part of it upon the sled. We had carefully saved all the blood for dog feed by dipping it from the abdominal cavity with the dog dipper into the dog bucket. After completing a little cache of meat, we set traps to guard it.

WE HAD TRAVELED HARD FOR many days from before daylight until after dark, exploring up the Kuparuk. The mountains had come closer and there were more willows which grew on most of the small side streams and even here and there in places upon the rolling foothills of the Brooks Range. We had seen caribou every day while the river bed was a regular avenue of trails. We had seen moose upon three occasions and many of their big wandering tracks.

I told Ook-sook one day before we left the Kuparuk section that I was going to climb the first low foothills. The climb looked easy and I expected to make it within an hour.

Tired and puffed, I reached the summit of the first foothills four hours later. The short day was drawing to a close as I once again pulled out the faithful binoculars to study the unexplored country. I had seen many caribou today but the sight that met my eyes surpassed even my fondest dreams. From where I sat the foothills rolled away in all directions, as smooth, rolling, grass-covered prairie landscape, partially bare of snow, even in February. The Kuparuk River split into many small channels here. They all seemed to come from canyons opening out of the mountains. The channels were easy to trace in the distance for they were all lined with the dark willow fringe.

For an hour I studied the scene before me, searching for the mythical big lake which is supposed to exist. We were many miles beyond the place where it was shown upon the map I carried. What we had found was an overflow in a swampy spot, but it would be no lake by summer by my estimate. Finally, I concluded that there isn't any lake there and later, upon having the opportunity to see an aerial map of this region, I can still contend that the report is a mistake.

The caribou I looked down upon were nearly evenly scattered in an area which circled me. I counted a sector of the circle and multiplied by ten, as I figured it represented about one tenth of the caribou in sight. My calculations came to thirteen hundred caribou in my test plot, which, multiplied by ten, would give a total of thirteen thousand animals in sight at once. This is a conservative figure as there were probably more on the lee side of hills where I couldn't see them. Therefore, I feel it is safe to estimate that there were around twenty thousand caribou in the area I could survey with my binoculars of about twelve miles in diameter. Three moose, a big roving wolverine, and a cross fox—half red and half silver—were seen during this study.

Lest anyone should start figuring the caribou population of the arctic by multiplying my estimate by the area of the grazing grounds, however, let me hasten to add that we had traveled over two hundred miles to see this sight on this particular trip. These particular caribou probably represented the animals drained from an area of between eight and ten thousand square miles. Practically any deer country in the United States at this time beats this average number of deer to the square mile because of careful husbanding of our game and the elimination of many of their natural enemies, particularly the wolves which seem to be the great controlling factor in the numbers of the caribou.

I was conscious that this was a rare sight few men have ever been able to witness in this generation, to see such a vast herd of completely wild untended game, uncounted and unknown. The sun was lingering upon the most distant mountain peaks to the south as I rose to return to camp. Darkness was spreading over the valley. A warmer breeze fanned my cheek, for the temperature was taking one of its milder spells at perhaps around ten below. As I was dressed for the sixties, I could loosen up my parka and cool off while walking back.

Like sentinels the peaks of the Brooks Range stood looking out over the lower plains to the frozen polar sea. What mysteries lay locked in those mountains which no man has ever trod? Perhaps the precious minerals of the world lie locked in here in north Alaska. But winter is no time for prospecting and in summer these mountains are nearly inaccessible. Perhaps wealth will be found in these realms yet someday when men come to realize that the arctic isn't a land of desolation but is one which only waits to offer up its treasure. Certainly, I felt it had offered enough to me by just giving me the chance to look at it.

Our trip of exploration in the caribou lands was done. It would have been possible of course for us to have lived here on caribou and continued exploring, but we decided to begin picking up our winter's traps to return to our base on the Itkillik with Connie and Ruth, and there prepare to return to Beechey Point. The arctic night had suddenly gone, just like that. Sunlight was now visible and would return with giant strides. It was almost March, and for the months of March, April, and May we planned an even more exciting itinerary to complete the chronicle of our arctic life. We were going to stop by Beechey Point and then move our household out to an island in the Arctic Ocean for the spring sealing and the hunting of polar bear.

LOADING OUR TENT AND ALL our supplies, Ook-sook and I struck overland for the camp on the Itkillik where Connie and Ruth awaited us. A blizzard had meantime carried most of the snow off the side hills. I never dreamed there would be a shortage of snow for dog-sled travel in the arctic, but so it was, and today we left our snowshoes upon the sled most of the day and pushed to help the sled over the bare spots.

All the landscape was tinted with a delicate orange light. We were traveling along the bottom of a small stream bed so as to be on snow when the dogs all pricked up their ears, looking at the sky line. From a long distance, first we saw four wolves. Three wolves were black, and one was white. Over the hill closer to us now came a band of around a hundred old bull caribou. They were walking single file with their antlerless heads bobbing from side to side. The low sun painted their coats a dull orange while their white neck manes stood out against the dull gray of the bare hilltop. I realized that the black caribou were changing daily into shades of gray, brown, and white as their hair bleached out in the returning sun. The animals couldn't see us for we were hidden in the stream bed. We watched while the band moved by. No matter how much game I have seen, it always thrills me to see more.

It was a dark night when we drew up at the Itkillik camp. But the place had certainly changed. The snow was all blown away except where held by the willows or grass. Our old sled trail along the bottom of the wash stood out like two raised white concrete rails laid over a desert of brown. Connie soon told me that she and Ruth had experienced a fierce blizzard and they had wondered how we survived it. But Ook-sook and I had met with no strong winds at all. There had been a little gentle breeze that didn't even disturb the soft snow on the willow branches of the upper Kuparuk, that was all. How a storm such as had passed here could sweep over flat prairie with such evidence of violence as was apparent and then slacken for no reason at all into a mere slight breeze when it reached other adjacent areas is a question I can't answer yet—but I understand that this is a frequent phenomenon of the arctic. There are some places which may have an almost chronic windstorm all year long while others may have no wind at all. The Itkillik and the Colville Rivers in their lower reaches near the ocean are subjected to wild winds, but the upper parts of these same rivers inland, which are separated only by flat prairie, are comparatively free of all winds.

Ook-sook was to take Ruth with a load of hides and accumulated meat and camp gear down to the junction of the Itkillik with the Colville, or what we called the Itkillik-pas, where Ruth's people had moved by this time for the late winter season. Ruth was in line for a vacation, for she, the slave who crouched in darkness in her own home, beneath the rule of a tyrannical mother, was *homesick!* Almost all white people, from what I can discover, who have had anything to do with hiring Eskimos find homesickness to be one of their greatest problems—and it may become a major factor in the success of their exploration. The Eskimo people are used to living huddled together in large families and they miss their families when they are away from them for long. We hoped it might do Ruth good to take a vacation with pay and visit her folks awhile before going out on the ocean with us this spring. After taking Ruth and the first load out, Ook-sook would return and the rest of us would move in due time. We all rested and feasted a day or two and on the third day Ruth and Ook-sook left.

On the eve of that day the wind started to blow, and Connie and I realized the last storm was not the final one of the season by any means. We scampered about gathering up the little sticks from the willow patch and making all as shipshape as we could for a siege which we were aware might last several days. Connie described the storm she and Ruth had gone through as being pretty severe. I chopped wood as if I were putting it through a mill and we stowed it inside, leaving another huge mound of it, half as high as the tent, right outside the door. Sometime before now an extra spare canvas had been hung on the front to make a double doorway.

There were no clouds in the sky, but it wasn't hard to tell a gale was coming towards us, for we could feel the wind increase steadily as the hours passed. Here was our first real arctic blizzard together. All night long it roared outside while the whistle of it had become a shriek as it tore through the willow patch about us. Yet inside our camp we were warm and snug. As Connie and Ruth had already been through something like this, we didn't give it much thought. The tumult outside was very effectively blocked off from us by our stanch, thick snow walls.

The following day when I brought in more wood to add to the pile inside which was warming by the stove, the wind nearly picked me off my feet. Yet the sky was clear and there was no flying snow except right near the ground; here, the granular snow and flying sand drove with the fury of a literal sand blast. And still the wind's velocity seemed to increase. How were Ruth and Ook-sook making out? We worried that they might actually freeze to death in their temporary camp on the trail. Ook-sook had had a brother of mature years freeze to death on the Colville near Matthew's camp. The body of the hunter was found just a half mile from home by his mother and Ruth's mother, his Aunt Alice, after the storm passed.

Near daylight the third day I awoke in the warm down bag to hear the outer canvas roof flapping like a bellows while the tent walls beside us were panting like things alive. A feeling of unrest came over me. Suppose our stanch snow walls did *not* hold! Suppose one of them, just one, which sheltered our tent, was blown down? Or suppose the outer canvas which was now flapping was borne suddenly off our roof never to be seen again? Would the storm be able then to scoop right down inside the snow walls and take our tent? If this wind should ever get a brace under one side of the tent, it would lift the tent out from over our heads in one swoop, and nothing on earth could hold it. Of this I felt sure.

Connie and I listened through the dragging minutes to the wind. It had become a steady roar like an airplane engine laboring at top speed and this morning in the darkness it was all too plainly audible.

"Do you suppose the snow walls will actually hold?" asked Connie. "I don't see how they can stand much longer." This was worse than she and Ruth had experienced before.

At about this time it happened. The canvas snow house roof snapped off as one snaps a dish towel. With the snow- house cover gone the wind flattened our tent in one puff. The snow walls around it which had turned to ice during the winter rebuffed the wind from shattering them, and how thankful we were now that they had been built well! As soon as our tent sank below these sheltering walls all was still, but the snow sifted down upon us slowly. Our stovepipe had vanished into the storm.

Somehow, I managed automatically to pull on my outer fur clothes from beneath the bag where I lay on them, and I dressed with care. I told Connie to dress as soon as she could, for I would need her help to get the snow house cover back on—if we could. Once I had plunged outside, I doubted if I would ever get that canvas cover replaced. Day was breaking with a clear sky, but along the ground the gale drove like stinging shot, blinding me and taking my breath away. Fortunately, the canvas cover and the stovepipe were lying in the lee of the snow house and I recovered them.

There was little use in cutting snow blocks to hold the cover on our roof because the snow was all blown away so that there was no material available to make blocks of. They would have been too light to use as weights anyway. Had not a score of blocks weighing up to one hundred pounds each been tumbled off? I crawled back inside the tent to get my breath, for I had found it very hard to breathe in the storm. We managed to right the tent. Snow was blowing into the flapping tent door and down the chimney vent, fast covering all the bedding inside the house, while the lantern which we had lit to dress by swung crazily from the tilted ridgepole, from whence we feared it might come crashing down any minute to set the tent on fire. A curious foresight taken before we both went outdoors together caused us to put out the lantern for fear it might set the tent on fire, but at the same time to put matches in our inner pockets just in case the whole camp should be blown away during our efforts and we should find ourselves without fire when we might want it.

Because we had had to dress in a cold house we were chilled to start with. Connie and I have been awakened on several occasions by some calamity like the house coming down, but the suddenness of the shock is one of the things a person never quite gets used to. I managed to get to the main river bed presently where there was very hard snow, and there I cut some blocks with the ax. The wind was so severe that I could hardly lift the ax for each stroke, and many of the blows were deflected. It was impossible to walk upright so I sneaked through the willows in a bent-over position, almost on hands and knees. The big blocks I cut would have made all others I have seen look small; I have no idea how much they weighed—around 150 pounds, I suppose. After two hours of crawling back and forth I had about a ton of these ice blocks ready to place around the top of the snow walls to hold the canvas down. The work had warmed me up but Connie was cold in the tent. I called her out of the house again and together we tried our luck.

By tying one corner of the canvas sheet to a strong willow with a length of rope I anchored it so that it could not get away. Then I told Connie to stand by and holding onto the snow wall for support to pull her end of the canvas over the roof. We could not hear each other scream directions except by putting the mouth close to the other person's ear; so, Connie held her end of the canvas down to the snow wall while I roped down the other end. With this done we had the wind bested for the moment.

I now started piling my great ice cakes on top of the canvas to hold it to the snow walls. Each cake had to be lifted as high as my shoulders, and without any breakfast yet I thought for a minute that I could never do it. And yet—the cakes were not heavy enough! The wind blew them off even though we had twice as many of them as originally, and in fact all the wall could accommodate.

We crawled into the downed tent and rested and thought again between operations. Finally, I hit upon the plan of pouring water on the snow wall and onto the canvas to stick it that way. Fortunately for us the water bucket inside the house was not frozen quite solid; a little water was found in the bottom of the bucket when we had chopped through the ice. Because we had no way of melting more water until we could get the tent up and the stove up, this water was to be carefully used. We didn't have a drop to spare. I poured it mighty carefully onto the top of the snow wall and then clamped a 150-pound block in place as Connie assisted, and the twenty below zero temperature froze it quickly solid. In this way we anchored down the ton of snow blocks and had a roof to our house once more.

The siege had lasted four or five hours altogether and we had had no breakfast so that we needed something to eat by this time. Fear and emergency are not met well on an empty stomach. Quickly I started a fire in the set-up stove and all was warm, and the snow brushed out of our house or melted within the hour. Our shaken nerves were reconciled with a big feast of boiled moose tongue and moose nose, which was all that was left of the moose brought to Connie as a present. We both recognized the danger there would have been had we not had our Eskimo clothing and our snow walls to protect our tent. With only a tent, that wind would have torn it to shreds and no trace of it, or perhaps of us, would ever have been found. A person's clothing would have gone with the tent had he been caught asleep in a sleeping bag. But by benefit of the Eskimo techniques for existence we could have curled up in our fur clothing and waited, even if uncomfortably, for the storm to blow itself out if we had had to. Although not a pleasant experience, even this could be done.

We spent a happy blizzard after that with a warm dry camp. We were short of food, but fortunately on a still day just previously Connie and I had taken advantage of mild temperatures and the returning sun to go out upon the prairie near the tent with our .22 rifle, and we had shot forty ptarmigan. The field was full of white, hopping, occupied birds, busily feeding and very tame just following the former storm—and we had gathered them quickly in gunnysacks and taken them home to pick and prepare. While our remaining caribou meat outside the house was sandblasted by the storm and some of it lost, we were left to exist altogether on these ptarmigan boiled without salt until Ook-sook's return for us.

Two days later the storm had passed, and a glorious day dawned. When we stepped out of our snow house it seemed like spring. Ptarmigan and black ravens were singing and chirping; there was a great stillness after the passing of the wind, and. the breeze was sweet, balmy, and warm almost to the thawing point. As a matter of fact, it occasionally does thaw in midwinter in the arctic! Mosquitoes have risen prematurely from the ground for a short time in February or in March. A thaw out of season is a very inconvenient thing and a dreaded thing, for the weather always turns severe afterwards, turning the land to ice with no snow left out of which one can build any shelter, while game may perish. Fortunately, this did not happen, but George "Woods and others have seen it happen. Connie and I prowled about and shot a few more ptarmigan. The passing storm had left the Itkillik River bottom a tunnel of mud, and all the earth for miles about was brown and wind-blasted.

When Ook-sook returned after a good many days he told us that he and Ruth had been able to get to Matthew's before the full force of the big wind struck. Ook-sook mentioned that he had killed a caribou one day's journey from the Itkillik camp. He had not thought to bring any of the meat on here with him, so we all ate ptarmigan again.

7

The day we broke camp and said good-by to the little spot on the Itkillik which had been our winter's home, the sun was bright, and we realized that soon we must use our sunglasses to prevent snow blindness. Spring is the great season for this malady, which comes on gradually if care is not taken. Complete "blindness" from the glare is probably unknown, but what one gets is scratchy feeling eyes and presently a splitting eye ache or headache which is a painful nuisance. This is what snow blindness chiefly amounts to. The greatest danger in getting it lies, strangely enough, on an overcast day of no sun and no shadows. On such a day one's eyes are under a strain in searching out the rough trail which is worse than that caused by a day of full sunlight. Another strong tendency to snow blindness comes from traveling or hunting entirely by night during this season, for the same reason. No shadows and the evenness of the dull glare cause some of the Eskimos to be troubled with snow blindness because of their staying up all night and being careless about wearing their dark glasses in spring. Dogs do not get snow blindness that I know of, but I have often wondered why they and other animals should not.

As we left the Itkillik camp ptarmigan hurried ahead of us, so busy pecking at buds that they could be driven in herds across the prairie, as they almost hated to look up and be bothered; the birds must have dieted considerably all through the several days' storm, for their appetites were keen. It was good hunting now for fox and wolf and all the animals.

At times we took short cuts across the bends of the crooked river. Although the ground was largely bare the drifts necessitated the use of snowshoes. For the bare stretches we quickly stepped out of our snowshoes and carried them under our arms, only to put them on again for the next few acres. Once we came to a place where the wind had blown straight down the river. We walked out on a drift and there, thirty feet below, emerging from under the drift, was our old sled trail. When we had come here three months ago there had been only soft fluffy snow over the river ice. When the winds came, all this loose snow had been swept from the river, and it left our sled trail standing like two white railroad rails. From this I learned that, contrary to popular opinion, winds do not always erase a trail in the snow of the arctic, but they may imprint such a trail more plainly than ever so that it will never be lost through all the winter to come.

But the greatest lesson to be learned from this study of our old sled trail was that if a novice had selected this site right here as his winter's camp on the basis that it would be "sheltered" by the cut bank thirty feet high nearby, he would now have his camp buried under a thirty-foot drift. A prime lesson in picking campsites on the arctic plains is *not* to choose them in the lee of some obstruction, as a "sheltered" spot, for the snow will collect here. He should build his camp right in the open. Many a former arctic explorer has learned this lesson at a great cost in equipment and sometimes of his own life.

All morning Connie and I strode chatting and exploring over a glittering world of endless prairie. Connie had got so used to the shelter of her home this winter on the Itkillik that, like many confined people, she had almost dreaded the day she would have to embark again on the 150-mile trip back to Beechey Point. But now that she had started, she was so ecstatic over the new-found brightness and beauty of the world that she wondered, she said, how she had ever found the quiet life satisfying. Travel does things to people: some people have only to start.

Near noon Ook-sook caught up with us and we traveled on with the sled, striding rapidly ahead of the dogs to encourage them. The sun crept behind the horizon as we came to the place where Ook-sook had killed the caribou he had spoken of. Where the animal had fallen were pieces of tom skin and blood stained the snow in several directions. The carcass of course was frozen. There wasn't a piece of skin as big as a dinner plate to be seen. The pitiful story was all too evident to me, although I saw no reason to mention it to Connie at that time.

I had often seen it written at a wolf kill and once in actuality when in hunting with Ook-sook the dogs had broken loose to swarm over a crippled caribou which had been shot. The dogs, with sled attached, had caught the caribou or Ook-sook had let them catch it before I could get there, I never knew which. The team had literally skinned the caribou alive. Eight dogs all tearing at a deer at once can quickly pull it right apart. A caribou will flee from danger but once it is caught by wolves or dogs it ceases to struggle and is actually eaten alive. I tried to convey to Ook-sook that he must always shoot a crippled animal again, yet he would always kill it with a knife or let the dogs catch it. I had plainly never succeeded in convincing him that I had plenty of bullets and didn't mind expending the extra one, and when he was by himself I suspected that he continued with his own methods regardless. The bullet that he "saved" would kill or cripple another caribou that neither he nor the dogs could catch. Ook-sook is a primitive man.

The next afternoon a solitary caribou was sighted in our path which I was tempted to get to take along. I thought it a little strange that this caribou was all by itself, but Ook- sook, looking through the glasses, announced it to be a fawn. Since we could use a fawnskin well, I asked Connie if she would like to try her luck as a hunter, but she declined.

Therefore, I went off to make a stalk of it while Ook-sook cast down the sled anchor and he and Connie waited by the sled. There was a convenient mound by which I could make my approach to the animal. But my telescope sight on my rifle was out of line—probably, we think now, from Connie's having jumped on and off it when she jumped off and on the sled during our travel—and the fawn was really a very decrepit or sick old cow which had not had the vitality to even so much as shed the velvet from its horns from the previous fall. Its sickliness and lack of vigor were the obvious reason why it was an outcast from any herd and wandered aimlessly by itself. Moreover, it was farther from my position behind the mound than any of us had realized from the sled. My second shot broke the animal's hind leg and knocked it down in so doing. It got up and ran on three legs out of sight around the far end of the mound. Connie was confident all the time that I would shoot again and get it before she and Ook-sook arrived, so that when Ook-sook took up the sled anchor in response to the dogs' impatient wails and himself climbed on the back of the sled, she sat composed enough on the sled load as the team tore after the fleeing caribou.

Had the caribou been left alone it would have gone off only to lie down shortly, when I would have stalked it and killed it with ease, but a caribou which is chased can run for endless miles, even with only three good legs. As the sled tore after the animal I was of course soon left far behind, and the riders themselves could only hang on for dear life and trust not to be upset. The dogs went wild and there was no stopping them now.

It was a wild ride. Still, Connie says she had no great misgivings until after a mile the sled rapidly began to close down on the crippled deer, whose shattered bloody leg could be seen flopping up and down as it ran. Connie now began to wonder just what it was her responsibility to do and concluded that she should shoot the caribou before the dogs got it, as they were certainly going to do. As the careening sled drew ever closer she realized to her horror that this was surely going to happen right in front of her eyes. She had always loved animals and the thought was unbearable. With one hand bare of its mitten she struggled to unstrap the frozen buckle which held her rifle in its case upon the bouncing sled, while still hanging on with the other hand in some peril. A glance at Ook-sook's composed and rather amused countenance as he skillfully rode the sled and made no effort to reach for his own gun told her at once the whole story that I had known all along: that Ook-sook was quite accustomed to letting his dogs catch and pull down wounded caribou.

As the savage dogs lunged forward, Connie asked Ook-sook to cast out the sled anchor, but Ook-sook was my boy and he was not used to taking orders from anybody but me, and he did not do so; he was a man and he did not even consider it. Still Connie cherished the idea that Ook-sook would presently halt the dogs somehow. As the dogs rushed in, the caribou turned to face them; its useless large velvety horns lowered to meet the pitiless enemy, it waited an instant that seemed an eternity, and then the whole team was upon it.

The unbelievable was happening. Connie had never thought she would be forced to be witness to such a sight. The pathetic deer was pulled to its back, its eyes wild with fright, while growls and gurgles succeeded howls of delight from the pack which tore at its belly. Ook-sook jumped lightly off his perch on the back of the sled and ran to the fore; presently he had the whole team in his hands, dragging them, and then he had the horns of the deer which he tried to drag away from them with shouts at them to desist. Dogs, sled, deer, and our primitive hunter in the middle of them were a confused blur while Connie tells me she was of no use whatever but still struggled with numbed fingers to get her gun from its frozen case. And this is how accidents with sleds and dogs can happen!

She got her rifle at last, pumped a shell into the chamber and let the hammer down on the safety catch so that the gun would not be cocked as she ran up to the melee. It was her duty to kill the deer out of mercy since Ook-sook just squatted there holding it, yet she remembered she must not shoot Ook-sook or the dogs. She left her mittens on the sled, as shooting is usually done barehanded.

But as she stepped out in front of the sled, just then the caribou broke loose from Ook-sook and was on its feet once more. Now was the time to shoot it if she could get a sight on it. It was just at this split instant that the sled struck her from behind.

Connie was knocked down, dogs ran over her, and here came the heavily loaded sled weighing about five hundred pounds. Connie was in front of the runners on her seat, plowing a furrow with the sled about to run over her bent back, as the dogs rushed forward heedlessly. Her feet were stretched out ahead of her, bracing the entire load against the strength of the uncontrolled dogs after the deer. Ook- sook grabbed the sled from behind in an attempt to hold it, and just as it got away from him, Connie flipped over onto her side in some unknown instinct of self-preservation and saw the runners of the sled slide by an inch from her face in the snow. Ook-sook had himself been tumbled into the snow at this and the two suddenly found themselves sitting upon the ground side by side, and one looked just as surprised as the other did.

Their first thoughts were now for themselves, not the deer. The dogs had got away with their sled and everything on it, and they were left afoot on the prairie. Getting to their feet, the one raced to catch the dogs and sled while the other raced back for her rifle, which had been thrown aside with some force and now lay a few yards distant. One of

Connie's mittens lay there with the rifle. The other was on the sled and gone, and it took no aid to memory to recall that it was forty below zero today.

As Connie picked up her rifle she became conscious that her fingers were turning to ice right there. She shakily saw that Ook-sook had caught the team again because they had caught the caribou, and all were in the same attitudes of absorption as before. Ook-sook was vainly trying to beat off the dogs. A rope of intestines was being pulled from the deer's belly. Faint with nausea Connie's mind turned to what she considered her duty. She could not stand it; she must shoot the animal. As though in a trance she jerked the stiff lever of the little carbine which she knew so well, and a shell came up in it and jammed. She had forgotten, you see, that she had already loaded it once before, and that a shell was in it. However, she stopped before she jammed it badly and she quickly dug the second shell out. It dropped from her fingers into the snow and she reached to pick it up.

Somehow, she must have thought that she couldn't afford to lose a shell. By habit and with some difficulty she got the odd shell into the hip pocket of her pants underneath her long parka. Meanwhile time was passing, and this just goes to show the things people will do in the stress of hurry under shock.

When Connie ran up this time Ook-sook was holding the deer by its antlers, and it lay calmly; the dogs, quieted now that the animal no longer struggled, were merely trying to sniff at it. Connie wondered, momentarily, she says, what Ook-sook must think of her actions. Securing her other mitten from the sled she decided to wait for me, since she could see me now fast arriving on my snowshoes. Some disinclination, inability to take action, had blocked her all along; it takes a lot of nerve for a white woman, even though she may consider herself an experienced hunter, to take command in an Eskimo environment. This was very fortunate because what Connie had not seen in her concern for the deer was that the muzzle of her rifle was so packed with solid ice from its fall that there could not even be thought of repair until we camped to thaw it out. Had she fired that rifle in that condition she would have blown it to pieces and possibly have blown her own head quite off.

Connie was a pretty shaken girl when I came up. She was almost unable to speak, and the tears streamed down her face as she quietly begged me, "Bud, will you please shoot this animal?"

I said I would. I strode to the deer which lay crouched back as far as it could get with its soft body pressed against the sled. I pointed my rifle downward, shot, and turned to other things. Smoke curled up in a little streamer; it had been necessary to shoot the deer in the heart rather than at the base of the neck as we usually do because I could not shoot into the sled. Connie kept looking in fascination at the deer, which blinked voicelessly at us. "Sometimes it takes them a moment to die when shot in the heart," I explained to her. But Connie was skeptical. A moment later the caribou saw its chance and leapt up, the sled plunged off, we were all knocked off our feet, and the delighted dogs had the animal down again. That moment I really cursed a dog team. Presently I was able to put a bullet into the deer's brain, and I felt a little sick myself. I had not seen any of the other occurrences, but now I fully realized all, while Connie wept, and Ook-sook looked sneaking and foolish. Then Ook-sook's mind turned to practical things and he busied himself at cutting out some chunks of the fresh raw meat for the dogs.

IT WAS A JOURNEY so long before we reached our habitation near midnight that night that none had time to brood upon the past unpleasant experience; the way it turned out we needed every bit of strength we had, and perhaps this was a good thing, for a few hours later, although she was nearly dead on her feet, Connie's nervous system was in perfect working order again and she was surviving well. This has to be in such a life. There is nothing like pushing and pulling a dog sled for miles on a cool day to work any surplus emotions out of the system in short order.

Our dogs were so weary that they would hardly go. Looking at them I thought sorrowfully how I had planned to improve their lot but in leading the Eskimo life in its vicious cycle had not been able to. The poor dogs had had a good many miles of trail and sadly needed a rest. I had come to realize that if these dogs ate up every seal and every fish and every caribou in north Alaska they could never be improved much beyond their present miserable state for they were degenerate mongrel stock to begin with, and in the second place our team, I knew now, was beset with worms. I had no medicine to give them to cure the worms with, and so it went.

I myself was the leanest of the lean. I was by build a much more powerful man than Ook-sook and I could beat him at all games of strength and skill except running; he had run me to death. While often he had double-tripped on our journeys and I had taken a day's rest in camp, he remained plump and compact as ever and his face seldom showed fatigue. One reason for this was apparent enough: his ability to get the best and the fattest piece of meat at all times and to eat ten pieces while I was eating one. I believe that the quantities of oils and grease and tallow he could consume during a hunt kept him in this fine condition, whereas those many nights in a snow igloo on the prairie this winter when we had had only raw meat and a bone to gnaw, or had existed on a boiled caribou head or the boiled moose head, as on one occasion, told on me after some months simply because the Eskimo consistently out ate me as man to man when it came to his native foods, to which I was not as well adapted yet as he. Little by little I had lost my appetite from sheer fatigue and living on nothing, but lean boiled ptarmigan the last two weeks had been a final privation.

Absorbed in his own dreams, Ook-sook gradually drew ahead of the dogs and disappeared in the gathering gloom of night, leaving Connie and me alone on the prairie trying to make the team go. The dogs would sit back and howl for that beloved figure at intervals, but once they had lost sight of Ook-sook in the distance they seemed to lose heart. I had great difficulty in forcing them to go. I would rattle the chain in the sled in threat of beating them with it, as I had seen Ook-sook do, and finally for our own preservation I even did some flailing. Connie, sitting on the load, now dizzily swayed while I hung onto the sides for support as I walked beside it. At last we both jumped on the sled and rode every time it started, so that all in all we must have jumped on and off a thousand times. Unfortunately, I was fast developing a bum ankle; perhaps I was so thin my joints needed oiling. It is a truth I know from experience that when a person gets thin in this life many small ailments soon develop and things go wrong. We were at the stage of two drunks when there came to us once again in the starlight that wonderful smell of wood smoke. Our dogs barked, rather feebly, made a very feeble rush forward, and there were Ruth and Cyrus and Alice and all their family, standing waiting for us outside an igloo. Ruth had been very "homesick" for Connie. She seemed to have shrunk to a tiny squat thing, smaller than we had remembered, during her absence from us, but I remembered her stubbornness well. We could barely see her happy grin as we gave her our hands.

Getting into the low doorway of the house in jackknife position was an excruciating gymnastic feat after the day's ordeals. Meanwhile our good Ook-sook, who had been following a trail in total darkness for the last ten miles—don't ask me how—was tying the dogs outside before he could enter. He would always be the first one out in the morning and the last one in at night, and he was loyal and true.

We sank down on the floor within. The people had been living upon nothing, but ptarmigan snared by Alice and the children, who kept the family going at this season, and upon a long, spotted fish, the *tictalirk*, several specimens of which were thrown upon the woodpile at this time squirming slightly behind the stove. Ruth squatted happily cutting up the *tictalirk*[2] for boiling in a ten-gallon pot, the house being full of visitors, as we soon saw.

The fish were caught by cutting holes through the five- foot ice of the Colville River at the junction of the Itkillik and jigging for them with a four-pronged barbless snag hook. A white piece of cloth was

---

2   It has recently come to the authors* attention that the fish herein described by us and known to the north coast Alaska Eskimos as tictalirk is now being hailed as a new medical find. Along the Canadian border at Baudette, Minnesota, our own *tictalirk* flourishes as *burbot* in the waters of Lake of the Woods and in other northern lakes; it ranges "from Labrador and the maritime provinces of Canada down to New England, New York, the Great Lakes and west to the upper Missouri, the Columbia River basin, Alaska and the entire arctic region," we now know. Formerly considered as worthless and but little known and seldom seen, this fish was discovered by young Ted Rowell, a graduate of the University of Minnesota School of Pharmacy, to have a vitamin content "four times more potent in vitamin A than the best cod liver oil on the market." The American Medical Association rates its oil as "eight times more potent than cod liver oil," especially the oil of the liver, which is now being produced on a commercial scale to supply civilization with vitamins. (From "Vitamin Harvest" by Robert Page Lincoln, *Popular Mechanics*, March 1947 p. 148. This is a resume of the material, not a quotation, except where quotation marks indicate.)

tied to the top of the shank, or a white ivory trinket was the lure. All day long the members of this family, including the smallest children, sit beside these holes cut in the ice, just as the Eskimos we have seen in the cartoons, jigging for fish. Giving little jerks on the line to cause the lure and the snag hook to bob, the Eskimo family sat on the ice, each beside his fishing hole. The lure would dance just off the bottom, where the blunt-faced, smooth-skinned *tictalirk* prowls in water six to ten fathoms deep. When the *tictalirk* comes to investigate the white bobbing thing he gets snagged on the hooks. The fisherman pulls up the thrashing body out of the hole in the ice, and since the hooks of the snag have no barbs, the fish flies off onto the ice, where he quickly freezes.

As for the caribou which chiefly concerns the adventures of this trip, it was but wolf bait when we found it. That is, it was—literally—waiting to be killed by wolves.

Its extreme emaciation when it was killed rendered it so worthless to us that we gave it to Ruth's family if one of them would simply follow back on our trail the next day to get it. The family had nothing to eat but the few fish and ptarmigan they secured day by day. Ruth's brother Johnny said he would sled back to get the deer, but we noticed that, Eskimo-like, he made no effort to do so. Something which was of more interest in his mind was the report we all heard of the coming of white men near by

8

It was from Ook-sook that we had first heard the arresting news that a caterpillar train had come along the Colville River going from Barrow to Umiat, right past Matthew's front door I At least we deduced from what Ook-sook said that it must have been an arctic caterpillar train. There were many white men. A white man sat in the cab of the leading vehicle and tossed cookies out the window to the Eskimos, who caught them, Ruth told us. She had never eaten any of this kind of cookies before and she wanted to know from us what kind they were called, but we were unable to tell her. We wouldn't have minded catching some of those cookies ourselves!

The caterpillar train traveled twenty-four hours a day steadily across the arctic, using regular headlights at night, and it had made a great road in passing that was handy for the traveling dog sleds of the people who went at once to visit each other's camps and discuss it. The white men who came, although they threw cookies, never stopped for a moment on their way, but bore steadily on.

At Ruth's home where this was discussed there were many people sitting. Besides Cyrus and Alice, with their children, Johnny, Wilbur, Thomas, Hattie, and Ruth, there were visiting overnight old Matthew and Harriet, and Ook-sook's sister, who had brought three of her five children along, making a total of thirteen people, which with our party of three more totaled sixteen people altogether to sleep on that one 10' X 12' floor. It was a good board house, but a very tiny one. Since there is no fuel at the mouth of the Itkillik, all of the sticks had to be hauled long distances to make survival possible. Some of the family and their guests slept out in an extra snow house attachment which had been built for emergencies, and as usual Connie and I were given the best and warmest comer for our own sleeping bag, where we had tried to make ourselves as small as possible.

All smiles and more delighted at seeing us than we had ever seen her, Ruth worked like a dog, being the only person to wait on this whole crowd; her chores at home consisted of bringing in snow blocks to melt her own water and packing in most of her wood for fuel, while attending to the butchering of the fish and serving and dishwashing. We were sure she wanted to go on with us, but we had a feeling in our bones as soon as we entered this dwelling that there would be unpleasantness before we got out of it. Therefore, we were not surprised when, the morning we were to leave, Ruth's parents began about giving Ruth a raise. She should either have had the raise or been sent home long since! But there had been no way to send her home, despite the fact that Cyrus had sent us a nasty letter about it to the Itkillik camp, carried by Koloyuk. She should have been sent home by her cousin Koloyuk who came by our camp at his trapping! We replied that Koloyuk would then have charged us for taking her, as he had other things to do; Koloyuk did not understand English anyway. We had never discussed wages with Ruth but had paid her and stuck to the bargain we had made. Ruth had been happy with us so far as it went.

Well, did not Ruth chop wood for Connie? We replied that Ruth had had most of her wood chopped for *her* by the men when we were at camp and that Connie had chopped a good deal of it when we were gone. Ruth had spent the winter with us with a sprained wrist caused by some overwork at home, and I had done it up in a sling for the winter, but it was well now. I explained earnestly that we never expected Ruth to do anything Connie didn't do, and that Ruth had eaten an equal share with Connie of all the imported foods, which Ook-sook and I had had to haul for them. But didn't Ruth sew for us? George and Nanny Woods got hundreds of dollars from us, so Alice had heard, for doing our sewing! And so on—a long, long harangue as the family of malcontents brought up one point after another on which they had brooded, hoping to get Ruth's wages raised so that it might accrue to the family.

Connie, a sincere advocate of raising the wages of domestic labor, was extremely attached to Ruth; she had taught her "school" all winter and the Eskimo girl had learned with remarkable facility. Connie gave Ruth personal gifts—a bath towel, scented toilet soap, a blanket, a comb, cotton stockings of the kind the women were so fond of, things given to herself for the most part by missionaries. Connie looked sensitive under the abusive accusations of Cyrus as he sought in every way to force his bargain. But I had told Connie how I had seen Cyrus at Christmas at the trading post and how he had bartered a revenue of forty dollars from foxes for flour and coffee which was consumed in the big Christmas fling during one week, leaving not one cent to improve the situation of the small children of his family for the rest of the year. Cyrus had not purchased one fish net or one box of ammunition! That had settled me right there.

"We are just young people," we tried to explain to him. "We are not rich."

Finally, getting threatening, Cyrus said: "You treat those fellows that work for you just like slaves!" and he added bitterly that he thought Connie would have had a hard time of it alone up there on the Itkillik but for the company of Ruth. He talked with Ook-sook then in Eskimo and we realized what was coming next: the family was going to put the squeeze on right here for a raise for both Ook-sook and Ruth at one time. This was bad. If the old man got our good Ook-sook discontented or used him as a weapon to advance Ruth with us, we could be in a difficult spot, and he knew it. "What would you do alone there at your house at Beechey Point with no dog team on this coast?" he sneered. "What you folks do for wood then, eh? You would freeze!"

We realized that he spoke better English than we had known. What had been his experiences with white men before now that he had such bitterness and thought the world owed him a living?

The ugly threats only made me mad, but I kept my temper. Connie and I knew enough about the arctic by now so that we weren't as afraid of it as the old man probably thought. He was trying to use a weapon to scare us. We never batted an eye. We knew right then that we would never give in to his insistence. A stand must be taken someplace or there would be literally no end! I replied, "Well, if the Eskimo people treat us no good on this coast, we can just go to Barrow and go live someplace else. Or we can go to the United States. We don't have to live here."

Old Cyrus tried to hide his disappointment; the Eskimos all along the coast would feel very hurt if we left, and it would be a disgrace on his shoulders, Cyrus knew! We were well liked everywhere and had developed a reputation for honesty and reliability. Cyrus hated Abraham and he hated even some of his own relatives, because they were more prosperous than he who yearly almost allowed his own family to starve. He tried to force his last weapon against us: "Ook-sook says if he had some ammunition he would go hunt caribou now." We took this to mean at the time that Ook- sook was telling us he was dissatisfied with his employment, but later I realized Ook-sook merely was thinking that he should lay in more caribou meat for me; thus, he expressed his loyalty to us. Ook-sook had never taken easily to learning English; his talents did not run along bookish lines, and he knew little of what the argument was all about. Ruth hung her head and looked away. Connie had been her best friend and the one who had always been the kindest to her of any person in all her life.

At the end when Cyrus announced flatly that Ruth would not continue with us, I myself didn't care whether she did or not; the jealous and greedy parents of the unfortunate girl had made the entire thought disagreeable. Ruth's main value had consisted in keeping Connie company and in keeping Ook-sook content by affording him someone of his own language to talk to: all in all, the four of us had had some chummy card games and some good times in camp! This last threat failing to elicit any regret from us, however, Cyrus said, beaten: "You will understand someday. You will understand."

His voice was so dead and lifeless that we were truly sorry. The bitterness of the family's poverty was as cruel to see and be exposed to in its way as was the killing of the caribou the day before. What did he mean, "You will understand someday"? When did Cyrus think the white people would ever be in such a position as he? His words and his tone cast the spell of an evil sorcerer.

Although these Eskimos profess to be orthodox Christians, they have ancient beliefs as old as the race which are common among many primitive peoples and throughout other cultures around the world: the Oriental's account of the inequality of men and their handicaps. Did old Cyrus believe that we rich white people might be born as poor Eskimos someday, like him? Perhaps he did not think it impossible.

When we left in the morning, Ruth and Ook-sook were again with our family, and old Duk, the lead dog, and his plumed followers were happy that we were all together once more. We could hardly wait to get started, for Cyrus and Alice had divulged that white men were camping in a tent with an airplane beside them just six miles down the river along our way. Were the Eskimos sure? What details could they give us? We didn't get much on this subject but hurried to see for ourselves before the mythical white men should fly away.

Down the middle of the Colville River this morning ran a trail that resembled a snow-covered highway. The river ice had been shoveled as though by a snowplow where tractors, pulling great boxcar sleds, had passed. Our dogs trotted serenely down this unaccustomed highway that marked the spot where the old dog team trails had been. Eskimo fishing holes cut through the ice were to be seen on either side. Ruth's kid brother Johnny, a beaming teen-ager, always ready for a handout, harnessed up his own shabby team and trailed along with us: he was going six miles in hopes of a cup of coffee. Our two shabby footsore outfits, the dogs only tied together by odds and ends of rope and even strings, strained in their old caribou-hide harness to pull a few pounds where hundreds of tons had so easily passed before. Connie and I had come here just in time to see the beginning of the change of the arctic.

Down the frozen river bed as seen through a white blur stood a sight: a brightly painted, tethered airplane. We saw the plane first and then we saw the little white tent. The tent was pitched beneath a sheltering bluff! Great dunes of snow were the background. Suddenly we were beset by a fear that the white men might fly away before we could reach them.

Crippled with my bum ankle I was lucky to hitch a ride on Johnny's sled. Ruth forged along with Ook-sook with our own load, and Connie tagged behind at the last. I saw two airplanes now, and the sound was borne to my ears through gusty snow clouds of one of them just warming up. Should I wait for Connie before approaching the camp? I decided to. We strolled into camp together and because of our Eskimo costumes were not recognized as white people until we made ourselves known.

One airplane which had been warming with the aid of a firepot was taking off just at this minute. This was the first airplane Ook-sook's dogs had ever seen. When the pilot raced the engine, they set up a pitiful wail and trembled, while some tried to break away.

We soon recognized that two of the men were in field uniform; they were soldiers and were awaiting their discharge from the war which had closed the summer before, and, as we soon found, they were here doing geographical work locating certain key points about northern Alaska with instruments, shooting angles at the stars each clear night. They discovered, for instance, that the present position on the lower Colville was five minutes of one degree off on all our maps. About all they did otherwise was to stay in their tent, and all things were furnished to them, including a radio for entertainment, and they knew little actually about arctic life, being not prepared by clothing or otherwise to venture out into it, even should an emergency arise. We had a hard time to convince them that the Eskimo clothing we wore was actually serviceable because they did not like the looks of it on the Eskimos they had seen, and besides, the hairs shed. On the other hand, we thought the heavy cumbersome shoes the government furnished them were the most unserviceable items that could have been chosen for men in the arctic, although perhaps it was all right if you considered that they did not expect ever to have to walk with them. They lived all the time just a few feet from their stove. A day later the three men— two soldiers and their pilot—were due to be set down at Cape Halkett, where they would continue to be serviced by the *two* airplanes which were necessary to supply the needs of life and scientific work. The expense to the government of getting the three men into the arctic was considerable in as much as the cost of chartering the two planes alone came to $1200 a week.

We were invited at once to come into the tent. Their oil stove was a powerful devil; no frost formed inside the large tent of the white men. But I had become so accustomed to the solidly built Eskimo camps that I was hardly prepared for this one. A few snow blocks had been stacked around the base of the big flimsy tent and this was all. The memory of our last blizzard was still so fresh in our minds that it could not be dismissed. Ook-sook was amazed himself. True, it was calm enough weather right now, but—Although Ook- sook and I showed them as tactfully as we could how to put snow blocks around the sides in the proper way, I don't believe the fellows ever quite believed us; they never quite saw the necessity of it. They had camped about the arctic in the big flimsy tent with their roaring oil stove before now and no especial gale had ever descended. They imagined they had the arctic just about whipped and that it was just something to play with.

Feeling a certain loyalty to our Eskimo companions which the white soldiers probably could not appreciate, we brought them into the tent with us. Presently Johnny got his coffee and Ruth went to visit friends who happened to live within the snow mound that was just across the river. Ook-sook remained, looking rather stern, as he sometimes did, and finally found amusement in playing at the Eskimo card game while the rest of us talked.

If the outside of the tent surprised us I must say that in many ways the inside fulfilled our fondest dreams. There was the radio playing music of the modern dance bands, the oil cookstove for which you didn't have to cut wood at all, air mattresses on the bunks, while a caribou skin covered the floor which itself wasn't so bad. Two bright gasoline lanterns flooded the tent and I could actually stand straight indoors for the first time in many months, although Connie and I and Ook-sook involuntarily hunched when we went into it.

We felt out of place in our Eskimo clothes around such civilization as the interior presented to our eyes, yet our common sense did not defer to appearances. The soldiers asked us many questions about how we camped and lived, and they could not believe it possible that we could find wood for fuel in this country or that we could exist as we did. For the past month now, we had been out of all food except ptarmigan and what odds and ends we could get, but here was a real feast coming up, a point in entertainment of concern to Connie and Ook-sook and me.

"What is the world news now?" we wanted to know. They couldn't think of any.

"There must be something," we put in.

"Not offhand. I can't think of any, can you?" said one fellow, turning to another. I don't know exactly what we had expected. There didn't seem to be any new news, or at least we gathered none.

As I have said, the group was composed of the two servicemen and an older man who was the chartered pilot for the present plane. You sized the servicemen up as the nice young one, kind of husky and chesty, with a three months' beard, just out of New York, and then his subordinate, only twenty- two, rabbit-brained and kind of a dandy by temperament. The best one, the one we found most agreeable and the one who did most of the camp work for the others, besides the fact that he was the boss, conversed very intelligently, it seemed to us, about what he believed to be the fundamental changes taking place in American society generally, and it was he who gave us our world news, what we got of it. This fellow and Connie together made the rest of us a big batch of spaghetti and meat balls, while the older man sat back and said little and the younger one said, "Oh, hell, spaghetti again?" He wasn't hungry!

Before the meal we brought in a bit of our one remaining chunk of raw frozen caribou meat so that everybody could taste this item. The men were game and said they wanted to learn what there is to it at first hand. But the experiment was no howling success. The men liked it all right or said they found it rather "tasteless" and non-objectionable, but when Ook-sook failed to do his part and plunged into the coffee with cream and the spaghetti, that rather let us down!

In the evening we concocted a good devil's food cake—two layers—from cake mix, for which I used the last of some chocolate drink mix they had in the camp to make frosting, and a plate of fudge, inasmuch as it was the government's food and the fellows would get reimbursements tomorrow. The rabbit-brain offered us all a drink from a bottle of whiskey he sucked on, but nobody liked it but him.

Near midnight while we were still talking hours on end a light gleamed along the Colville, which was becoming quite a traffic route. I recognized it, for so often I had seen the same sight far away on some desert highway in our West. It was the glow of headlights from an approaching vehicle. Half an hour later, Morris, a Barrow white man of many years' standing, and his Eskimo companion drew up driving a Weasel. We were all in bed when Morris arrived—Connie and I and Ook-sook bedded down in our bags on the floor—and the conversation was conducted from bed. Morris wouldn't stop for coffee. He was on his way from Umiat, following the trail left by a caterpillar train, traveling in a heated cab.

The next day being clear, our surveyor friends were to leave for a new location. At breakfast time Rabbit-Brain announced he couldn't stand eggs and he seldom ate butter and why not just have coffee? The pilot laconically started some bacon just as I was afraid nobody was going to want breakfast. "Let's just eat the left-over cake," suggested one. Of course, Connie and I had rather had that in mind, but we wanted something else to go with it, because after all, there was only a small half cake left for six people, so I announced brazenly that I am a dickens of a good biscuit maker when given the trimmings. Looking at our favorite trouble-bum who had such a lagging appetite I said seriously: "What, cake with bacon?" in a scandalized tone, and he admitted that when he thought about it cake and bacon wouldn't go well together. Consequently, I made biscuits and got down ten myself, along with syrup and butter and the bacon and cake. Connie thought she would get the remains of the cake herself when we broke camp, but I felt softhearted and slipped it and the candy out to the Eskimos who came by to watch—the last and only chocolate on the north coast of North America. I almost regretted it later.

Connie was washing the breakfast dishes when the pilot of the second plane came in. Eskimos had come from all directions like magic, attracted to the sight. I suppose we were a colorful crew all in all, what with sleds and slant-eyed, furry dogs, papooses and gaily painted airplanes beside the tent piled with snow blocks. The assembled Eskimos had been shy and very polite to the white men. One used to them could observe that they had come dressed in their best, whether the white men recognized this or not—which I don't think they did. The white men had seen the Eskimos as human beings only very vaguely, as a kind of scenery at which they had tired of looking long ago during their enforced arctic sojourn. And, too, it is surprising how little curiosity people have about other groups as people.

At so many dollars being spent for the airplane service the camp must be upended and everything packed in a hurry. As usual, the new pilot grumbled audibly as he began pitching snow blocks from the tent helter-skelter, while Connie ran to dump the left-over coffee into the snow; she was too ashamed to pour it out in front of the famished eyes of the watching Eskimos, so hit upon the expedient of mixing it with the dishwater so that what she did was disguised before our friends. In half an hour all was ready and the first plane and then the second plane took off on skis. Women and children scurried back from the roar, while our dogs wailed and struggled at their tie ropes. Ook-sook stood stolidly and unblinkingly by me and after the last white man had gone away he said, "Strong! Lots of wind!"

We were really in luck. The surveyors had left some stove oil behind which it was not convenient to haul out in the little planes. Because there was absolutely no more fuel oil at Beechey Point we would have been out of both heat and light in our coming hunt out on the ocean ice unless we could learn, perhaps, to use seal oil in the way the ancients did. That the crude stove oil could be used in our primus burner we found by experiment.

It was now permissible for the Eskimos to look about at the strange things concerning the camp of the white men and to pick up things that might be useful. They had stood back respectfully while the white men were here, all dressed in their finest fancywork, to me a charming group. But now they came in and Connie and I realized they were not shy with us but considered us almost as one of them: people who share the same lot soon become close. The Eskimos picked up used tea bags, which I have no doubt saw service again in another teapot not one hour after the white men had left the scene. They picked up cigarette butts, and one woman, Mr. Lynd's daughter-in-law, arrived promptly with an empty five-gallon gas can into which the garbage of discarded food was thrown and taken home to be thawed and picked over for what could be gleaned. The white men would have been surprised if they could have seen us all five minutes after their departure.

Ook-sook turned up with the left-over spaghetti of last night in one of our camp pans frozen solid on the sled; he had been instructed to "feed it to the dogs" but our dogs wouldn't eat anything but meat—fortunately. Good old Ook-sook had saved the cherished spiced food for us and our family enjoyed it at a later date. Part of the fuel oil we got we arranged to trade at once for the blubber of several seals towards fattening up our starved dogs. Empty bottles and cans were fingered lovingly and hauled away by the holiday crowd. Several months later we recognized cans from this overnight camp in use a hundred miles farther east along the arctic coast.

Now we made up our sled and quickly departed, for we had a long journey to make this day. It was good that we didn't fully realize how long—clear down the Colville and out to an island in its delta in the middle of the night.

We were a tired and frozen, not to mention famished, lot, that trudged along under the not very efficient moon, peeping through rifts. At midnight we came to the Lynds' in a land where it takes a certain know-how to tell igloo from ice cake.

Lynd was away picking up wood and only his blind wife Mart and the small children were at home. There was nothing to eat in the house, or rather the family had been living on what we would call starvation rations. They had some biscuits made of flour and water, and they had some seal oil to dip the biscuits in. Weeks ago, they had run out of last fall's catch of fish and apparently old Lynd was no caribou hunter of skill. Although they had money coming from the store on some foxes, Mart explained that they couldn't get any food until the store opened again after April first, inasmuch as Abraham, having been starved out and frozen out there himself, had been obliged to abandon the store and take his family inland to the Kuparuk to camp and hunt caribou for a few weeks. Of course, even if the Lynds had had plenty of store food, this was not what they needed—they would still be on a starvation diet with that alone; this situation shows to what extent the Eskimos are dependent on their native meats to supply food. Mart explained that she and old Lynd and the kids would just take a tablespoonful of seal oil several times a day and this would keep them going. "You cannot take much at one time," she told us, "for much of it makes you vomit." These times had come before in early spring and the privation was nothing new to the family; it was considered by them to be one of those inevitable things. Somehow, they got by.

The family inside the igloo was in total darkness when we found them for they had no kerosene and of course they could not afford to burn the oil which they needed for human food. Ruth lit our lantern. We could see that only a half dozen sticks remained for the family's fuel supply. Should we as guests consume them? But the blind woman, with Ruth to assist her, seemed happy to start a fire in the stove; we drank hot water then and all ate a few of the biscuits set before us in spite of ourselves.

Debating inwardly if we should divide up and cook the last caribou meat tonight for the destitute family, Connie and I decided in the affirmative, except that we voted the meat might go best for tomorrow's breakfast; old Lynd himself would then be here to enjoy it, while our own family had to think of its strength on the morrow's trail. Midnight rolled past, and old Lynd wasn't home yet when we spread our sleeping bags upon the floor and called it a day.

The Eskimo children shivering in their thin bedding were made very happy by Connie with a stick of gum each, brought from the white man's camp. Mart told Connie that her children sometimes cried because they were hungry and that the littlest boy could not play outside all winter because he had no clothes; most of the time the child had to crouch behind the stove or must stay in bed to keep from freezing—and so the poor family got through each winter. Upon their roof next morning we saw several caribou hides which had never been used, and we could not answer why these were not sewed for clothing except to say that here is one of the many evidences that the closer they get to civilization the worse often seems the condition, during the period of their transition, of what have formerly been a hunting and fishing people—a transition, in fact, from which some of the people of this earth have never emerged but have completely vanished in the process.

Next morning Lynd returned after his all-night trip, pushing his sled load of wood across the frozen bay. A package of cigarettes brought to his face that old smile that I knew so well. Ruth carefully cut equal portions of meat and served it up from the boiling pot while all eyes watched; she had learned this past winter from Connie to be clean about her cooking and seldom boiled up things any more with floating feathers or hair in them. We all thought her a dandy cook. Lynd had walked all the way to George Woods's to borrow some tea, which now appeared for breakfast: for the moment we were all in luxury; life seemed complete.

As we left for Beechey Point old Lynd started out for wood again. He told me it kept him busy rustling wood. I realized this was true when I later saw the spot from which he rustled it. The place was eight miles or more from his house, and to borrow the pinch of tea the old man had walked thirty miles just last night. Probably fifty-five years old, he had made that trip in the dark all night long and now was going again without sleep. Well, I guess you could not say that he was a lazy Eskimo, and it will be noted that I have never applied the term "lazy" to these people. Lynd's little supply would last a day or two at most, depending on how much the family stayed in bed, and then he would have to get more. He had caught six white foxes with a value of $126 for his year's income, which amounted to only about $40 in buying power here as judged by standards in the United States. Desperately the Eskimos need better trades on their fur, cheaper goods, and more buying power. They can't go back; they must go ahead. Old Lynd and his wife and the children hoped to move eastward near Foggy Islands to live with an older married son who was a strong trapper of foxes, and there they would find easier times. Yes, I hope so, Mr. Lynd!

THAT SPOT WHERE WE HAD first met Ruth, Oliktok, a place distinguished from sea ice at this season only by the sod icehouse erected there, came and went, sinking below the level horizon, while at the same time George and Nanny's camp rose ahead of us. In the clear air you could see miles; two hours after we had sighted the familiar camp of George Woods, we were inside it, drinking George's good hot tea.

After a single biscuit and the tea, we noticed that everybody was sitting around dressed up in his best and that everybody seemed to be waiting. Some of our fur boots and socks needed new soles, and as Nanny always took care of our sewing, I began explaining about the work that we needed done. But Nanny, in contrast to the last time I had seen her, seemed indifferent and even indignant. Finally, she said sharply, "Tomorrow I fix."

Not until then did we remember that it was Sunday! I had got Ooksook so that he would travel and hunt on the Sabbath with me when necessity demanded it, because by nature he was not as "religious" as the Eskimo women, and Ruth had come along with our party today, rather against her will, although sew or "work" she would not. As Nanny pensively began to hum a religious hymn under her breath, I got the idea. "Are you going to have church services?" Connie asked. "We go to church all the time in the United States" (exaggeration) "so go ahead." At this signal Ruth and her favorite girlfriend, her cousin Hester of Richard's People, rushed outside and returned with hymnals and Bibles which smoked with frost as they were brought indoors. The spirits of the whole assembly, who had been waiting for Connie and me to come around, soared in gladness, and we breathed a sigh of relief. Connie and I joined in the hymns, lustily sung in English, not a word of which was understood by most of them, and then George, rapidly making a few notes with a pencil and tablet, delivered an enthusiastic short sermon in Eskimo.

That more food other than the tea and biscuits was not to be forthcoming was presently apparent. What was wrong here? We had never come to the camp of George before that we were not fed lavishly. We soon learned. They didn't have any food I Early spring, you see, is a hard time for all the Eskimos. This whole assembly of eighteen or twenty well- dressed people sitting here didn't have anything to eat and hadn't had anything much for some time. Eventually a half dozen frozen Arctic Ocean fish of a kind called "herring" (and presumably a kind of herring) were resurrected from some snowbank and served our party of travelers, and we ate them while the others watched. Although herring is much less to be preferred than whitefish, I noticed that even Connie ate one down with no ado at all in the frozen state, whereas originally, she had never been much of a herring eater at all. I enjoyed mine a good deal, or at least the hunger pangs were relieved.

Bad news awaited us about our sewing. Practically none of the beautiful outlay of Eskimo garments for our collection to be sent to the United States was forthcoming. We were promised—oh, such promises I—last August, three quarters of a year ago, and had been waiting months for the most elementary garments to put on our backs. While such garments would be merely articles of curiosity to people in civilization, a truly primitive people were not able to procure them easily for these purposes. The people didn't have the skins, which must be summer-killed. The fancy house boots which I had ordered ready in midwinter for a birthday present to Connie appeared on the trim feet of Nanny's daughter, little crippled Martha, when we looked around this evening. We curbed our impatience. A glance at poor little Martha, most popular of all among the young girls, would have told anyone that she deserved the small happiness of the boots that had been intended for Connie, for probably she was not for this world long; she had always been frail.

By the coughing I heard at George's camp I realized we were in for trouble, too. George explained that Jacob and Carrie, with their new baby, had brought the cold on their return from Barrow. Ruth and Ook-sook, happily dipping into the seal oil can from which the fingers of coughing individuals had just retreated, would soon be ill. A woman carefully wiped a baby's running nose on her fingers and dipped them into the seal oil after Ruth, letting the excess oil run off into the can again as she licked.

The next day at Richard's camp we were fed some beans and bread by Hester. We noted Hester to be a very neat, conscientious, devout, good girl, perhaps lacking in Ruth's merriment, but also lacking in Ruth's slight streak of the unscrupulous. How could we know at this time that Hester and Ruth, the shy and the bold, the gentle seamstress with the placid smile and the little vixen who couldn't or wouldn't sew a good seam at all, were in love with the same young man? Hester and Ruth both loved Apiak, who was George's favorite son.

We arrived at our own Beechey Point house early in the day. Connie lagged far behind on the last lap coming across the sea, but that suited her well; she liked following the sled tracks at her own pace just as well as shivering around the cold house which would have little or no fuel waiting at it; It would take an eternity to begin to warm it up with

Beechey Point's bum fuel. I no sooner got in myself than I sadly saw that Abraham, who had moved into our house himself before he had been forced to vacate entirely, had taken down a little drum heater I had made and put up the old Sears, Roebuck cooking range again. I guess he liked the looks of it, but that range had burned-out grates. It was exactly forty degrees below zero on the beam by the wall thermometer. We would remain here as short a time as possible.

I thought something was missing at Beechey Point. One of the little driftwood houses was gone. Abraham had burned it for fuel to heat his dwelling during a storm.

Dogs in a blizzard

Hester

PART TWO

Sea Ice Hunting

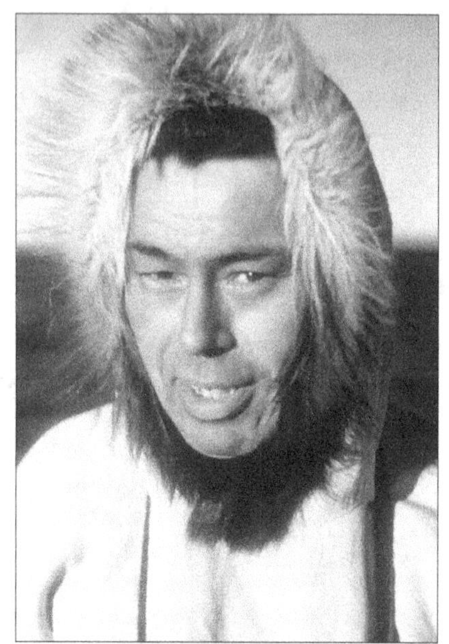

Abraham

Thelma

1

The clapboards banged on the house at Beechey Point. True to custom there was no wood left in the woodshed. After much scraping around among the old bones in the shed we got enough soggy, urine-soaked wood to fill the stove once, and this, assisted by our primus stove filled with the fuel oil of the surveyors, warmed the room a bit. We lived in the house with our parkas on.

Ruth was beginning to sneeze and the next day she was sick. While Ook-sook went after a sled load of wood, we tried to get everything in order to move our family to Cross Island thirty-five miles away in the Arctic Ocean. Near dark Ook-sook came in and we had supper. Although Ruth consumed her usual amount of meat, Ook-sook ate little.

"You feel strong?" I asked him. He admitted he wasn't very strong but felt like a paunch-shot caribou.

We took their temperatures. Ruth had a temperature of 102 while Ook-sook had one of slightly over 103 degrees. Connie and I were alarmed. We remembered how many Eskimos had died of the "cold" about this time last winter, from the tales of it, but we said nothing except that they must do no work and must stay in their beds. They went to bed rather unwillingly but in trust. We had some sulfa tablets the hospital at Barrow had dispensed to us, so according to directions we dosed our patients. The next day I had to harness up and drive the dogs out on my first time alone several miles across the arctic sea ice to get wood to keep us going; I just followed Ook-sook's old trail and had little trouble except that of making the dogs go. Ruth and Ook-sook were cured in twenty-four hours by the marvelous sulfa drug, big medicine for Eskimos who succumb to the little germ.

We kept them in bed awhile, hauled ice for our cooking water, cooked the food, fed the dogs, and I hauled another sled load of wood. Then Ook-sook declared he was "strong" and he would be an invalid no longer. Abraham came by with twelve white foxes he had caught and then returned to his trapping camp. The winter had got us accustomed to living with many people, so that we thought nothing of just putting the extras on the floor. We had dispensed with formalities, as the saying goes.

On March 20 we left for our arctic sea ice spring hunting. The hunting of polar bears must be done at this season, and we had waited all year for this opportunity which comes to few white men in all the world. Dog feed was fast dwindling while our patients recuperated, and in order to save our last few quarters of caribou to take out on the sea with us, we had been existing mainly on our old last fall's ptarmigan and a couple of last summer's brant, which Ruth boiled up, inclusive of the two heads with their long bills sticking out of the pot, but *that* only lasted one meal. In this life where you have nothing else to eat but flour concoctions to go with your meat, you instantly feel privation if your meat runs short. A person can't live on just flour and tea! When Abraham happened in the final evening at Beechey Point we were very proud of our table and the manners of our kids before him. He who usually fed them raw meat on the floor inside the trading post when the Eskimo people were held there by an east wind must have been surprised at "Please pass the butter"—our only hoarded pound of it from Barrow, going and gone!—and the grand flourish with the serving fork, lifting asparagus delicately from a solitary can. The conversation at the meal was conducted in both English and Eskimo with Abraham as go-between; our culture had become a hybrid of both peoples. Abraham had left his girls with six caribou down and had come in on a quick trip with an empty sled for store grub. Of concern to us all was the store's lack of most of the items we had counted on strongly for our orders. There was no more corn meal, no more tea, sugar, tobacco, needles, no more anything again.

A beautiful smiling sun beckoned as we lashed down our sled and turned our steps toward a little spot which we had been told lay some thirty-five miles across the expanse of sea ice.

To the land dweller the ocean is a strange and mysterious realm. But when that ocean is frozen to ice of some five feet in thickness, and it is strewn with large cakes of old ice that survived last summer's sun to freeze into the level ice of this year, it becomes a queer study in delicate pastel shapes and phantoms verging really on the exotic and the weird. For three quarters of a year we had lived beside this ocean and looked out upon it during the various seasons, yet we had never been out far from shore; we had never been out upon the sea ice. The arctic of spruce and birch Connie and I knew well. The arctic of willows and prairie we also knew. But what of the Arctic Ocean? As our sled and dogs wove in and out I reflected that no knowledge of the arctic is complete until we have seen not only the land and the land-dwelling animals, but the frozen ocean beyond the continent and the things of the sea. Here a set of rules govern life and nature which are different from all others. Here is something else again in arctic travel. These two writers do not pretend to have more than touched the edge of the mighty ocean; there are not more than half a dozen white men, or perhaps one should say men of *any* race, in the world today who know anything much about it.

Ook-sook had hauled a hundred pounds of flour, a hundred pounds of sugar, and twenty-five pounds of beans, besides caribou meat and most of our camp gear, out ahead. After a twenty-five-mile walk to a reef known as Little Cross Island, I ate two biscuits (we had a gunnysack full, half cinnamon rolls) and then seemed full. I explained lamely to Connie, which only made her mad. You see I was pretty jaded and I couldn't seem to get rested up. But we couldn't remain at Beechey Point; the only thing we could do was to go on and trust for an easier life at the next camp. We would have to learn the tricks to sea hunting or else.

Ook-sook had made us a snug snow house with our tent pitched inside in the usual way. We all walked about searching for driftwood to burn as soon as we arrived. The little reef on which we had landed for the night was washed over by severe storms in summer, as it was only a few feet high; winds kept its sands swept bare of deep snow except where drifts had formed. There was wood here for a few hours' burning or say for a limited camping time. This island is sometimes called Reindeer Island.

Since the east wind is the prevailing wind of the north coast of Alaska, its regularity enables one to read the snowdrifts for direction as dependably as a compass. If the east wind hasn't made the most recent drifts the west wind has, and it is just as reliable. It was by the drifts that Ook-sook had found Little Cross Island, which he had known only from hearsay.

After gathering enough wood to run Connie and Ruth a couple of days, Ook-sook and I took our course by the drifts the next morning and headed for Cross Island proper, out further into the ocean. The most westerly of the Midway Islands, Cross Island may sometimes be found as a little dot on a big map if you look close.

None of us had ever been out to Cross Island except Ruth, who had been there when she was a very little girl one time before she could remember, and Abraham had suggested it as a base for seal and polar bear hunting inasmuch as we needed some island where our main camp could be located on solid land and where there was a chance to get driftwood for fuel; yet we needed a base far enough out in the ocean so that we would be well into the ocean's hunting grounds. Abraham said there were two old Eskimo driftwood igloos on the island. We planned to spend the next three months in one of them as home or stay until the summer progressed enough so that it was time to go ashore.

Meanwhile, today found Connie and Ruth encamped in the snow house tent on the reef mentioned, and Connie was sitting most of the day with her feet in a pan of hot water. That twenty-five-mile jaunt yesterday on the hard sea ice in moccasin-like skin boots had practically broken her feet down, added to a week or so spent in moccasins on the hard level floor of the house at Beechey Point. She had always had a tendency toward foot trouble which had to be watched. It was nothing too serious: as soon as we reached our destination I massaged her feet and put the bones back in place and bound her feet with bandages for a couple of weeks. She would merely have to start out polar bear hunting riding on the sled—an embarrassment, but it couldn't be helped. She was glad to be here and the arctic was her home.

Our situation, it seemed to me, necessitated that we get game within the next ten days. Now that we had turned to the sea, this meant seals or polar bears. Connie and I had by now caught the Eskimos' colds, after resisting them for some time, and so it happened, as it does sometimes, that good hunting was off to a poor start. Ruth was supposed to chop some wood for Connie on the little reef where they waited for Ook-sook and me to find Cross Island, but the first thing Ruth did was to break the ax off at the head. The girls bound it with wire for the time; presently I made us another ax handle out of driftwood.

As I had the sleeping bag with me Connie sat up a good deal of the night to keep the little stove going. When she finally rolled up inside her parka on a single caribou blanket and a canvas stretched over the snow floor, she says she knew she was in for one of those nights. Ruth too was cold, but somehow the night passed, and they slept. They had fought it out together many a night before on the Itkillik—for Connie had slept without a sleeping bag all winter since we only had one sleeping bag in the arctic, due to lack of carrying space. Sleeping in your parka is a tactic which is possible if the house or tent is well insulated, although it is ruinous to a good parka in no time.

As soon as the little stove died out, Connie told me, the camp on the Itkillik would freeze pretty hard each night, yet by sleeping in her parka rolled up in our old caribou blanket she survived nicely if grumpily. Her fur boots came to above her knees, but a draft would hit her legs, she said, as the night progressed, and as one garment would slip one way and one another the cracks and the drafts grew ever wider. Her pillow was her duffel sack. She would sleep on one side only in a certain position to hold the covers down. Her unmanageable hair, having lost from it every last bobby pin in our part of the world as time went on, she tied straight back native style in ribbons and rags; it would escape its confines in sleeping and would fall over her face, where the condensation of breath would freeze it into a sheath of ice as she slept. In the middle of the night she would awaken at least once to light the stove and thaw out. Hot tea and some silent midnight contemplation over the cozy little stove, and she went back to bed again: it wasn't too bad. Ruth slept on, a halo of frost around her breathing hole from her own thin and desperately shabby covers.

That Connie had slept in this way during the coldest part of the arctic winter in those periods when I was absent with our sleeping bag on the trail probably shows more than any other words on this subject the excellence of Eskimo clothing. But winter was almost whipped now, and this was about the last of it.

The girls awoke late, a somber day. Just as Ruth was frying whole-wheat pancakes for breakfast, Coaly, Ook-sook's pup tied outside, commenced to bark uproariously.

Ruth's eyes met Connie's across the skillet. *"Nanuk!* Polar bear!" she gasped. Then, collecting her wits more quickly than Connie—for Ruth had seen a polar bear come at her whole family once when they were traveling on the sea ice with their sled—*"Sapoort, sapoon!* Heaven's sake, get the gun!"

"Where are my mittens?" Forgetting all about her injured feet in her first desire to get at and kill a polar bear—a sort of automatic reaction to the word "game" after experiences with herbivores—Connie sprang out of the tent door. Even though it was only Ook-sook arriving with the team there stayed in Connie's memory after that the unforgettable expression on Ruth's face. Ruth, you see, had seen polar bears.

Thus, it was that our lives all changed very decidedly as soon as we had left the land for the sea ice. We were all on the lookout now, for polar bears will stalk camps and the hunter finds that he may now become the hunted. It was in fact Connie who was destined to deal the most intimately with polar bears of any of us on our entire trip, although none of us could know this beforehand.

The girls were relieved to see Ook-sook; the fool pup Coaly, still barking, didn't know our own dogs. Where was Bud? "Get wood."

Instantly Connie divined that I was at Cross Island all right, that I had found our permanent residence for the spring months of sea hunting, that the island could not be very far, and that the empty sled had returned to bring a part of our duffel and herself on top of the load. After pancakes and coffee (the latter for our Eskimos) the three travelers embarked. It was warm, perhaps five degrees below zero, and the trip was pleasant. While Ook-sook ran ahead, Ruth played driver and the girls had a fine time navigating dogs and sleds over the level sea ice between the hummocks and snags.

OOK-SOOK AND I HAD FIRST looked for Cross Island from the top of one of these upended ice cakes which we had climbed for a more extended view. These big cakes, which drift in the sea by summer and which solidify into a mass by winter, are not icebergs although we often hear them referred to as such and although we may use the term "iceberg" loosely in this narrative. Icebergs correctly are large chunks which have broken from glaciers coming down to the sea and so have been set adrift; one sees them, so we understand, in the North Atlantic, coming down from Greenland where many glaciers lie. Some icebergs are also born from the glaciers of southern Alaska. But remarkable as it may sound there are almost no glaciers in the arctic, and certainly none that come down to the ocean in north Alaska, and therefore there are no icebergs. These chunks of ice that we find in the Arctic Ocean are really pack ice, some of which, to be sure, is very impressive in its size and height because formed by pressure. These ice cakes frozen into the sea consequently became more numerous as we left the coves and bays of the mainland and approached the outer islands which guard the coast, and as we entered the pressure areas.

As Ook-sook and I stood on a large cake we could see rough ice beginning out to sea, and far in the distance was a little slim dark pole standing in an expanse of white with jumbled ice all about it. The pole we knew was a driftwood log of some size set up on the highest point of land to enable travelers to see the location of an island either by winter, as now, or by summer, when such a pole would rise out of the sea. The sandy island reefs, built up by ice action, are so low and flat that to a traveler in a small boat they are invisible from a couple of miles away; in winter when such a traveler journeys with the dog sled they are snow-covered except where blown bare by the winds, so that it is hard to tell land from sea ice.

The Eskimos themselves take little pains in marking an island, although they may stick up a log in the sand. But the pole at Cross Island, one of our most northerly islands off the Alaskan coast in United States possession, was set up by whalers, for it had been described to me as a big pole solidly braced, which could be seen for many miles. It proved to have two crossbars near its top at right angles to each other and on them were carved the dates of 1886 and 1890. The local legend goes that Cross Island was so named because it was at this island that the whaling ships used to cut out from land and go straight across the sea towards Herschel Island, Mackenzie Bay, Canada.

The Eskimos may be poor at setting up permanent structures, but they are quick to see them; Ook-sook saw the big crossed pole that marks Cross Island through the binoculars, but I never did see it from that particular ice cake when we changed our course and headed for it.

Two hours later our sled was grinding across an exposed sandy surface and we were on Cross Island. There the cross pole stood, like an ancient guardian, before us, and five hundred yards beyond it were two snow-blown driftwood houses which leaned badly. Letting closer examination of the pole go for the time, I headed for the old igloos to see what could be made of them.

One of the old houses was in good shape although its door was gone, and it had been blown as full of snow as ever a house could be. The people in this land seldom close a door. The last people in moving away had left the door wide open and thus the wind was able to pack the house full of snow. Of course, we had brought along our shovel, and while Ook- sook busied himself cutting the first blocks to make a snow- house around the igloo, I began shoveling out the snow from the skylight, standing on top of the roof until I could work down inside.

As I shoveled I studied the old house. It had belonged to an Eskimo named Muagyuk who died last winter of pneumonia at the age of around ninety. His house was a very good example of the well-built driftwood igloo dating from olden days. It was twelve by sixteen feet inside, with a maximum height of six feet at the skylight that was set, Eskimo style, in the roof for lighting, since, as I have mentioned, Eskimo houses have no wall windows. The walls were nearly five feet high where they met the slanting roof on the sides, and they themselves slanted somewhat by design, because slanting walls enable the better placement of sods in this type of architecture. The slanting wall is an arctic housing feature which white dwellers might adopt very beneficially. However, this island was a sand reef, and no true sod was available here. The boards which composed the hut were ax-hewn planks ranging from four inches to two feet in width and placed with the flat side in and the natural curve of the log to the outside. The roof was made of the same planking and covered with scanty, sandy sod. Large cracks between the planks had been calked with oily rags, but most of the calking had fallen out. There was a six-inch square ventilator hole in the roof in addition to the large skylight and a hole for the stovepipe. The opening of the door was small, being only four and a half feet high. The old *ugrug* intestine skylight covering had long since departed and was represented only by a hole two feet square.

After much shoveling and bumping of my head on the ceiling I managed to dig down to the beach-sand floor. The shovel had uncovered an old copper seal-oil lamp, a four- prong snag hook used to snag seals with, called a *manak,* and a pair of seal net sinkers. Evidently the last occupants had lived almost entirely on seals. Ook-sook nailed a clean flour sack over the skylight, and except that our wood stove and flooring materials had not arrived, the house was just about ready to live in, when we calked it. Connie and I and Ook-sook and Ruth had made a lot of different kinds of camps livable before this one.

That night as Ook-sook and I cooked our meal of hoarded boiled caribou meat freighted from the Itkillik, over our primus stove in the unheated igloo, my Eskimo comrade told about the people who had once lived here, and it seemed to me as if ancient seal-oil lamps still sputtered in the darkness out beyond the reach of our own tiny flame.

Snow fields sparkled as Ook-sook left to bring Connie and Ruth next day and I started walking along Cross Island, or Nepahalik, as the native people call it, to make stacks of driftwood.

Cross Island resembles an apostrophe in shape and it is two miles long by a quarter of a mile wide at its widest. It is composed of sand and small gravel entirely and nothing else. During violent storms one can well imagine the waves of summer washing over practically all of the island except the few square yards where the houses stand, and they are perhaps threatened at times. The boundaries of the island are determined by the jagged broken ice forced against its shores on the seaward side; the landward side, sloping off gradually into the deep, one can only surmise. The water beside the island is deep enough so that a vessel can be brought right up beside it, we understand, and this in turn means big ice cakes alongside.

With my rifle on my back and my shovel swinging over the other shoulder, I walked along the seaward side of the island poking at likely looking sticks or digging at some suspicious bulge under the snow that might harbor burnable drift. I would carry those sticks I found until I had an armful and then would make neat piles of the drift, stacking it in windrows along the length of the island from which they could easily be picked up later with the dog sled. As I walked along, I tried to piece together the history of the wood I found.

This stick here now, I know its history well. The tapering ends showed it was cut by a beaver, for I know the tooth marks. It is cottonwood and drifted into the Arctic Ocean from some mighty forest far to the south where beavers live; it could be from the Ipikpuk or the Killik, but the Mackenzie over in Canada is my guess. Most of our wood on the beaches of north Alaska comes from Canada on the westward drift of the ocean currents.

Here is a log nearly four feet thick and twenty feet long. It has the marks of a good woodsman's ax upon it and a crosscut saw severs its top. A picture comes to my mind of a man clearing land. Or maybe it got away from some logs which were being sent to a sawmill a thousand miles away. Its growth rings are wide apart, showing that it grew in some warmer climate where there is a long growing season each year.

But driftwood is not plentiful. I walk the two-mile length of the island and find only some three cords of wood in all. Where the tail of the apostrophe comes to an end in sea ice there are a few willows washed up. All the branches and roots are yet intact; even the bark is green. Most likely last summer's floods tore them loose from some bank of the Kuparuk or Sagavanirktok or Hulahula Rivers, who knows?

Driftwood is my main concern but in hunting it I find other things. Suddenly, from among the other trash, I pick up a child's wooden boat! How did it get into this ocean? It certainly made quite a journey from somewhere.

Much can be told about an arctic island, even when all is frozen in the wintertime. Near our house stand stalks of Iceland poppies. This island is covered with flowers in the summer.

Piled a little way off are two poles that resemble telegraph poles. They are arctic spruce, I know at a glance; their tree rings verify it, as well as their texture. It took several hundred years to produce these trees inside the Arctic Circle, but now they represent the best in firewood to me.

My walk around the island has confirmed my suspicion that storms wash over nearly all the island except where the houses stand. There are old tent pegs protruding from the snow in two places, showing Eskimos have lived here in summer some time ago. None have lived on the island for eight years—that I know from the people I have talked with.

I know quite a lot of things about this island now. On a peg inside the house I found a sort of lariat affair. It was made of rawhide thong three feet long with a rock the size of a baseball tied to each end in a rawhide net cradle. This is a weapon. It was used for killing ducks. When a flock flew over some point of the island in summer, the waiting hunter whirled this affair about his head and threw it into the flock. Some birds were struck by the stones and knocked down while others were wrapped up by the rawhide and brought to earth. The hunter probably had to be fast to pick up his birds before they got to flying again. But the weapon proved ducks were here. My subsequent search now uncovered several balls of eider-duck down that had once lined nests upon this island, along with a few balls of old squaw-duck down. That loons, snow buntings, phalaropes, ptarmigan, song sparrows, and horned larks also nest out here on the islands of the Arctic Ocean in the summertime I was to learn. I knew from reports of the Eskimos that large trout may be caught from these desolate sands in nets set along this beach.

Right near our house I saw one more pile of drift logs, I thought. When I got close to these I changed my mind for it was part of the skeleton of a whale. The great vertebrae looked like stumps lying there in the drifted snow. A new polar bear track led right over them. The Eskimos had killed two whales here one fall eight years past, but these bones spoke of being here fifty years or more. Probably this was a carcass left adrift by some of the old whaling fleet farther to the east. Unbelievably wasteful methods of whaling were practiced all along the arctic coast fifty years ago when baleen sold for five dollars the pound, but the rest of the whale was considered worthless. Let us hope whaling is never resumed again except for food, or that all of the great body will be used for some valuable purpose.

A walrus had once been killed here but walrus are rare anywhere east of Barrow until you reach the Atlantic side of the arctic. *Ugrugs* are fairly common as some scattered bones of this animal testified. The bones of seal, polar bear, fox, and fish covered the sandspit.

As I stood presently beneath the pole which marks Cross Island, I thought how it had seen canvas give way to steam and how today it looked down alone upon a world of white broken ice in all directions, a small sand island, two ancient igloos and just me. And I wondered who might come here or what might happen to it in its future days.

What of the future of Cross Island? I mused. "There certainly will never be any farming here. No real estate broker could make a profit. What then? Well, the eider ducks like it. The birds and the animals like it. The Eskimos like it, and anyway, does everything have to have a future figured in dollars and cents or power politics?"

Far out in the broken ice I heard, "Go ahead!" and I knew that Ook-sook was coming with the girls and that old Duk was loafing again. I walked to the house and put the teapot on the primus stove with snow in it to boil.

The old snow house canvas cover which was used on the Itkillik formed a floor for our new home; our bedding made a couch. We set up the woodstove and the cracks were chinked. Connie set up her little wooden box of writing materials beside the wall where she sat. As an artist and a naturalist, Connie literally wrote her way through the arctic and she found plenty of original material there. The little cookstove, with a new damper and improved oven, heated the place well, while there was an abundance of wood and plenty of light from the skylight. Again, it was daylight for almost twenty-four hours a day.

Three hours later the dogs slept curled up in the snow, and a plume of blue smoke climbed above our house of snow blocks, while the merry shouts of an Eskimo card game could have been heard by a passer-by. Cross Island was inhabited once again.

Making camp at Little Cross Island

Connie on the arctic pack ice

We arrive at Cross Island to spend three months

Bud builds a wall of snow blocks

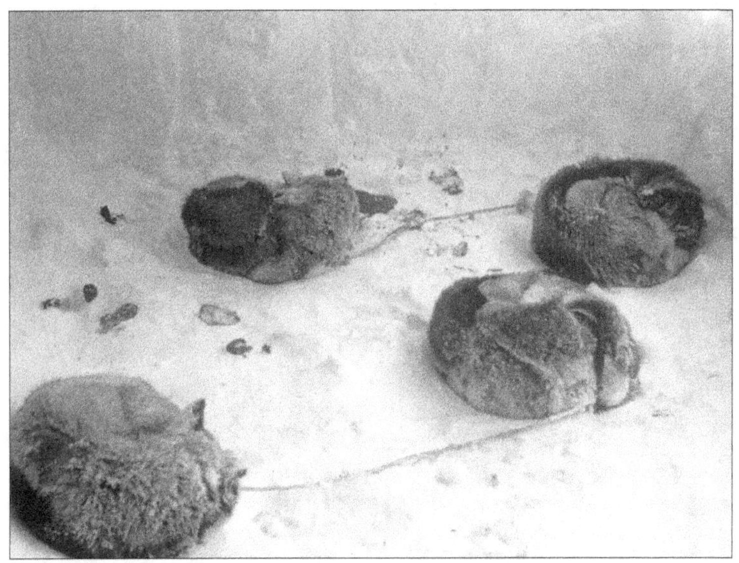

Dogs shelter behind a snow wall

Bud and Ook-Sook stop for lunch on the sea ice

Bud and Ook-Sook dig a path through the jumbled ice

Camping on the sea ice

2

For five days high winds kept the hunters confined inside our Cross Island home. Then it calmed, and we pulled out to hunt. We took the last of the caribou meat with us and left the girls to subsist on biscuits, cookies, and tea. Dog feed was the thing which was ever and eternally on our minds and we had to get some, and we had to get meat for all of us.

Since we were existing by hunting and fishing just as the native does, we depended upon our own exertions to survive, and this had become a commonplace thing. We must hunt out from Cross Island, our base, for there were no animals on the island itself in the winter except for a very few field mice and lemmings or a rare wandering polar bear or white fox. The seals and the polar bears were our concern now; of these two animals the seals were by far the most likely. Polar bear hunting is much a matter of luck. Connie and I have made an estimate, jokingly, of the number of polar bears which may inhabit the enclosed frozen ocean to the sportsman's concern: if you just start out walking and looking for them you will find that there is probably one polar bear to each 100,000 square miles. At the present time there are no closed seasons or legal limits on these bears, and if it is any satisfaction, they are perhaps the only American wild animal whose hide can today legally be sold on the market. There seems no immediate danger of their extermination. The trick in finding polar bears at all lies in going to certain areas which are more prolific in them than other areas; this is the main reason we chose Cross Island.

Our location was on the edge of the Beaufort Sea, which has been termed the area of the heaviest polar ice known. After finding the island, Ook-sook and I were pretty skeptical about sea ice hunting, because it was new to us, and especially I might say it was foreign to Ook-sook because he was from inland people who were caribou hunters. He had never hunted seals in his life! He had never seen a polar bear!

We both realized that there are associated with good sealing and good polar bear hunting certain dangers which are inherent in the sea ice itself and which are enough to alarm any landsman with good reason. All of the Eskimos on the north coast of Alaska are very wary about going far out on the sea ice from the continent's edge. Ook-sook could not have been induced to go out to Cross Island at all in all probability except that he liked the wages and had confidence in me. Our party was safe enough all this spring in our little home on the island or anyplace on the ice to landward, but from here out there was always the possibility of a gale springing up which could cause the land-fast ice to crack off. If hunters were out sealing at the edge of the floe on the ocean, they could be drifted out to sea with a danger of not being able to get back to the continent. This danger is especially acute in spring. If a party should get stranded on ice fields that moved out and separated them from shore, such a party could well feel some apprehension about having to spend the rest of the summer out there until winter came again, or even could feel some uneasiness about having the ice break up or melt from under them.

George Woods got drifted off like this one time for four days and he said he was mighty scared. His party got ashore again to land-fast ice when their floe drifted in on the winds some miles to the west. There is known to be a current going in the direction of Siberia.

Let us be more explicit still. At no time in the winter can a person walk out upon the ice of the Arctic Ocean for many miles without eventually coming to an open crack or "lead" between the great ice fields. These cracks are caused by winds and currents and possibly by tides; they open and close at will. Such cracks dividing ice floes may be as far as three hundred miles apart, but they can always be found even in the lowest temperatures. Our purpose in coming to Cross Island was to go out from the island to the nearest crack, called the "edge of the floe," in spring. We would walk out to the edge of the floe on the ice shelf which was attached to Cross Island, or upon land-fast ice. This ice is safe so long as it does not break off and join the moving pack.

We knew that open water could be expected only a few miles out from the island as spring progressed. Here there would be seals swimming which we could shoot and they would float at this time of year; they would be shot when the wind was favorable so as to drift them into the ice on the side of the lead where we stood, or if they were shot at fairly close range they might be secured by the *manak,* a wooden float on a line, with hooks, which is hurled from the hunter's hand by whirling it first around his head somewhat as a cowboy throws his lariat.

Not only is it like navigating a granite quarry to get through the indescribably jumbled ice blocks of these pressure areas out to where the land-fast ice meets the moving pack, and not only do the hunters return with black-and-blue shins, lamed dogs, and the sled battered and broken to splinters in a dozen places from a trip to the edge of the floe, but one who ventures far out into it is playing with terrific and unknown forces.

Another reason, however, for our coming to this area to look for polar bears is that the very movement of the currents out beyond Cross Island would imply the presence of polar bears in the vicinity! This movement, with the upsetting of the great ice ridges and pushing them about, as a human hand might push checkers about in a mass on a checkerboard, makes for fine polar bear hunting! The bears like the areas of the greatest currents with their shifting floes and open water where they can catch the seals upon which they live. Wild polar bears do not eat fish as they do in zoos, but seals only, as a rule, and then mostly the blubber. This is why, then, few white men have ever seen a polar bear in the wild. Polar bears are sea animals which rarely come to land, and their environment is almost inaccessible to man. Even the Eskimos do not get many polar bears; they do not usually search for them or hunt them.

Our dogs were new to sea ice; they were suspicious of the strange environment as Ook-sook and I and our furry safari left Cross Island and headed straight out north to try to find the nearest open water. Connie and Ruth were entirely content to stay at home on the island; they wanted none of the hazards of sea ice travel, and the impediments in taking four people with our sled would have been doubly great. Connie and Ruth watched the smoke from their chimney anxiously, waiting for the least change in the wind. A change in the wind would bring Ook-sook and me back to Cross Island on a dash.

"Now keep your eyes open, hunter," I encouraged Connie as I left. "A polar bear could just as likely as not walk right across this island sometime again this spring, as we have already had one visitor by the tracks. Then you'll want to be ready for him. Yes, I think there's about a fifty-fifty chance one may come right here to the house to you." Connie didn't quite believe it, and I hardly believed it myself. Nevertheless, Connie's rifle remained by her side, never far from reach, and she never so much as gathered a stick of wood without carrying it with her. Taking Coaly the pup, she went first for a walk about the island to explore its dimensions. That little dog would see any bears that she might miss. To discover a bear would probably mean suicide for Coaly, of whom she was fond, but she added in explanation: "Maybe I'm getting toughened."

The ghostly white bears of the ice have been known to stalk their human hunters from behind; an Eskimo was killed by a big polar bear some years ago just a mile or two from Cross Island in this way. The poor man was catching seals in nets he set under the ice—a method we never used because we had no seal nets—and he had no gun when the bear came upon him. The polar bears have no fear because the only creatures they have had experience with are the seals on which they feed, and other bears. If they stalk a man, it is probably in the belief that he is a seal and good to eat. More often they have been seen walking boldly up to a camp with no attempt at concealment at all, for they are curious and aggressive; the sound of a dog barking or of people shouting, or the smell of smoke from a house, is more apt to draw them than the reverse.

Connie was thinking some of these thoughts when soon she saw Ruth coming along after her. Connie thought at first that the reason Ruth, in staying in the house nearby to sew, didn't want her to take the pup was that Coaly was Ook- sook's pup and Ruth was responsible for him. When Connie rather absent-mindedly started off with both the gun and the pup, Ruth followed behind and joined in on the walk too. Ruth looked rather sneaking. It occurred to Connie, "Is it possible that she is afraid to stay alone inside the house when I and the rifle and dog are not a half mile away in broad daylight on this barren island?" Yes, Ruth was scared. As the sun slipped down the horizon, both girls and dog strode for home with seven-league boots. After the sun set Ruth wouldn't peep outside the door alone unless she saw Connie go out, and the two girls took to staying close together. Now Ruth left Coaly untied to roam the island as he wished, but the timid pup didn't roam far. Connie saw that Coaly was to sleep right in front of their door in the snow alley rather than in the snow doghouse we had built.

As the two girls made ready for bed Ruth suggested: "Rifle— inside tonight? Tomorrow—outside!" Connie had to admit Ruth's nervousness was making her look over her own shoulder by this time, and despite the fact that we never bring rifles indoors because they frost up with moisture when they are warm, Connie brought her carbine in, unsnapped its case for easy access, and lay with it beside her head all night, while valiant Ruth, taking capable survey of the tiny driftwood door, with its high sill you had to step over and its hinges made of thongs of *ugrug* hide secured with a few nails, latched it as best she could from marauders with a piece of stove wood thrust through the ancient iron door latch. Both girls lay with one ear tuned all night, but all was still. They had to laugh at themselves, too, because remember, Connie had *wanted* to shoot a polar bear.

Four feet above where they slept, of course, was the two- foot-square Eskimo skylight which screened them from the dangers of the outside by a mere piece of flour sacking. Last winter at Barter Island, Andrew the minister's family had had a polar bear climb up on the roof and peer down through this hole at the inhabitants. The bears do not know they are on top of a house but probably imagine the house to be a snowdrift or ice cake; the fact of a stovepipe sticking out of the top does not enter the province of ursine speculation. "Listen," I reprimanded Connie sternly, "whatever you do, don't bring your gun indoors of a night anyway. With that moisture on it, if you had to take it out to go after a bear, it might freeze solid, and you wouldn't have any gun at all! *Then* what would you do?" She admitted of course in the arctic we have to leave our gun outside in its case.

Ook-sook and I and our dog sled had wound a few miles through a friendly maze of old ice whose rounded domes rose on either hand, and we were confronted by our first real pressure ridges. The young ice of last fall, a foot thick, had been squeezed and splintered into a million sharp fragments. The piles of fragments lay ahead in ridges and hills in every sort of shape. When the wind blew out here sometime last fall, indescribable chaos had taken place to cause this. Actually, the ice moves very slowly when it does move, but one thing you can say about it is that it is inexorable. The pressure caused by the wind when it starts the great ice floes in motion is unimaginable and unmeasurable, for each ice pan that rears up into the wind is turned into a sail. The pressure caused by the wind blowing against the millions of ice sails in their aggregate force is infinitely great. This comparison of the ice to sails is not original but it is still the best description that I know of it. In this way the great floes, often hundreds of square miles in area, strive to drive before the storm like giant full-rigged icebreakers. The younger ice near land is crushed and ground by the monsters into a tumbled mass, occasionally rising as high as seventy-five feet above the general level of the sea. Nor is the young ice the only victim of these rigged battle cruisers. When they catch a smaller member in between them they grind it or crawl upon top of it. The storms sound the battle cry and the sluggish ice monsters answer. Neighbor crushes neighbor and the weaker are annihilated. The biggest ice floes are split and cracked by a wedge driven into them, while the smaller fields are telescoped by sliding under or on top of one another. When the war cry of the storm is stilled the fury, it has caused lives on in frozen music as the great floes solidify in death embrace. The cold turns the ground-up slush to solid walking for the pedestrian, who chops now through the ridges with his pickax to make a trail for a sled to pass, and the pressure area rests until the next storm. Young ice forms over the recently opened sea and peace reigns that is utter and complete. The seals pop up through the slush ice until it reaches such a thickness that an upward butt of their heads can no longer make a breathing hole; then they quit traveling the leads and take up the job of keeping their hidden breathing holes open by gnawing from under the ice.

I have never been out upon the moving ice in a storm, but I have seen the results of these forces when I ventured out at calm times for periods of a few hours or a few days. The most hazardous pressure area is known to exist only the first fifty or one hundred miles out from land, after which the floes become comparatively level on top and ice movement is more sluggish and safe.

To travel through the pressure area on a nice day you try to find the lowest places to cross the tumbled ridges, just as you would look for a mountain pass. The winds have smoothed these down somewhat by drifting snow over them, but it is no easy task. A trail must be made with pickaxes if you intend to haul any load—and of course one wouldn't dare go here without a load: he must have complete camping equipment with him at all times. Our sled was loaded lightly with the bare essentials of a three days' hunt, and by much effort and many upsets we managed to get along. The dogs would jump from cake to cake and often a dog would hang in mid-air over some crack while his companions struggled forward. The harness and ropes would catch on the ice snags and I would step into cracks just large enough to admit my big tender feet, but several feet deep, and thus would almost break a leg any moment. When it happened that one of us got his foot stuck, the dogs heedlessly ran ahead and the sled upset. The sharp edges of the ice cracks always managed to scrape our shins nearly to the bone— or so it seemed.

Once we were up on top of a pressure ridge the dogs would scramble down the other side at a gallop to keep ahead of the sled which bore ruthlessly down upon them unless a man could hold it. Ook-sook and I would fall in trying to keep the sled upright. It was a common sight to see the sled race down a steep incline and crash into a solid cake at the bottom or jump off a sheer six-foot ledge into space. At times a person would stub his toe through his soft deerskin boots against some little snag that reared up while he was trying to run. This happened to me so often that it reminded me of my barefoot days. One main reason we had not taken up sea hunting until this season was the lack of visibility in this rough ice and the difficulty of seeing these treacherous snags. During the winter darkness when the sun is below the horizon the daylight is too brief to make such venturing very safe, particularly due to the fact that no shadows are cast to tell one the height or depth of ice boulders and their sockets; a person would run too good a chance of breaking his neck entirely in this granite quarry.

We had made ten miles and the sun was setting when we came to a place where the ocean had been open a while ago, but now showed only a crack tending east and west approximately paralleling the continent. We could see water down below within the crack and in places young ice a foot thick covered what had been the open lead of a hundred or more yards wide. But we couldn't get seals now in such a place and find open water we must.

There was nothing to do for the present except build a snow house and travel on tomorrow, I thought. We had a small primus stove made out of a gasoline lantern to heat our camp with; accordingly, I decided to build a round snow- house igloo of the type many people think the Eskimos of Alaska use—that is, the kind usually drawn in cartoons by humorists, if this will identify it. This is actually the dwelling of the Coronation Gulf Eskimos who live nearly a thousand miles east of here, but I had never seen it except in the *New Yorker* magazine.

We took a string and using our knives for pegs drew a circle eight feet in diameter. Ook-sook cut the snow blocks with a saw and carried them to me while I built the structure. Ook-sook was good at doing things he had always done but he was awfully slow to learn new ones. The Eskimos of Alaska make only square snow houses, using driftwood rafters to support the roof or a canvas roof. Both Ruth and Ook- sook would eagerly try new food and new inventions, like the lipstick Ruth now used regularly, and the phonograph they played at Beechey Point, but they were laggards at learning the principles lying behind material inventions. This is likewise true of the mass of people inhabiting our big cities and is not peculiar to Eskimos but is indicative of the primitive or the unlearned in all men. Neither Connie nor I ever succeeded in teaching Ruth or Ook-sook *why* anything was done. They judged by surface appearances and as an illustration were much impressed by fine clothes and white man's food, but had we not possessed these we would have had no influence upon them whatsoever; as in our own society, unless we were well supplied with material goods achieved by one method or another, we simply would not rate with the Eskimos.

Ook-sook thought it was rather plebeian of me to be interested in building a snow house out of snow only, when we had white man's canvas for a tent! I had been convinced of the working principle of the domed igloo for certain occasions in arctic life because I had read about it from Dr. Stefansson. Ook-sook, who had never heard of Dr. Stefansson (although his parents had), did not think building a round igloo was possible and he thought I was crazy to even experiment.

Briefly, I got Ook-sook to cut the snow blocks about twenty-four by eighteen inches and six inches thick. I undercut them so that they leaned inwards and shaved the corners so that they formed a tight wall about the eight-foot circle. When the first tier was finished, the circle was seven feet across the top. With my snow knife I smoothed the blocks off, so they were all even. I then cut one block diagonally nearly in half. Here I laid the first block of the second tier. Ook-sook handed the blocks to me while I stayed on the inside and fitted them carefully into place. The nice snow blocks cut easily and by trimming them a little each slipped solidly in. At low temperatures the snow is very tractable. The blocks quickly freeze solid.

After four tiers of blocks spiraled upward the snow house was done. A final keystone filled the remaining hole in the roof. So far there was a complete dome of snow with no holes for entrance. I was inside the thing and Ook-sook was out. Had we been able to build the snow house upon a drift a few feet deep we would have dug a hole under the snow wall, making an air trap through which cold air couldn't enter, but as it was we had to build the house upon soft shallow snow due to a shortage of suitable snow for blocks. I cut a small hole at the floor level for a door with my snow knife. We later cut a snow block to serve for the door and blocked the doorway behind us when we crawled in to sleep.

Ook-sook and I chinked all the cracks and shaved the roof down to a thickness of about four inches. We made one mistake. A snow house of this design must be chinked from the inside.

A hole some two inches in diameter is cut in the center of the dome for a ventilator. This sounds strange, but never neglect this if you build a snow house for habitation, for a snow house is nearly airtight and when the primus stove or lantern is lighted it will give off carbon monoxide fumes. A snow house which is not ventilated thus becomes a death chamber. Carbon monoxide is odorless so that its victims never know what happened until they keel over. The hole is always cut the first thing and you are careful to see that no blizzard blows it shut.

We had chinked our snow house from the outside. We crawled in and lighted the primus stove. As the snow house quickly warmed up we discarded our clothing down to shirt sleeves. The snow dome began to melt but it did not drip because the snow acted as a blotter, absorbing the moisture. But the irregular contour of the dome, because of its being chinked improperly, grew more and more irregular, until at last there were points in the very top from which a little water began to drip. This was our mistake: we should have chinked it from the inside. Had it been built with the inside smooth we could easily have shaved down the outside until melting was checked by the outside cold. However, even unprogressive Ook-sook, who was only impressed by the pretentious, had to admit this was a pretty good snow house. He would have come to like it if we had ever had other opportunities to build this kind. But this was our last chance to get good materials this spring.

The temperature was slightly lower than thirty below zero; yet we slept quite warm in our bedding within our snow house. It was much more roomy than our 7' X 9' tent had been and far warmer than the tent's thin roofing which allowed the heat to escape. A round snow house is the safest, warmest, and strongest structure which can be made for an overnight camp in the real arctic. I wished that we had tried it before now on our caribou hunts inland, but I was new to the arctic and it had taken me this long to become my own experimenter. Next morning when we prepared to travel on, I climbed up on top of the snow dome and finally persuaded Ook-sook to join me, just to prove to him how strong it was. The round igloo had grown so solid from interior heating and then freezing that it would have supported a dozen men standing on its roof just as easily. Once a snow house has been glazed inside, polar bears may walk over it and still it will not break down; it possesses unbelievable strength to carry loads. Only a sharp blow will break it easily.

Since we had found no open water we started seaward again in stubborn search for it. We took no camp gear with us this time; we would not dare go farther than one more day's travel but would return to our snow house for the night. The ice was rougher than yesterday with belts of pressure ice a half mile or more wide to get over. The surface as far as one could see across the frozen ocean reminded one of cube sugar that had been piled in long windrows with the cubes being six-foot blocks piled from thirty to eighty feet high. From the highest points we studied the surrounding ice looking for open water or wandering polar bears. We saw neither—only more ice.

The day was unusually clear; we had to wear sunglasses all the time now. As we got farther out from shore the ice gradually was beginning to get smoother and we began to find aged unbroken fields from years gone by. Two features easily distinguished this older ice. Old ice is worn smooth from the summer's sun. Its pressure ridges resemble hills and valleys of some prairie land, while it is not salty in taste but fresh. From this old ice as well as from drifts of fresh snow, water for drinking may be obtained anywhere at sea with no difficulty. New ice which is salty is contrarily distinguishable at once because it has the contour of broken glass, while it is sticky, and the snow adheres to it because of its saltiness.

Around 4 p.m. we climbed an especially high ice hummock and searched with the binoculars. Far to the north a dark line appeared trending east and west—water sky. Water sky is caused when the dark mass of open water is mirrored in the overcast sky or clouds hanging above it. A traveler on the Arctic Ocean soon learns to use the sky ahead of him as his map, for often it reflects the terrain beyond his horizon of vision. From the position of the streak of water in the sky, we knew the open water to be at least fifteen or twenty more miles away and felt that it was too far for us to venture.

We were now twenty-five miles north of Cross Island. As we started to retrace our way, Ook-sook stopped and started examining what looked like an old polar bear trail. When the sea ice forms it is sticky and damp on top. This, combined with a little slush snow that may fall during freeze-up, makes a layer around an inch thick of glazed snow. The wind blows all the other snow into sheltered spots or makes drifts of it. In this way the arctic ice and its sand islands are kept swept bare in places except for this thin crust of snow. A man or a bear sinks through this crust or dents it and you can follow his trail all winter long thereafter, whenever the wind keeps the loose snow blown away from the indelible footprints. It was such a trail Ook-sook was following and by his surprised look I saw something was queer.

"People!" he finally said. "No dogs."

It was true: his "people" was really a person, and he had clearly been an Eskimo hunter all alone. There had been no one out in this vicinity all year, since everybody living along the coast knew where every other person went at all times; everyone's comings and goings were common gossip which it would be difficult if not impossible to hide. Yet here were the tracks of a man out in the ice and they were quite plain. A novice might have taken them for tracks of yesterday.

The explanation is not dramatic, but it brings up an important point. The tracks may have drifted to us from another area in the polar basin as the ice pans moved. For instance, they might have been tracks made last fall on a field of ice by some Eskimo of Canada to our east.

Back beside the clean gleaming snow dome Ook-sook and I talked about our dogs. Duk caught his chunk of frozen meat with a snap and looked for more; the expression in his eyes never changed, and the fact that he was licking his chops was the only indication that dog-feeding time was over. Our dogs had been fed on too much lean meat without fat all winter; soon now their diet would be bad in the reverse by being composed of all fat with no lean. This is almost as bad, for it does not build strength but merely sustains from day to day—a starvation diet for dogs as well as humans. The team, bedding down, complained long and mournfully to the gods above. That is, all except Netsig.

His name means "hook" in Eskimo. It came from a pink mark which might be seen on the roof of his mouth when his jaws were pried open wide. Netsig, named for the hidden mark, according to typical Oriental observation of small things, was nearly full-blooded hound and his song was a sonorous bay.

The subject of arctic sled dogs is one upon which we find people in the United States to be much misinformed, and this applies to many people in Alaska too, I think. They seem to have the notion that sled dogs are all of a special breed: why, of course—they are Malemutes or Huskies!

You will note that our dogs were never called thus in this book. Long discussions are waged in the dog world about these two mythical "breeds"—corruptions, originally, from the names of Eskimo groups from which these dogs apparently sprung, but the distinguishing characteristics are very vague. Sled dogs in general, call them what you may, are merely all kinds of dogs that pull sleds. One of our dogs was apparently part collie while others showed strains of terrier and Saint Bernard. One was definitely a mixed German shepherd. All had come from known dogs imported by white men, according to Ook-sook. All sled dogs are not large; one of our hardest-working dogs was scarcely larger than a fox and didn't weigh over twenty pounds. Connie and I would have gladly traded for larger dogs had they been available; with the Eskimos small scrubby stock is the result of lack of attention to the breeding of the dogs, just as scrubby stock results with any other animals anyplace where attention is not given to developing the best traits in the stock. But the practical fact is that whatever the faults of these mismatched and scrambling teams the dogs which are actually pulling most of the sleds which are pulled today are mutts of all colors, sizes, and descriptions, and it is surprising what can be done with them quite as a matter of course. Most of them develop the "wolf howl" or the "call of the wild" when they get together—even the Pekinese—but I don't know why.

When we broke camp Ook-sook wanted to leave our camp gear at the snow house. He thought, "What's the use of hauling it? We'll soon be back here again on the next trip." But something told me we might lose it while we were gone, and accordingly, when we packed, we took everything. It was lucky we did, for a few days later when we returned a pressure ridge had moved up and buried our snow house under tons of ice so that nothing was to be seen of it.

The dogs looked dejected, Ook-sook looked downhearted and sulky, and I felt downhearted as we neared the island and home. Unsuccessful hunters were we. I could see plainly what Ook-sook thought: "Why should we come out here when there are plenty of caribou to eat on land?" The trip held no purpose for him. As for polar bears, Ook-sook was nothing if not unheroic; they were something to be avoided.

Three dogs out of our team were limping painfully; they were almost cripples. My feet were sore as boils and Ook-sook's feet were sore I knew. It was time to don our spring sealskin boots with *ugrug* soles, for the soft winter caribou boots would not stand up to this long. The poor sled had suffered most; every one of its floor boards was broken while the first three were torn clear away. Even the handlebars and rails were smashed. If we looked quite beat up at least Connie and Ruth were glad to see us, and they had hot tea and cookies on the floor when we arrived. The first puffs of an oncoming storm rattled the little stovepipe as we gratefully sipped our tea.

Some people might call it a blizzard. We called it an east wind. Visibility was soon not more than one hundred feet on the ground, and we were of necessity house-bound again. On this kind of day of no shadows sunglasses are more than ever imperative to prevent snow blindness if one is on the trail. There was nothing to do but sled over to shore to Beechey Point and get some caribou meat we had left there. It would tide us over for human and dog feed for a while. We would be gone two nights at the shortest, battling head winds to get there, and we would have to pick up a load of wood along the shore to supply the Beechey Point house with fuel in order to exist when we got there. Ruth's face fell a foot when she learned for certain that we were to leave and travel; she didn't look as if she would forgive us, for it was a Sunday.

Connie hunts seals at an open lead with Coaly

3

I t took us sixteen hours to travel the thirty-five miles to Beechey Point, for soon after we left Cross Island the wind increased its fury and blew straight into our faces. The world vanished and on we ran through blinding snow. For the first time all winter it was snowing, too. I would ride, and Ook-sook would run behind the sled so that he could see where he was going by keeping his eye on it; then we would change about. It was more than we could do to make the dogs face the storm, for our leader kept turning sideways by imperceptible degrees. Darkness came and with it we struck land. But we were off our course several miles. For a while we were both puzzled. "Me loss," said Ook-sook, for he couldn't pronounce the *t* in "lost." Then we realized we were outside the Jones Islands and that we had been traveling at right angles to our course, which means we were heading out to sea when we discovered our error. Old Duk caught it from Ook-sook, and after this he faced the storm with an almost audible sigh.

From the darkness the trading post lights suddenly gleamed. As soon as we stopped, the miserable dogs huddled behind the sled in a tight mass. Gone was their old fighting spirit now. They shivered, and their teeth rattled, so to speak, as the temperature rose to zero in the gale, causing the warm snow to stick to their fur until they were masses of ice. We beat the snow from our own furs, stamped our feet, and trailed in. I thought of the frozen music of the ice pack out to sea and wondered what it was doing tonight. After I had once been out there, I would always think of it on nights like this.

People from the westward had taken the opportunity to travel in to the trading post on the wind and trade their fur catch. It was the first week in April; the trapping season had closed for white fox on the last day of March. Dog teams continued to arrive until every trapper to the west was here or was represented by some member of his family. There are really few Eskimos in all the world, supposedly 15,000 altogether in Alaska, including the Aleuts of the Aleutian Islands. On the north coast of Alaska beside the Arctic Ocean there are not more than 250 Eskimos all told. The nine families we knew intimately lived adjacent to Beechey Point and they totaled 50 people. Because many of this number were half white with various nationalities thrown in, one expects that they will presently be called, not Eskimos, but simply "our arctic coast population." Perhaps the term a Barrow schoolteacher applied to these people is pretty exact. He called them not Eskimos but "whalamos."

As the trappers came in we talked about their trapping. The highest catch this year for one family was 49 foxes. The price on each fox took a slump this year in the United States market and $18 was the average pay-off for each white skin. These particular 49 foxes had a value of $1029 for a family of six. This was Richard's family. The next highest was 47 foxes, represented by George's son Apiak, and after that the catches fell to 20, 9, 6, and at last 1 fox represented by the obsequious presence of Ruth's father, our old friend Cyrus. As a few of the foxes were red foxes and blue foxes worth but $12.50, this brought the total amount of dollars down.

Beautiful white skins hanging in bundles of ten foxes each—I helped Abraham to hang them up in the warehouse. The total fox catch, including Barter Island's catch and all along the north coast except Barrow, came to 250 pelts. If we multiply this by $18, which is a high average, we get $4500; with an added $1500 for foxes that might have been traded off privately on a trip to Barrow, and miscellaneous income, we get an estimate of $6000 as being the whole arctic coast's yearly income. Divide this by the population of 200 people and we get an average yearly income of $30 per person. This doesn't go far, with coffee at $ 1.40 a pound, needles at 70 cents a package, a box of .30-30 ammunition at $4 for 20 shots, and so on.

I was reflecting that this income represented the entire money derived from an area as large as one of our whole Western states, when: "Dog team come," and we all ran to a window. Sure enough, here came Leffingwell. He must have our mail from Barrow this time! I had promised Connie he certainly would have it.

"It's always that way," explained Abraham to me, presently, as my face dropped. "He forget it." Our Eskimo friends kept making their sled trips to and from Barrow, but they kept forgetting to bring the mail back, and this continued for the year we were with them, while there seemed little that we could do about it.

Ruth returns home

Connie remains alone on Cross Island

4

The foxes were counted, and the last store products had been rationed out to the trappers. These were flour, oatmeal, and beans. Ook-sook and I loaded our sled with the caribou meat for which we had come and left. The sun was bright and the day not much below zero so that the ice shoeing upon our sled runners came off and the sled pulled hard. Finally, we had to cache half our load on the sea ice in order to make it to Cross Island that day.

On the way back, Connie had heard us coming far out in the rough ice and had walked to meet the sled. All the way back I had dreaded telling her I didn't have the mail. I could see she thought I was playing a game and keeping the box of it hidden under the sled cover. At last I blurted out: "I didn't get it."

"Oh," she said. Just, "Oh."

Ruth had got one of her spells of homesickness while we had been gone and closed her lips, refusing to speak or answer. Ook-sook had had occasional tendencies towards homesickness too, but fortunately he did not have the time to brood on these things as Ruth did, inasmuch as he and I were almost constantly out in the open journeying upon the trail, struggling just to keep our family alive. During the brief times Ook-sook was in camp I had to think up chores, play cards with him, and keep him constantly amused.

Connie had written in her diary at the beginning: "None of that friction, I hope, between Ruth and me which is so typical between 'white mistress and native servant girl.' These Eskimos have never been in contact with any white people other than the missionary and a kindly trader, so that they have never been trained, like the rest of the world, in habits of servitude or discipline. That's what I like about them! They have never worked for anyone before, so that the process of submitting one's will to another, I am sure, would be an entirely new experience. Knowing this, and knowing how hard it would be, I never ask Ruth to do anything, and I interfere very little with what she does. This might not be possible to abide were we living the conventional life in a house, but so far as camping life goes, it works fine."

In that Connie had never told Ruth to get up or to cut wood or given her an order in her life, she had probably conducted a unique experiment. It worked well for a while, but after a few months with us Ruth thought that she had learned everything there was to know. She had always been stubborn; now she was discontent.

After a day of rest on the island and small portions of caribou meat for all of us, Ook-sook and I pulled out again to hunt for seal and polar bear. I had stomach trouble. I felt a little gassed for our biscuits had got some gasoline on them from the primus stove tipping over on the sled; I had had a good belly-ache for the last five days. There was trouble in the air in our camp. There is not an explorer in the world who has not had these bad times when employing natives. It seemed a kind of minor crisis upon which hung the Eskimos' respect for us. I must get meat and get it soon. We had educated Ruth and Ook-sook to a lavish standard of living this winter and this had but trained them to expect more and more because we had always been very indulgent with them in all things; there was no end to it. It had come to the point where Connie and I could do more gracefully during hard times than they could. I had brought out $300 worth of store grub to Cross Island, but after this was gone, no more was obtainable. Of course, if Ook-sook and Ruth actually went home to their own people they would regret taking this step after they got there. They would be "homesick" for us again. Yet, without meaning to, we had educated our "children" to snobbery and insolence: they just couldn't take it. I have no doubt that since Connie and I left the north coast of Alaska those two rogues of ours have been almost unbearable in their snobbishness. Well, unless we got a break soon I was just afraid that our long-awaited spring polar bear hunting with all the colored photography of the sea ice life would be called off entirely and we ourselves would have to part ways with our kids and go back to our own Beechey Point house to live out the rest of the season. We could do that now, at least—and reconcile ourselves to failure in getting along with Eskimos.

It had got so I couldn't talk with Connie any more without their wanting to be in on the conversation. They might be talking in their own language, but they would stop, and their ears perk up at once as soon as Connie and I said a word to each other. They were jealous and wanted to be played with all the time! They wanted constant attention, as spoiled children do, and would not be excluded from anything, yet they would exclude us whenever they wished. A very unpleasant habit of theirs which had grown more unpleasant was to grab up and handle things which were not their property and then throw them down again. We had put up with a good deal of this, never reprimanding, realizing that it was but innocent primitive curiosity—but sometimes even this can go too far. Ruth would get into Connie's manuscript papers while Connie tried to write and would just sit and pick and pull at things. I had brought pencils for Connie; therefore, Ruth and Ook-sook had to have their pencil and papers too, but they weren't satisfied. Now when I gave Ook-sook his bullets for the hunt, he threw them upon the ground in front of our house. I wouldn't pick them up, Ruth wouldn't pick them up; we needed every bullet badly—finally Connie picked them up. I had no idea what was the matter with Ook-sook and his long face.

Then Connie and I hit upon the idea of telling them that we were going to go back to the United States. We could always reach Barrow or Umiat by dog sled and fly out, and they knew it. Accordingly, we would have a farewell party. Tonight, at least, we would forgive and forget. Rare roast caribou meat from our last forty-five pounds (Ruth knew how to roast it frozen, and come out with it just right, something which I have never seen in any cook book yet), mashed dried potatoes, green fresh-frozen peas (that carton which we had hoarded all winter from Barrow), snow ice cream and a cocoanut jelly layer cake for dessert. Could you believe it? Not bad at all! I'll bet that's the best meal that any human being has eaten on bleak Cross Island! Ruth commenced washing dresses for herself for the trip home, while Connie baked to get supplies ahead for the trail. We were through with Eskimo life! Would Ruth wash Connie's single dress, her snow shirt? "I don't know,"

Ruth rebelled. When I spoke, however, Ruth did it. Ook-sook was sulky even when stuffed on pancakes, which he called "pod cakes."

It was a considerable satisfaction to us to see the really long faces on our two companions as they became convinced that we really meant to leave. Smilingly I told Ruth she could go home and there would be no more hard work but there she could of course play all the time. And now that we were going away, Ook-sook could have cream in his coffee every day since we would not be here to prevent him. Weren't we going to discharge Ook-sook as soon as we could sled to Beechey Point, and was not our responsibility over to him and his hounds from this point on? Well, when I thought about it, the dogs deserved a good meal, they had worked so hard all year, and Ook-sook deserved a vacation. We would have to have a supply of caribou meat before we could do anything. Of course, those little slim dogs would never get back to us with so much as a whole caribou because the amount they would eat while they were gone on the hunt would go faster than Ook-sook could get it. I knew Ook-sook wanted to be off hunting caribou with the other young men at this time of year, and that was probably half of what was the matter with him. Therefore, once again we saw that intrepid hunter start off: a pinch of tea in a jar, some frozen biscuits; he must secure game or starve on the way. Could any white sportsman that you know do as well? For what he was, you had to admire Ook-sook. And as for me—ho-hum for a rest from Eskimos.

Just before Ook-sook left, Andrew's two boys, Thomas and Peary, from Barter Island dropped by across the sea, bringing a saddle of mountain sheep meat from their father, and our problem of domestic help solved itself. The message they brought was that Ruth's mother, old Alice, was ill and Ruth must go home at once to take care of the family.

Ruth was half glad and half sad to go home now that events were out of all our hands. She was scared of polar bears and she didn't like life out on Cross Island. Ruth slept under the six-inch-square ventilator hole and we had told her jokingly that a bear would think the ventilator was a seal hole and Ruth a sleeping seal. Ook-sook even pointed out that Ruth was a little fat like a seal. Homesickness was forgotten in jolly Eskimo laughter enhanced by crude gesticulation describing this event. The bear if it came would reach down the hole and hook Ruth and pull her up through the little vent, and so the story would run with minor variations, but perhaps the person who laughs last laughs best.

Ook-sook took Ruth to Beechey Point and her brother Johnny picked her up there with the family sled, after Abraham had had her on his hands to feed for a few days. Ook- sook returned alone to finish out the spring hunting with us, sunburned, crippled, and nearly snow-blind because he had lost the sunglasses I had given him, as I had more or less supposed he might do, and very content. He had killed three caribou a long way inland. All were cows with unborn fawns, more's the pity. He brought news of seeing three other young hunters at different places. Their kills ran up to nearly twenty in some cases. Ook-sook reported, "Ruth homesick for Cross Island." Be it ever so humble—! What, Ruth, already?

Abraham wrote a letter explaining why Ook-sook had thrown his bullets onto the ground. Ook-sook had got the idea gradually throughout the winter that I was not pleased with him because he shot so many bullets. Where he got this idea I can't possibly guess, but it shows upon what things his mind dwelled and how it worked. His prowess as a hunter had been touched because, while a good shot, he often missed his mark at the same time I often hit mine. Remember, I had a telescope sight. Of course, he couldn't hope to compete with a man using a telescope aid; nevertheless, he had brooded upon this until, when it came to sea hunting, which he didn't like anyway, he exploded in a temper, and of course I didn't know what on earth was the matter with him. I now transferred Ruth's five-dollar wage over to Ook-sook in the form of a raise, and everything was cleared up, while Ook- sook had come back resolved to put new heart into the sea ice hunting.

Now we set to work to rig up a device the Eskimos called a *pesitwack,* a trap gun, and after this we began to get seals without trouble. It is a modern method of sealing.

First, we must explain that seals are swimming all the time in this ocean underneath its ice, even though they may not be seen. There are other ways to get seals than to find them in the open water. Each seal has several breathing holes through the ice scattered over several acres of territory. But the human eye is not often able to discern them unassisted; they are small as a pencil's end at the surface and are usually covered with snow. Often seal holes will be located under even deep snowdrifts at sea. The seal may have a snow- house under the drift where he sleeps when he is not swimming beneath ice, or he will have a sort of cave gnawed into the ice itself, where he can haul out and be quite inaccessible to the outside world all winter long. The young seals are born in these caves or snow houses in late April.

For years seals were not even known to exist here. Arctic explorers of the ice called it the "lifeless polar sea," for they were able to find nothing to eat, not knowing that seals existed. Even if they suspected it, they had no way to get them, inasmuch as seals never appear on the surface all winter long, or for most of the year. But the Eskimos of various groups about the northern world have known for thousands of years how to secure seals under the ice; they depended upon this animal alone for their fuel, light, food, and clothing during long periods.

Failing to find open water for sealing, I decided to try the system used by the Eskimos of Coronation Gulf. We would lead a dog around on a rope and let him smell out a seal's breathing hole for us. Our old dog Netsig, the hound, became our sealing dog; as Ook-sook said, Netsig had a "strong smell."

In the old days just a few years ago, over Coronation Gulf way, the hunter would sit beside such a seal hole which a dog had smelled out for him, for hours on end with poised spear, waiting for the seal to come up to this particular hole to breathe. This is the hardest work in the world: just waiting, completely motionless. Because the seals have very keen hearing, the hunter would not dare to so much as move an eyelash, and he must crouch behind a windbreak of a few snow blocks, attentive through the hours of storm and cold, his eye on an ivory indicator below. The more hunters that could be stationed about at several seal holes in the vicinity, of course the more likely they were to be able to spear the elusive seal. After the seal was secured by a downward thrust of the spear, the hunter would enlarge the hole in the ice, pull the round seal out like popping the cork out of a bottle, tie it to one of his waiting dogs, and home the dog would run, pulling the slippery seal over the ice like a bouncing ball. This method of getting seals is still widely practiced throughout all the northern world except that today's hunter uses a rifle and shoots the seal. Getting seals by waiting at seal holes is something every far arctic traveler should know.

But there is a better method even than this if you have an extra gun in your crowd. Although many professional explorers scorn the shotgun and the .22 rifle and will not take these guns along on their expeditions, we have found them very handy, and always will try to take them for the two of us, as they work very well for odd chores. One of the most valuable chores that either of these extra arms can perform, but especially the shotgun, now owned by every Indian and Eskimo that can afford one, is to be of use to the hunter as a trap gun while he sits at home warm and waiting in his igloo.

Today in this kind of sealing the Eskimo still uses a dog to smell out the seal holes in the ice, but he sets up an extra gun (if he has it) on a frame or tripod. If a party were marooned out on the ice several guns could be set in this way to get food in emergency. If I had only two guns in my party, I should still risk setting one as a trap gun in such a case.

Here is the way you set a trap gun for seals. When you have dug the snow away and set up your gun on a tripod so that it will shoot straight down into the seal's breathing hole, you take a long slender stick and freeze a flat piece of ice to one end, about the size of a teacup in circumference and an inch thick. You place this stick so that the ice hangs a half inch above the water level and the other end of the stick rests against the trigger. You can tie it with a string to the trigger guard so that the stick can move up but not down. You now cut a snow block two inches thick and big enough to cover the entire seal hole. Cut it in half and make a groove in the center for the trigger stick. You place this carefully over the hole so as to shut out all light and make it air tight, for if the seal sees light coming into his hole or suspects it has been disturbed he will never come up here again. Cover the edges with soft loose snow and smooth off the surrounding snow. You next make a small snow house to cover the gun so that the wind won't make it vibrate and scare the seal. If the seal hears the sound of the wind blowing against the gun, he will use other breathing holes. Just before you put the snow-block roof on, you examine your "set" again and cock the gun or push the safety off. When the seal comes swimming along underneath the five-foot ice and noses up into his breathing hole he bumps the trigger and shoots himself. He floats in the hole and freezes there, where he will remain all winter or until you come along with pickax and shovel to chop him out.

By the time we had secured two seals in this way to tide us over, a light west wind had opened a lead and we could see water sky to the north. Ook-sook and I took surveillance of it from the island and cut a cord of wood and stacked it in the house with Connie. Connie would still stay at home on the island while we hunted. Ook-sook looked surprised that we should leave, as he put it, "one people" alone on the island, but I assured him Connie was "strong" and anyway she had her rifle.

The cutting and hauling of wood according to the rules of our family had never ceased to amuse and amaze Ook-sook, but he was agreeable. According to him, people rarely chop more than enough wood to cook one meal. They get some more when the first is gone. This wet, soggy drift burned poorly at best, even when it was dried out, I had found, but a piece of it frozen to below zero was enough to stop any stove. Connie naturally liked to have a big pile of it chopped ahead and stacked inside the house in order that it might at least thaw out.

The driftwood was hard upon both our saw and the stove. Evidently the salt and other chemical agents from the sea had become concentrated in it. When it was burned, the chemicals ate up the stove. The sand in the driftwood would fairly grind the edge from a saw.

I have often marveled at how much these people can do with so little and how little they can do with a lot. An ax is an ax to Ook-sook. He uses it to chop wood, frozen meat, and even rocks; to pry off planks, hack loose dog chains that have become frozen in the ice, or to cut up sheet steel with it as if it were a cold chisel. If he has a pickax, cold chisel, crowbar and hammer, he merely throws them aside and uses the familiar ax for all purposes. I had two axes five years and never knocked a chip from either of the handles, but Ruth and Ook-sook broke both handles in two months, while it was impossible to keep the axes sharp after they came to work and live with us.

Now our dogs were full of fresh seal meat and they were quarrelsome. Half our team was crippled from fighting as we started out to the edge of the floe. In a short distance Ook- sook vanished in the broken ice ahead and at the same time one of the dog's traces caught on an ice snag. The dog was pulled back into the following dog as the team lunged ahead. This was the chance the rear dog had dreamed of, for he dearly loved to fight. The fight broke hard and vicious. In a moment the whole team was a tangle of snarling, fighting, screaming dogs. Separating the dogs and untangling the traces was no easy job. Sled dogs fight like wolves, and that is one analogy used by novelists that is hardly an exaggeration of the truth. These dogs often kill one of their team mates or maim it so that it has to be killed.

∽

AFTER EIGHT MILES OF TRAVEL we reached the lead. The amount of damage a wind will do to the ice cannot be determined, because currents, tides, temperature, and direction of the wind all enter as factors. The last wind had been nothing more than a strong breeze from the west. Yet the floating pack had moved out a mile from the edge of the land-fast ice when we reached it. We gazed delightedly upon a big lead of a mile of open blue water before us. Probably this crack would never close permanently again until next fall's freeze-up, for it was now the month of April.

"*Natchuk*—seal"—Ook-sook pointed, using both the Eskimo and the lately acquired English name.

Yes, the first thing we both saw was a seal swimming about in the placid blue ocean depths and calmly eying us as we stood on the white ice shore. I did a flip and came up with my rifle ready. At its report pieces of seal scalp flew high into the air and an oily film widened around the inert floating form. Ook-sook struggled with the *manak* while the dogs set up a clamor of highest treble voices. This was always their reaction to the sound of a rifle shot.

A *manak* is a wooden ball about the size of a grapefruit. There is an iron ring fastened to it, and by a short piece of sealskin a four-pronged snag hook is fastened to the ring. The sealskin is fastened to the lower shank of the hook in such a way that the hooks point away from the wooden ball. A five-foot piece of rawhide is tied to the eye of the hook and from the other end of the rawhide run generally around forty yards of cod line.

You throw the *manak* by coiling the cod line on the ice so that it will play out freely after the flying ball. You are always careful to stand on the end of the cod line so as not to throw your line away. When all is ready you take a grip upon the end of the five-foot rawhide thong with the wooden ball and hooks attached and whirl it around your head until it gains as much momentum as you can give it. Then you let the line go. If your aim is true, the wooden ball will sail out and fall beyond the floating seal. You then work the line until it passes directly over the seal. You slowly draw the line in and just as the hooks are ready to pass over the seal, you give a sharp jerk that sets one of the hooks into the seal's skin and the seal is easily pulled in to you.

Ook-sook whirled the *manak* in the approved fashion and let go. Outshot the flying ball and the cod line made a beautiful arc, except that it landed short. The seal had been at the extreme range of our *manak* to begin with, and the current was now slowly carrying it to the other side of the lead where we could not get it.

So, goes the other method of seal hunting which we here describe. It is heartbreaking to see your game drift slowly away while you stand helplessly by—but this is quite typical in sea hunting. All day we waited and hunted. Ook-sook killed two more seals, but they drifted away before we could get a line on them. I killed one more and it, too, floated off beyond reach. At midnight Ook-sook killed a seal that came up near some congealing slush ice that had formed, and it stuck there. We would get that one next day when the slush ice was hard enough to walk out on. I never shot any more, for there was little use in killing seals we couldn't get.

I suppose that for every seal that is secured in the arctic, there must be five seals lost. In the fall, out of thirty-eight seals I shot, only eight floated and were retrieved by boat; they sank at that season. In the summer out of twenty-four shot, twenty-four sank. In open water in the ice now, while we were very careful, we yet lost as many as we managed to secure because they drifted out of our reach.

For three days we waited at the lead for seals but got only the one. There were plenty of them swimming by all the time, but none came near enough to the edge of the ice where we crouched to secure them with our *manak*, so we didn't even shoot. Before we started for home Ook-sook went out to get his seal that was frozen in the young ice. At every step the thin ice bent under him, just sagging. Unlike fresh water ice, salt ice bends quite a way before it will break, but if it once does give way, it does so suddenly, and one goes straight down through it without a crack, just as though he plunged through soft ice cream. Hundreds of feet of water lay beneath Ook-sook while he had to keep moving or he would sink through. He secured his seal, dragged it gingerly over the rubbery bending ice to shore, and I held my breath. Ook-sook had proved to me many a time before now that he was quite a man when he didn't have the sulks; one couldn't ask for a better. The hungry dogs greeted the seal's arrival with whines of delight. While Ook-sook fed them the unaccustomed seal meat which at first, they would but sniff suspiciously, I started back over the trail through the rough ice for the island, home, and Connie. The day was warm and balmy.

By mid-April the sun was shining eighteen hours a day and by May Cross Island was just about bare of snow. It always had been bare in some places because of the wind. The sun beating down on this brown earth was absorbed rather than being reflected back in light, so that the snow actually began to melt on the dark surfaces of the island even before a thawing point was indicated by the thermometer. We had taken to going to sleep of nights as late as eleven or even one and awakening near noon once more. A succession of glorious days found it ten degrees above zero at noon with all of us roasting in the balmy zephyrs. Sweat cascaded off Ook-sook now at the chopping block, where the two of us shed our parkas to work in shirt sleeves.

While he and I contentedly foraged about the island's edge with the "best-smelling" dog in tow to locate seal holes and to watch our locality for fresh polar bear tracks, Connie had fun running her own household once again, and found herself quite capable at it. Breakfast was coffee for Ook-sook, who arose first and simply made his own, boiled meat, which boiled itself, having been chopped out frozen and placed in the cooking pot ready the night before, and some excellent whole-wheat pancakes with sugar syrup.

When we came in for lunch Connie fried eight or ten rare steaks from a long piece of loin which held dozens of choice ones similarly attached and ready sawed there; with this she had raised whole-wheat rolls, rice, and gravy. Ruth had always started the rice boiling at the same time she started the meat and we had endured it. You couldn't break her of the habit, so that for months we had eaten rice cooked into such a mush as wasn't fit for a dog to eat. Supper, in the evening, was steak again, a great pot of soy beans, and hot sweet prune dumplings with the last of the vanilla ice cream on which we all practically burst. Food now must be split only three ways. Connie washed out Ook-sook's orange snow shirt with soap and melted snow water and hung it up to dry. She wanted to have it bright for his colored pictures. Then she washed his green bath towel for him, for she had noted that he had recently resurrected the comb and hairbrush we had first given him when he came to us at Beechey Point, and if Ook-sook would stop being so careless and losing things all the time he might have all the refinements the rest of us had.

Out of the corner of my eye I saw Ook-sook using his new green towel as he performed his ablutions in the long tin tray we had made for his own wash pan out of a gasoline can. This consisted of vigorous scrubbing of the face, missing the neck and ears entirely, soap in the eyes you may be sure, and a blind lunge, as of a walrus, for the first bath towel he had ever owned in his life. These people have never washed any part of their bodies that I know of, since they live so crowded together that I cannot imagine their ever having opportunity to do so, but to wash the hands and face has become a sort of ceremony, especially with the women, who may wash their hands many times a day, due to the missionary influence which has reached them. You can't say that washing has improved the state of the Eskimos so far because passing around the towels has only helped to spread communicable disease. While Ook-sook had been with us several months, he and I had been on the trail constantly, and as hunters had small use for towels. Ruth got a towel for her own, but somehow Ook-sook got left out. The hardships of the winter generally, combined perhaps with its darkness, had left little inclination on the part of either of us for these refinements. It was a good thing not to wash our faces because washing only chapped them dangerously as it made one's face the more inclined to frostbite. Of course, I shaved about twice a week of necessity, but Ook- sook never had to shave as he grew no whiskers.

Now with the warm sun bathing our snow house in splendor on Cross Island, and plenty of meat in camp for once, we could luxuriate in these things. What Connie and I didn't realize was that this was really the nicest season in all the year that we were now enjoying. It is warmer on the sea ice in May for all purposes of comfort than it ever is again for all the rest of the summer to come, for after the ocean opens the damp fog comes, too.

Of course, there were still days when the wind howled. Old man winter was on the run and he was merely complaining at his banishment. Ook-sook and I worked at planing new sled lumber inside the house on such a day. Connie huddled in her parka sitting on top of the upturned dog bucket with her writing.

One day we had scalding tea and squares of a cake she had made with real canned milk and powdered eggs, while the wind whistled through the house that had lost its calking again. We had come home today with a perfect balloon of a female seal, dragging it by a rope passed through its lower jaw. In between eating the cake with hot prune and whiskey sauce we skinned the latest seal in the house, after she had thawed a bit, and using the dog ladle dipped up the blood and passed it into the tub for dog feed, boiling, with its many redolent odors of course, upon the stove.

The seal itself, inside its encircling casement of blubber, was a rather small creature whose flesh was dark red or nearly black. Its milk glands were full of milk and Ook-sook explained that some of the people like these boiled up; Ruth had long looked forward to the sealing season, we recalled, because she was so fond of boiled seal intestines. Inside the mother was an unborn infant seal of a most delicate pale yellow or pastel shade, definitely not of this world. It had white, needlelike claws on its flippers, which were folded beneath its chin in a prayerful attitude. The curly-haired hide, Ook-sook told us, was valued at a dollar at the trading post, as against only fifty cents for the skin of the whole mature seal, its mother. Delighted with the little unborn ghost, we tacked its skin out on our wall to dry, wishing that we might get Nanny to make something pretty of it.

None of us would eat the seal meat unless we were brought to it—not as long as we had a scrap of caribou left. Even Ook-sook, the caribou hunter, would not eat it. Connie and I never stayed in this part of the arctic long enough to get used to eating the sea animals, which have a flavor different from all else. Presumably the meat is extremely nutritious.

Such were the things we learned of seals and sealing before we had the opportunity to take up the study of the polar bear.

Ook-Sook at Beechey Point

We hunt seals on the melting sea ice

5

I t was spring on the sea ice, and I walked at a brisk pace coming home along the familiar trail we had chopped from the edge of the floe. When I was only a few miles from Cross Island I climbed a large ice hummock to study the ice about. To the south I could see smoke curling above the horizon. To the very distant southeast rose peak after peak of dim, snow-capped mountains stair-stepping into the sky; these mountains were somewhere on the coast of the mainland towards Canada. A black spot behind me was Ook-sook winding among the tumbled ice blocks.

Connie came to greet me as I neared the house. Her eyes were wide.

"Did you get anything?" she first asked.

"Only a seal."

"I just shot a polar bear!" she said.

Then she paused and looked away, and finally said, "Well, you will have to find him for me."

ABOUT SEVEN IN THE MORNING Connie was sound asleep inside the igloo on Cross Island when she was awakened by the pup Coaly, barking wildly. Coaly slept just outside her door, in the snow alley. Always before, the barking of dogs had meant a sled load of people arriving. But visitors at this hour? An awful premonition stole shiveringly over the roused sleeper, as over whom wouldn't it? The dog outside kept barking, barking—frantically.

There was good daylight to see inside the house as the sun had been up for many hours. It was ten degrees above zero outside. The house still held heat within.

Connie shot bolt upright out of dreamland, slipped her parka on over long-handled underwear, crawled out of the caribou skin sleeping bag, and made it to the door in the fur stockings in which she had slept. Another grab secured her mittens; with misgivings she timidly unbarricaded the door by taking down the double-bitted ax which she had wedged across it. There were only two things which it could be: people or a polar bear. There was no other alternative. There were no sounds from people. Opening the door a crack, Connie looked right smack into the broad furry white face of a real honest-to-God polar bear inside the snow alley not four feet from her own face!

Oh, she closed that frail little door in a hurry! Her gun was outside in the snow alley where the great bear was!

It seems a very wonder that the tremendous bear did not kill the dog he had cornered with one sweep of the paw. But, attracted by the seal blubber up on top of our roof, the odor of which had drawn him to the island from the surrounding sea ice, he left the dog backed up against the door inside the snow alley, and presently Connie could hear him on the roof. She was held at bay inside!

Was this not some crazy dream? Could this really be happening? Connie had never seen a live polar bear this close except in a zoo, and that at the age of around five, but it's one of those things you know when you meet it. Here's one for the psychiatrist to ask his patient: "Are you ever troubled when you first wake up in the morning by the suspicion that a polar bear is up on your roof?"

If Connie had first doubted the reality of that specter which looked into her face at the door she was soon convinced of its actuality. It sounded as though the house were coming down as the white monster began dragging meat from the roof. Besides seals, we had a whole caribou up there, which Ook-sook had got for human food, when he hunted recently on the mainland.

She opened the door a wedge and in shot the dog; the ax barricaded the little driftwood door again, and Coaly, planting himself between his benefactor's legs, stood barking. Connie kicked and cuffed the little dog and even grabbed him by the muzzle at last and held his jaws between her shaking hands to shut him up, but he continued his excited yaps as though to entice the bear right into the house to get both of them. For a minute Connie just stood there with her hair hanging down in her eyes, she said, not knowing whether she should make a break for it outside the door and try to get the gun or try to strangle the dog. Four feet above the girl and the dog there was only the Eskimo skylight or window in the roof, covered with a flour sack, which the bear might accidentally step through at any moment.

Yes, Connie got the gun. She had to. This couldn't go on any longer. Even if the bear didn't fall through the roof, he was eating up all our meat, and Connie might be imprisoned indefinitely. She reached out the door with a long arm and dragged her rifle butt first in its case into the house, got it out, got a shell into its chamber, and then, led onward by some imp of daredevilry, crawled out the snow alley to go after the bear. What if she failed? she wondered. It was the day before our wedding anniversary and she couldn't help thinking what an anniversary present it would make for both of us, if she didn't succeed. This bear, according to what I was able later to make of it from the tracks by our house, weighed around a thousand pounds.

Just as she had feared, the bear heard Connie creeping out of the house through the snow alley, as the door closed irrevocably behind her. He heard the door squeak, or perhaps he decided just then to get that dog. Leaving his savage foraging on top of the roof, he came down from the house with a bound, rounded the corner of the snow house with a kind of amiable, happy-go-lucky expression on his face, and Connie fired at his head at six feet, later measured. And she missed.

Was she a little nervous? She could hardly lift the gun. She knew that she was attempting to do something that was beyond her abilities; to her it seemed that she was meeting sure death. Bear fever is something which puts buck fever to shame.

Connie had had in mind that as soon as she shot once she must shoot again and again as rapidly as she could and never stop shooting. The fluffy bear, really a very beautiful creature, whirled back in surprise at the explosion, which gave Connie time to get another shell pumped into her rifle; then suddenly he was at her in a rush on all fours as a cat goes for a mouse. There was no amiability in his snapping small black eyes this time.

This time at four feet Connie was able to hit him in the face, at which he turned, streaming buckets of blood onto the snow. To illustrate how fast he could move, he galloped off forty or fifty yards before Connie could fire again. She was in a daze. That was a close call she had that day.

We give all this data carefully, for even in her extremity Connie was a good observer from long training, and every detail was engraved upon her memory with accuracy.

What I found hard to believe was that Connie could then stand at the door and empty the whole gun, five more shots in all, at the lumbering bear, and not score another hit. It sounds impossible that anyone could miss that huge form, but this is what bear fever does to people; they become helpless.

Now a head wound on a big game animal is either fatal at once or the animal gets well. This was one of the most difficult situations we have ever met in hunting. The reason Connie had aimed for the bear's head—and a polar bear, a swimming animal, has a small head for the rest of his body—was that she was afraid to try a heart shot from such a close range. Shot in the heart or chest cavity with a rifle as light as merely a .30-30 carbine, the bear might easily have rushed and killed the hunter even as it died itself. Connie was probably correct, therefore, in having aimed for the head, trying for a brain shot. Later examination proved to us that a polar bear's skull is paper thin in the temples and a .22 bullet would shoot clear through it if a person were calm and knew the right spot. If Connie's bullet had been placed just three inches different from the way it landed, the bear would have dropped instantly right in front of the door and that would have been all there was to it. Such things are very simple, or they aren't.

Feeling so ill that she was about to collapse, Connie went into the house, reloaded her rifle, dressed, and went out on the three-foot-broad blood trail to see what hopes there might be of finding the bear nearby. Pieces of teeth and jawbone correctly told her, as they told me at once when I saw the signs three days later, that she had shot the bear in the mouth. That's all she could see when she shot, as a matter of fact, she relates. The bear had had the advantage of elevation when he charged, for he was up on a drift while she was down in a hole, like a mouse in its burrow. This was because the wind had drifted snow outside our door as it always did at any camp. Of course, there was no time to aim for the second shot.

Perhaps she would find the bear dead nearby, Connie thought. So often together we had found game thus. With gun cocked and outthrust before her she prowled the tiny island; Coaly ran ahead, sniffed the air, and barked like a fool, but as a trail dog that pup was a false alarm. Each step Connie took forward was such a strain on her vitality that she could hardly walk at all. Yet she was remembering that it has been our creed never to let a seriously wounded big game animal escape to suffer and die, and we had kept this vow all these years. Mostly now she hoped to merely read something of the bear's condition by the trail; she had almost been killed a moment ago by him, and it would be just plain suicide for her to risk again the charge of the bear in the state she was in. Therefore, she did not dare to leave the friendly island and follow the big tracks into the ice. The bear looked yellow, not white, against the snow, but still so white that it would be plenty hard to distinguish him from a snow block among those other snow blocks amid which he moved and waited.

Later, when I got home, I was able to show Connie where the bear had lain, expecting her, just a few yards off the island out beyond. She could have got him easily if she had had self-confidence, or at any rate I knew I could have got him had I been there. But perhaps there is something in not pushing one's luck too far; she turned back to the house with the dog. What a path of blood led out from the door of our house over that little island! Except for that, and the ejected empty shells lying on the snow by the doorway, at which Connie placed small sticks to mark the spots for authenticity, the appearance of the white visitor from off the ice might have been a dream.

By the time I got home the blood splashed before the door had turned to brown, and it had even dried up and blown away like sand in the wind, while the toenail scratches of the galloping great feet were scarcely visible to tell that a polar bear had really been here. It was an odd thing: I saw a bear trail showing scattered drops of blood right out near our camp on the morning of our return and said then to Ook-sook: "Maybe Connie shoot this bear." But since this was miles away from Cross Island it had hardly seemed probable, and I had almost fallen for Ook-sook's song that the bear was bleeding from sore feet.

Almost, but not quite. I had thought then, "That's funny. I believe that bear's bleeding from the mouth." I deduced this on account of the fact that the droplets of blood swung from side to side of the bear's prints, exactly as a bear would swing his head on the reverse side of his stride.

"Well, he must have got into a fight," was all I could think of then. It seems quite plausible that polar bears on the ice sometimes maul each other up quite badly.

The tracks of this bear followed along our old outgoing sled trail where he had been eating snow. I backtracked him just about all the way home as well as one could guess. That bear had hoped to meet someone in his present mood. As it was, he had been within three hundred yards of our camp on the edge of the floe where we were sealing and looking for bears, and Ook-sook and I had barely missed him without realizing it.

I was mighty thankful that Connie had learned how to use her rifle as well as she had, and we talked over what to do. After I had studied the trail and Ook-sook and the dogs came up and sniffed over the blood and the big tracks, I had forebodings that we would never see that bear again—but we would try. If only Connie could have had the steadiness to hit him once again as he ran, even in the ham, or inflicting a body wound, we would have got him. As it was, we had very little to go on. Ook-sook thought to find the bear dead or frozen, but I had had a lot of experience with different kinds of game, and I was pretty sure that we would find him, if we did, very much alive.

It stormed; we rested at home a day and then started out tracking. It was a day of no shadows, overcast, with a blinding glare. This was on the fourth day after the bear had been wounded. He had many advantages on his side: the rough, almost impassable country in which polar bears live, the forty-foot ice precipices, mountains and angles and hummocks of ice. He would head for the roughest country he could find, as all grizzlies do. Connie and I both felt sorry for the bear, but he was one animal that had come marauding right to our house, and he had certainly asked for it.

The tracks led straight for the moving or unattached ice; we were able to cross where the lead was closed, and we followed. Although the bear bled freely at first, it was plain to see he had suffered no fatal injury. Polar bears sleep in the daytime in summer; for the first day he had slept on top of the highest ice hummock I have ever seen. This was his instinct to watch his back trail for approaching enemies, once he had learned the meaning of fear. By using the range finder of the camera, I was able to figure the height of this ice hummock as around ninety feet. His bed was bloody here, and yellow belly hairs were stuck in the frozen blood among the green ice boulders.

For three days Ook-sook and I followed the trail of the bear along the edge of the moving ice pack but on the third day we gave the bear up. The trail had led us along tide cracks that resembled miniature canyons with only a very thin film of ice formed over their open water beneath. The ice bent perceptibly under Ook-sook and more perceptibly under me when we crawled down into and sneaked along such a crack trying to follow where the bear had gone. Presently it burst upon us why the bear had followed these cracks. He was hungry. He was hunting, trying to secure seals. He had stopped bleeding almost entirely by the seventh day of his wound and seemed to grow stronger. We believe that he recovered after his encounter with Connie and her little .30-30 carbine, except that he may be going around right now with a few teeth missing.

It was a lead of open water that finally decided us to give up the hopeless chase. Our chances of losing the bear had been resolved: he would in all likelihood cross water where trackers could not follow, or the tracks on the moving ice would become turned all around so that they would not link in those areas which are forever changing.

Now we reached a crack about twenty feet wide which separated us from the land-fast ice. Clearly, the floating pack was slowly moving out! This crack had slowly opened during the few hours since we had crossed over to the moving pack. We ran along the crack, trying to find a place to cross. We had left our sled and dogs on the safe side, and now had only ourselves. In one place I noticed some floating ice cakes the size of washtubs. Maybe we could make a bridge of them to get back. Ook-sook and I threw in some more loose cakes and fragments to form a bridge, and we were not slow about it. The deep green of the cold ocean water lay placidly waiting for us to cross on our bridge to its farther white ice bank of safety. It seemed almost like some little river or perhaps a still lake hemmed in by white marble, only this lake had a temperature of around two degrees below freezing and it was bottomless, so far as we were concerned.

Ook-sook crossed with slight difficulty, but I weighed a little more and the ice started to sink and turned over under me. Only by some fancy jumping was I able to keep from falling in. Ook-sook laughed, and I laughed, but then we always laughed, no matter what.

We went home to Cross Island.

Bud kills a polar bear

6

T he next polar bear story has a different ending and one which I am happy to relate. Ook-sook and I had chopped a nice trail through the rough ice eight miles out to the edge of the floe as spring progressed. As the weather became warm and beautiful beneath the circling sun, Connie decided that she might as well go out on these hunts with us to camp at our regular hunting spot at the edge of the floe as to stay alone with polar bears where she was.

The edge of the floe Connie found to be a remarkable country, as I had already tried to tell her. Piles of great ice boulders become at sea the outcroppings of rock and the hedges and bushes of any rough country. This country has its own mountain ranges and its little pleasant valleys, too, only all of ice, so that it is hard to believe that its geography is not permanent but in fact very transitory. The only difference between the ice country and real country is that here the coloring is all monochrome. Especially does it remind one of the southwestern desert, for there is the sameness of color, or rather lack of color, that the desert has at bright midday, and yet the same delicate pastels of evening. You wear sunglasses just as you would on the desert and you realize before long that your complexion is going to take it hard from "snow burn."

All of the time the ice floes are silently changing out there.

You walk along your own foot trail at the brink of a quarter of a mile of blue water, which has become like home, and you think of it as a kind of winding lake set in a pasture rather than as the bottom of the Arctic Ocean—but the next day something is different. You can't quite decide what it is that is different; then you see that a part of the ledge has moved out in the night like a ghost, has joined the drifting pack, and is nowhere now to be found. Your own footprints of yesterday went with it! You must watch that this does not happen to your camp!

The ghostliness of the pack on a quiet day is not lessened by the wonderful, magical displays of all kinds of life to be found there in the spring. There are seals. We shoot them in the head when they pop up in the lead and retrieve them by throwing the *manak;* the seals floating dead on the surface of the pond look like blimps. These seals are full of millions of small shrimps which can be seen in the upper strata of the exposed ocean everywhere. Great rafts of king eider ducks with immense orange noses have arrived to float between the floating ice cakes, also apparently feeding on these shrimps—and what a singing and crowing and cackling they make!

To my amazement I saw three ptarmigan, a land bird, a *grouse,* out in the ice pack miles offshore. Another strange visitor Connie and I saw far out to sea as we waited for seals beside this lead was a solitary wild swan. It flew with long wings silently over our heads, following the crack of open water miles down the ice with long slow wing beats, looking as it went; it, too, would taxi to a stop in some icy pool to feed contentedly on the floating shrimps of the sea. One finds the most unexpected array and conglomeration of land friends out here in this place of the endless ice!

The white fox is of course a permanent, year-round resident; he is another sea ice animal, not a land animal. A good many white foxes are trapped on the islands or on the prairies adjacent to the ocean of course, but their main abode is on the moving ice, from which they have come. I was not too surprised when I saw one of these, a ragged creature now turning to "blue" or muddy black for the summer season, because I already knew that the white arctic fox spends more of its life at sea than it does on land—but I was extremely curious in my wonderment of how the little creatures could live. White foxes follow the polar bears and eat the leavings of their feasts; probably the bears pay them no attention. The foxes which are trapped at sea or which have recently come from the sea ice can be told at once from the land-living foxes because they always have a yellow spot on the fur in the corners of their mouths and perhaps dribbling down their chins which cannot easily be removed—the stains of eating seal blubber. These foxes are not "smart" like our land foxes but seem brainless, being so tame at times as to follow and bark at the heels of a man walking across the ice. This is probably because the ice-dwelling foxes have no enemies which habitually prey upon them.

We had loaded our sled for a five-day hunt this time. The dogs' tongues lolled out as they trotted along, panting. Every mile we would stop and let them cool off, as we labored through the rough ice. Sometimes the dogs would howl with fright as they were jerked from some ice ledge or would leap frantically; trouble always came when part of the foolish team went on one side of some ice post and the other half tried to take the other side. We were hot, too, and shed our fur pants and outer parka. Connie didn't have any fur pants or outer parka to shed, for she had never had any—a consideration which had colored her attitude towards hunting all winter; I told her she could wear my outer pants now when waiting for seal.

The dark line of water sky came slowly toward us until it stood nearly overhead, and we were at the lead. Connie was overcome by the beauty of the monochrome tones of ice with its unending variety of conformations. "It looks as though a person could wade out a ways into the river there," she said.

"Don't try it," I cautioned, and we stood looking down into the translucent green depths. Eight or ten feet below us a sharp snag of ice protruded like a tooth from the bottom of the ice shelf on which we stood, giving depth to the perspective and wiping away any visions of wading that a person might have. After traveling over the ice for several weeks I had begun to think of it as a kind of land, and it was interesting to me that this was exactly the same impression which Connie got at once. We no longer remembered, except vaguely, that under us lay oceanic depths. We regarded the cracks in the ice as deep prairie streams one must never step into, while the open lead was a chain of lakes with a river connecting them here and there. The ice ridges were broken hills and the flat places were pastures hedged by boulder-strewn walls. The shades of color were brownish or gray as seen through our dark glasses at midday or a blinding white glare if we took our glasses off. At midnight, or one might say for several hours before, the colors were like a sunset on the desert. The various shades of white, blue, and green in the ice were very receptive to colors from the sky. The country about us burned then with orange and purple in the setting sun and sparkled under the sun of noonday like billions of diamonds. Under a leaden cloudy sky, the ice looked somber, but stray shafts of sunlight would filter through the clouds to fill some rocky little valley of ice boulders with a sprig of rainbow. When you could see only the very peaks of the distant pressure ridges touched by sunlight, they became the lights of some distant city shining in early morning.

The fact that we were living by hunting out here was what interested me most of all, for I guess I am at heart a hunter almost like Ook-sook. In the arctic you must take advantage of each harvest. You can't hurry the harvest or slow it up, for here opportunity knocks but once. The seals we could get now would feed the dogs all summer; if no seals were secured, it meant hard times ahead. Accordingly, we each took a station at near-by protruding points of ice. The surface of the lead lay like green plate glass and the sun shone warmly upon our furs. I was nearly ready to fall asleep when Ook-sook came walking by. I roused myself and we moved down the lead.

We had pitched our tent at the edge of the floe and tied our dogs by running their chains under ice. Now seals are as likely to appear in one place as another in the open lead, but they generally travel, and you will meet them coming from either direction. The large leads are seal highways; the seals follow them, I had observed, not exactly in groups, but where you find one seal there are likely to be several more nearby. We were walking a little way back from the edge in order to miss some rough ice, and anyway there was a pan of foot-thick ice drifted against our shore here, a half mile square. Except for a few small open ponds in it there was no open water near shore.

In one of these ponds swam a seal. I saw it, but Ook-sook, being shorter than I am, didn't. A seal shows only his head when he swims unless he is playing; then part of his back line may show as he rolls. When seals come up to the surface to breathe they may stay up only a few seconds. This seal was playing when I saw him, and I ran for a place to shoot. His big glassy eye saw me as I climbed up on a pressure ridge a hundred yards away. When seals are in the water they are more curious than afraid. A hundred yards distance seems a safe situation from their point of view. But their judgment is wrong where a rifle is concerned; an oily film spread over the water following my shot, and the seal floated high as a blimp between the ice shores. Ook-sook was happy as he hauled the carcass up onto the ice. A team of eight dogs or, yes, nine dogs here with Coaly will consume a seal within three days.

We walked a mile farther on to where there was plenty of open water again and took up our stations, leaving behind us little bloody trails with the seal at the end as it had been dragged from the water, along the edge of the lead. Ahead of me in open water a flock of squaw ducks came flying in, their hoarse musical cries echoing from the many-sided ice ridges. Ook-sook tried his luck at two more seals and scored misses. I had killed three seals and they drifted in to an ice point. Ook-sook had the *manak* with him and thus he came up to help me retrieve my seals. We managed to get one, but in order to retrieve the other two that were now against the opposite point, we would have to skirt a half mile of open water.

"You stay. Not much strong rifle, me. Bud strong," Ook- sook said, and started around the bay to retrieve the other two seals while I would stay and shoot some more. Ook-sook had been gone a few minutes and I had seated myself on an ice chair to wait for more seals. I could see Connie walking toward me along the lead a half mile away and surmised she had got lonely for she didn't like to have us get too far away. By the shots she knew we had secured seals. I looked out over the open water but there were no seal heads showing, so my gaze wandered idly toward the rough ice Ook-sook had just disappeared behind. My neck fur rose on end in that moment. A large yellow form was rapidly following Ook-sook!

Polar bear! It was evening and there was no doubt in my mind at all that the bear was hunting. My first impression was that the bear looked small among the great ice cakes; this has always been my impression upon seeing big game in its natural habitat: the habitat itself is so large, the very background is so immense, that a polar bear seen on the sea ice, for instance, is small. You get used to large things and great distances. So, the bear looked, in fact, rather tiny and nothing about the whole situation seemed real.

It is remarkable what a lot of impressions can go through a person's mind when he has to act fast. "This may be the bear Connie shot," I thought, for he had hung around in this vicinity. Then I thought, "Ook-sook is hidden in the ice from me, but *he* would look even smaller to me than that bear looks, and that bear is pretty close to him, while he doesn't know it." In another instant the bear had so changed his position that I could only see him by standing erect upon an ice pinnacle, and accordingly I aimed ten feet above his back offhand and fired. The range was around four hundred yards and I figured my .30-30 bullet would drop about ten feet at that range. I also knew that if I shot twice in rapid succession Ook-sook would run up on the nearest high ice pinnacle to look, and if the bear was after him he would be warned. To hit a moving bear at four hundred yards offhand would be pure luck, so I had rather expected to miss.

What surprised me was that the bear turned around and looked in my direction. I moved a little to see better and possibly the bear saw me. He came straight for me faster than it takes to tell! I was so surprised that instead of waiting for him to come closer, I fired again, holding as before. I had nearly completed reloading when the bullet landed, and the bear did a flying flip-flop. Yet he landed on his feet running, at a ninety-degree angle through very rough ice. I could only catch glimpses of him as he passed between ice boulders. In these instants I fired three times more but saw the bullets plow into ice blocks between us. I must have used up all my luck on the second shot.

But the bear was bleeding badly; its chest was bright red as it vanished for good. It was a doomed bear. As I reloaded on the run I was shaking all over from excitement, and the events were real enough by this time; there was Ook-sook blocking the bear's escape to the west where it would have to cross an open level ice field. Connie had it cut off from the water, or at least I thought she had, and from every side we were all ready to shoot the moment the bear came out. But the bear never came.

Ook-sook closed in from the west and I came in from the east and found the bear's bloody trail with the claw marks showing deep. The trail wound through the ice blocks; we followed cautiously, step by step. At the end of the long gory trail lay the bear before us. Its great yellowish form looked angular against the white snow. It had fallen between two cakes of ice and lay as if asleep. Here where it had dropped in its tracks it had bled out its life until the great amount of hot blood had melted the ice beneath and made little rivers and channels. We walked up to examine our prize, and Ook-sook's eyes were as big as I expect mine must have been. I poked the bear with the rifle barrel and it gave a low growl. Its eyes blinked once and gazed out over the vast field of ice it had for so long called home. They never closed again.

With this polar bear I had now killed one of almost every major species of big game on the North American Continent, a project in which I had been engaged from the time I was big enough to hold a rifle and which was now more or less finished before Connie and I were twenty-eight years old. Connie also had contributed to the project, the hobby of big game hunting. We had had some great experiences while we were still young.

We shall now tell of the killing of the bear as it affected Connie. As it neared nightfall of our first evening together out at the edge of the floe, Connie stepped up to the tent which was pitched on the ice, carrying the caribou robe on which she had sat all day, waiting for seals. She had looked around nervously before now, and it had occurred to her that the tent would not be much of a protection to hide within if a polar bear should come. There was no shelter out here, no trees either. She lived around bears all the time. Well, she was getting used to it. She got the camera and started down to where she could see Ook-sook and me at our more successful sealing three hundred yards away. "Well," she thought, "it's just a step. They have two guns between them, and I'll leave my gun in the tent and just use the camera."

Could any person have such mistaken judgment? Being a naturalist is all right, but safety comes first. Connie was doing something here of extreme potential danger in being separated even for a minute from her rifle at the edge of the floe; this holds true whether one is inside the tent sleeping or is feeding the dogs or filling a bucket with snow nearby. A polar bear on the prowl can and will invariably appear from any quarter when least expected. The dogs chained nearby may not even smell him. The bear may stalk the dogs thinking they are seals on the ice and kill or maim the whole team, and that is why it is not safe to leave the camp unguarded at any time. Some arctic authorities even say that it is not safe to leave your camp and dogs unguarded on land, because of the wolves, but I can certainly concur that this is true in regard to the dangers from polar bears out on the sea ice. I had kind of talked Connie into staying right at camp because somebody should be there.

Now as the foot trail we used wound in and out through the ice hummocks and piles of ice slabs, Connie lost sight of me as she came towards me and soon she heard me shooting on up ahead, for I had moved my position meanwhile and gone on and left her! Still she did not return to the tent for her gun, for she thought: "I'll catch Bud in another minute." Although the sound of the fast shooting was audible to her, she thought we were shooting at seals. She should have known better. A hunter can pretty well tell what another hunter is shooting at. Catch me she did at last, a half mile away from camp.

"What in God's name are you doing without your gun?" was the first thing I asked her, in a tone I usually used for stopping dogfights. After a short lecture I decided to give her a lesson in such a way that she would not forget it. I told her to follow on ahead a few steps farther around the turn and I would come along right after: there was a view I wanted her to see first. "There's the prettiest patch of ice and water to photograph you ever saw in your life; even Ook-sook praised it."

She fell for that, and all enthusiastic over a possible picture, she proceeded as directed, quite trustfully. What a shock when her eye lighted upon that blood trail! She had seen that kind of trail before, and not long ago! One would think she would have no trouble in recalling it. A seal carcass dragged up from the water's edge like those others down the line? No—huge, immense, frightening bloody footprints, the claw marks of the first cousin to the grizzly, made by an angular animal that had a big hump on his shoulder, too.

"What is it, Connie?" I asked her innocently, coming up. She followed the red trail excitedly now, like a hound. Fifty yards further on lay the great yellow carcass which she trusted would be there, the animal we had come out into this ice to see.

When she saw the size of the bear and felt him over she had a moment of thought for the danger she had put herself in, wandering aimlessly around enjoying the view where monsters are afoot. Then she went into her war dance of happiness and could do nothing but jump up and down and grab both me and the great bear around the neck for a while. Connie in her mild way is as great a little killer of big game as anyone: at least she has been in on many an exciting event.

Connie has the temperament of a naturalist and an adventurer and the examination of new things never fails to interest her. She gets tired of one location or one scene before very long; she is domestic only by interludes.

This polar bear was a grown female with no cub in evidence. It was shot at 340 paced yards. Of four shots, only one shot struck it, and this near the heart. After receiving this shot the bear turned and fled until it dropped some two hundred yards away. The bear had come wandering along the edge of the floe from behind all of us, just as Connie left the tent; it had somehow missed smelling our camp by a few yards and had passed Connie without her gun among the ice cakes and gone on with neither of them knowing the difference. Ook-sook, who was between Connie and me, never saw the bear at all until he came up to the dead carcass with me. Ook-sook was to get a five-dollar bonus for every bear I killed, but the poor kid was having a hard time of it so far to win my watch, which I had promised him as an additional bonus for the first polar bear he could show me. The bear had small black eyes and a black nose and—a point which most people don't know—when we turned it on its back we saw it had black soles on the bottoms of its feet.

Ook-sook went back to camp to get the sled and dogs and complete butchering and photographic equipment, where after we all posed for pictures with the bear. It was one of the most beautiful evenings on the sea ice that an artist might imagine, but a wilder scene than even he might dream. Beside the blue-etched pressure ridge we three humans exerted our strength to haul the bloody bear out of the boulders and roll it onto its back; we got out the dog bucket and the dipper and stood them nearby. Ook-sook had parked the dogs with the sled tilted at a forty-five-degree angle on an ice boulder in the background. It was the first polar bear our dogs, except the pup Coaly, had ever seen. One imagines that Coaly himself will never forget that grim apparition by which he was awakened from peaceful dog dreams that day to see a great monster's face blocking the doorway. He would never sleep in the snow alley after that!

The slant-eyed dogs waved their plumes and lay down in the snow. Coaly wagged his own young stem and barked. I traced the path of the bullet through the bear. It had entered the chest about six inches directly under its chin, square in the middle, and it had passed just above the heart, cutting that big artery there, and emerged in front of the right hip. The bullet had passed clear through the bear and never expanded, although it was of the latest design supposed to expand at all ranges.

After the bear was cut up and hauled to the tent with some difficulty we dined first upon cookies and tea and then upon polar bear meat boiled over the primus stove. It was twilight and the middle of the night. I noted that the current was still flowing slowly toward the shore of the lead so that our camp seemed safe and the seals we had killed would drift in to us.

That night was one of those unforgettable experiences in a lifetime that remain to enrich memory forever. There is something wild and mysterious about the ice pack that defies description, and from all the explorers who have ventured upon it we have heard nothing of its beauties, nothing of what it really is like. It is a cruel place. It can be ugly, frightening, menacing, and tiresome to struggle over. But it can also be beautiful, friendly, entrancing, and productive of food and life. It is strange because there are so many things we don't know about it, yet for all its strangeness it is the realest thing I have ever met.

Tonight, as we settled into our bedding inside our former winter's tent, unbanked with snow, because no snow was available now, the country of the ice had all of these qualities and more too. We heard the water softly lapping against our ice shore a few yards from our door, and our clothes and our guns were within reach. We slept with ears alert and one eye peeled. A big white swan came flying low over the lead, giving its low inquiring call that should come from a wren instead of a lonely swan. Spring on the ice pack by the continent's edge was the craziest and most wonderful season for adventure that we had ever known. Poets may sing of other springs, but this was a really good one for two tramps and an Eskimo named Ook-sook.

7

I sent Ook-sook to Beechey Point with a sled load of seals to put into our ice cellar there for summer and Connie rendered our polar bear fat and fried several dozen doughnuts in it and made oatmeal cookies and ginger cookies with burned sugar syrup, which helped to cover up the bear flavor. We had found the fat on polar bears to be unlike that of land bears but similar to the seal blubber on which the bears feed; when Ook-sook got back to the island he and I ground up a deal of the polar bear meat with our little meat grinder, which Connie made into meat cakes, camouflaging these with some hot sauce she had; still none of us liked this, and experimenting proved that polar bear meat just plain boiled, Eskimo style, was most palatable for every day. We all missed our caribou a good deal.

Ook-sook was mighty quarrelsome one day and we stuck a thermometer in his mouth and found he had a temperature of over 100 degrees. Sulfa for him, but next day, not obeying our orders to stay in bed, he insisted on getting up half delirious, and hitching up all his dogs he left for a week's vacation with pay. We gave him sulfa to take along with him and he apparently ate it. What he was after in his delirium was fresh caribou meat, and when he came back a week later to the island, he had it, too.

Connie and I walked out to the lead trailing two polar bears recently arrived in our vicinity. The bears had discovered a seal which we had planted along the trail, and the seal was gone. One of the bears had dragged the 150-pound carcass into the neighboring ice hummocks, but there he had left it and had not eaten it. Later we recovered this same seal.

Then after a sixteen-mile hike Connie and I returned to the island to find smoke belching from our chimney, indicating an inhabitant, and four tents bloomed nearby on the sandspit: a whole new colony had arrived on the island in our absence! The person in our house was Ook-sook come home; he greeted us just as ever with a big smile and radiant health. He had tried to reach the home of his parents but had not been able to because the Colville River had broken out! This was such exciting news that our grins widened to his own. The Kuparuk River also was running, and many ducks were there. It was hard for us to realize here on the island that summer had arrived during the last week on the mainland. Ook-sook had shot two cow caribou and returned with a load of fresh meat, having cached much of it in the ice cellar for us at Beechey Point.

The four tents pitched in a row on the bleak sandspit jutting out into the frozen sea meant the Lynds and their party, who were moving from the Colville delta to Brownlow Point, a distance of around two hundred miles. The elderly couple were many times grandparents. Their worldly possessions were small, and they owned but one dog. Lynd's son-in-law, Alfred, was helping them move. They had just arrived here an hour ago, yet they had all the comforts of home set up. Fires burned in the sheet-iron stoves and children played about. The day could hardly be called "chamber of commerce" weather, as snow was falling, hurried along by a keen wind. The temperature was thirteen degrees above zero and this party had faced into the wind for many miles of open sea ice to reach the island.

Their lean dogs lay along a tie-up chain, with eyes glued to a seal that was being cut up. The dogs weren't very strong, Mr. Lynd said, and of course the people had to walk all the way while the dogs pulled the sleds with their belongings. They had managed to secure two seals that day that were sleeping on top of the ice beside the holes which the seals were now commencing to gnaw through. The seals furnished food for man and dog. The ease with which this group of people—an old man, his blind wife and small children—traveled and made camp in comfort with such meager equipment should prove to the most skeptical that the arctic is friendly to those who understand its ways.

"Oh, but they were Eskimos," someone will say. That someone will have missed the point. Connie and I had just about turned into Eskimos ourselves this year, living in a tent and wandering about, and we had come to know that Eskimos suffer just as much as anyone does if they must endure suffering: the principle of the whole thing is to avoid it by living intelligently in one's environment. Furthermore, Connie and I even liked the Eskimo life—for a vacation. Today many of the Eskimos are even now wandering away from their native way of life; some Eskimos live in California, Arizona, or New York. These of course are just as helpless about living in the arctic as we are on the average, and they would have a hard time of it there.

The next day Connie made an immense pan of sourdough doughnuts rolled in sugar. These could be fried in the bear oil which these people think very good. Then she made oatmeal cookies and ginger cakes which she cut into squares and frosted with white sugar icing. Here went the last of the salt, too. The little assortment looked very attractive when she had finished. It took her all of the day to prepare the party by baking the dainties in our 6" X 8" oven. The guests were invited late in the afternoon; each brought his own cup.

When all had assembled, we had nineteen people in our 12' X 14' house, including two nursing babies which nursed meanwhile. And with these people was our favorite orphan Hazel, age eleven, of the reddest cheeks we have seen in the world and the widest grin, and whose hair had never known a comb and whose body nothing but hides to wear. Now Hazel's adopted family were heading east along the ocean to even wilder land than here, farther yet from the white man's haunt.

In this group there were several small children who had never seen a mirror, so Connie dug out our old cracked wall mirror and they all had a look at themselves as a part of the entertainment; even the old people enjoyed looking in the mirror. I interested the men in the usual game of Eskimo cards and Connie passed picture books around for the others to look at while the coffee came to a boil on the top of our little stove in two buckets. Then the surprises were laid out on the board. I think the people all got up to a half dozen pieces each. We noticed that some of the women were carefully picking the frosting off their cookies. Evidently the cookies were too sweet for them. They would then use the frosting in their tea. Most of these people were habitually without sugar all year. We always tried, therefore, to serve some sugar when we had guests. But the only use the Eskimos know of sugar is to sweeten their tea.

The little band of pilgrims left for the next island along their route, Pole Island, in one of the worst winds we had had all spring. They had to face it, so that the sail for their sled was of no use to them. They had waited until late in the season so that the wind might be tempered to the shorn lamb, so to speak, considering the number of small children who must walk, and now they must travel by the sea ice, without delay.

The wind was driving straight towards Beechey Point with a velocity of around forty miles per hour, but the wind, if wrong for the Lynds, was right for us. "Let's sail to Beechey Point today, Connie," and suddenly we began preparations to leave our own island home.

I had never seen it done, but I knew vaguely that the Eskimos at times like this use a sail on their sleds on the sea ice. I managed to rig a mast from our old tent pole on our sled, and a boom from our tent uprights. We used a tent cover (now a part of our igloo flooring) for a sail, folding it triangularly. When all was packed and loaded, we pulled up the dog anchor, jumped onto the sled, and were off.

The sled shot over the ice while the dogs had a hard time to keep from being run over by it. Finally, one dog which was lame fell behind. He was pulled backwards for a way, but since we could not well help him, he presently got loose from the harness. At last he was lost from sight in the flying snow and we sailed on, thinking he would follow our trail. As a matter of fact, that dog got lost on the sea ice, and three days later Ook-sook had to go back to Cross Island. He found him there, hanging around our vacated camp, starving.

The sky above began to clear, and a brilliant sun shone down. It all seemed like a fairyland to us on the bouncing sled with the broken ice hummocks flashing by when the colors were suddenly turned on by the sun. Our usual time with a loaded sled was between twelve and fourteen hours from Cross Island to Beechey Point. On this day we made it in four hours fifteen minutes—quite a ride.

Now at Beechey Point all we had to do was to wait for the Arctic Ocean to melt and we would be free to canoe over to Canada, and our long arctic sojourn would be ended by returning to civilization.

PART THREE

To Canada's Great Mackenzie

Meltwater pools on the ice as spring advances

Bud builds a canoe from driftwood planks

1

L ife along the arctic coast is one round of following the seasons, with an emphasis on winter. It is true there are hot days in summer, but when the wind blows from the north over the polar ice it brings with it freezing temperatures. Snow may fall at any time of the year along the arctic coast.

But the people, birds, and animals of the arctic view the seasons with a very different interpretation of them. When you are dressed in a full suit of winter clothing of caribou skins a temperature of zero seems quite warm and you must shed your fur boots for waterproof ones of seal. The birds return long before the last snow is gone and sing their spring songs, while what a southerner would call a "blizzard" is blowing. Dogs lie panting in the snow and the caribou begin to shed. Eider ducks and brant and snow geese and pintails have passed over Cross Island by now, to tell sea ice hunters it is time for human beings to get back to the mainland. The sun shines twenty-four hours.

There were no people living at Beechey Point as the Eskimos were all camped on some islands a few miles away where drift was plentiful, and this was still their season for hunting seals on top of the ice. True to Eskimo ways, there wasn't a stick of wood at Beechey Point when we got there, but we had brought some carefully hoarded fuel oil back with us. As we began unpacking the sled in the keen winds which whipped about the old trading post, we learned that somehow during that wild ride under sail our fuel oil can had sprung a leak and the contents were gone!

We searched the high drifts which almost obliterated the buildings for something to burn and came up with a gas can full of seal blubber which had been meant to feed our dogs. We would have to burn it. It made a hot fire in the cream- enameled Sears, Roebuck stove which quickly warmed the house. What really warmed us most of all was our year's stack of mail waiting for us. Two great boxes of it were sitting on our table, with more yet in the warehouse. Richard's boy Aivuk (Walrus) had brought the mail from Barrow!

Connie and I couldn't wait, so we pulled up the first chairs we had sat on for almost a year, sat down beside the sputtering blubber fire with a bucket of blubber between our knees and in our parkas began reading out loud. Ook-sook couldn't read, and he amused himself playing the phonograph. The needles for playing the records were worn out, but Ook-sook sat patiently sharpening them on a piece of whetstone.

Finally, Ook-sook got hungry and boiled us all some caribou meat for supper. It was old meat he found around the place, left by somebody else, and a little sour, but not too bad. The snow continued to drift, and the sun swung around into the north and rolled on east. It was nearly six the next morning before we decided to call it a day, stuffed on sour caribou meat and last year's Christmas candy—and news from our families.

Mail is a big event when it is your first news of the outside world in such a long time. One of our main worries was about our pictures. Were we using the right exposures? Would our badly outdated film still be good? Were the two cameras working properly? Or was all this work of two years in vain? It was therefore a tense moment when we began to examine by hand viewer our colored work which had come back from the laboratories; it had been taken this winter by dog sled by the Eskimos, who mailed it at Barrow, and we could see the results now of all but our most recent work. Yet, our fears were in vain, the results were more than we could have dared to dream. The very fact that our film was outdated had preserved us from certain errors of overexposure which are the tendency of the inexperienced with snow photography. The cold temperatures of the arctic had refrigerated and preserved the film from deterioration at the same time. The pictures we had got, however it happened, were a miracle beyond belief.

Our families now eagerly awaited our return to them. And here we sat waiting for the Arctic Ocean to melt before we could get out of this part of the world! If you want a lesson in patience just sit around waiting for the Arctic Ocean to melt.

The next day Abraham came in from his own sealing camp; he and Thelma were out on Leavitt Island. Dora, pregnant now, had gone to Barrow by sled to have her new baby.

When Abraham saw some of our colored pictures of himself and Dora, taken when they were married at Barrow last fall, the word soon spread of the wonderful show to be seen at our house. The Eskimos had never seen colored slides through a viewer before and they were thrilled beyond words. They would come to our house after that in ever-increasing numbers to sit by the hour taking turns looking through the viewer at themselves and exclaiming in Eskimo about the pictures. As I wanted to be sure the precious slides didn't get thumb-printed, I sat with them patiently, putting the pictures one by one through the viewer myself. In this way I was kept busy upon several occasions.

Connie had almost dreaded moving back to Beechey Point for several reasons, all of them involving work. There was not a day Eskimos would not come in to the trading post and, when we were at home, straight to see us—a burden which we must share along with poor Abraham, who has it for life. Abraham sat these people on the floor and fed them nothing but tea, meat, and bread as a rule—but somebody always has to be getting the meat, there are the dishes to worry about, and loaves upon loaves of bread must be baked ahead. Now that Dora had gone to Barrow, there was a strong possibility that Connie might take Dora's place as the great hostess of Beechey Point. The Eskimos, even the smallest children, never really imposed on us, but there were so many of them and they were so poor and so desperate for any kind of entertainment in their lives that we ended up doing always more than we had expected. In summer the people would come and go at all hours, even more by night than by day. Every time they walked into the house in their sandy mukluks, a housewife would have to get down on her knees and scrub the floor to keep the place even decent, said Connie, so that by summer a housewife would be in this position most of the time. Life was easier in a tent, Connie had found. In a tent, when the house needs cleaning, you just move the tent over a few feet. Well, we had lived with the Eskimos for a year and shared everything with them, even to their germs.

"Ook-sook," I said one day, "you and I are going to build a new boat." We would call it *Little Willow Number Two;* something began to tell me, as I saw summer approach, that our original *Little Willow* was not designed to be a seagoing vessel. Of course, Abraham had promised me that as soon as the ice broke up enough so that ocean travel along the edge of the land was possible, he was going to make a trip with the trading post cargo boat eastward two hundred miles or almost to the border of Canada to get a load of good wood for the summer; we and our canoe could ride that far, perhaps even all the way. For a while I thought I had Abraham almost talked into going clear to Aklavik, the Canadian settlement which was our destination. Our Eskimos had some curiosity to see the place and many of them had relatives living there. But I was taking no chances. Experience told me not to wait for Eskimos to make up their minds about anything. In the end, we made most of the seven-hundred-mile voyage in our own canoe.

I don't believe a person ever appreciates a sawed board until he has to make the board by hand. I had anticipated the need of building a canoe last fall by doing my best to supply us with the proper materials at Barrow. These consisted of a gallon can full of small nails and some canvas and a little white lead paint. For wood I found a twenty-four-foot length of three-inch plank, very rough and sand-covered, lying along the beach, and one piece of good hickory plank three inches wide by twelve feet long. Believe it or not, I had been able to save this wood all winter long and had never burned it up.

For tools there were a very dull ripsaw, a crosscut saw, a carpenter's plane, square, drill, and two hammers in the Eskimo workshop at Beechey Point. There was plenty of room in the old warehouse to work. Sawing and planing all of those thin strips of wood which a well-built canoe requires was a job I hadn't looked forward to all this winter. Ook- sook didn't look forward to it either, as he had rather hunt, but here it was time to make it, and so we began. To describe the countless hours of sawing and the thousands of tiny nails that went into our craft would be dull to say the least, so I shall describe it roughly and let it go.

The craft was twenty feet long with the lines of a light whaleboat. It had a square stern with a well for the kicker. This well was extremely important to protect the outboard motor from being flooded by the combers of the open ocean. I am sure that this well subsequently saved our lives several times. The boat was rigged for sailing and it carried a mast and boom just in case the motor quit. The construction was that of a regular planked canoe with a canvas-covered hull, painted with white lead paint, spread thin.

It took us a month to make the canoe but when we were finished we had as proud a craft, we thought, as ever sailed the Arctic Ocean.

As THE WARM WEATHER HELD, the people began returning to Beechey Point for the summer's activities. Even Connie and I, who once thought this coast cold, now thought of it as the Eskimos did after our year of residence in this section.

It was too warm to hunt caribou with dog teams and the ice was still in the ocean so that it was impossible to set fish nets. Thus, the people turned to ducks, geese, brant, and the eggs of birds for their livelihood during a period of about one month of the year. Ptarmigan figured and also seals which the people had got on the ocean, but the three waterfowl and especially their eggs were most highly favored; they were eaten all at once in season, and never tasted again the rest of the year, according to the way of primitive existence.

In primitive tribes the children and the old people are the gatherers. Here the eggs are gathered in gunny sacks, carried home to the tent and hard-boiled. Brant especially are depleted by the egg hunters, for the brant nest in the delta of the adjacent Colville in great numbers. An even mightier nesting ground, also molested by Eskimos, is the delta of the Yukon which enters into the Bering Sea; a missionary post is established there, but it countenances the primitive practices of getting food and does not interfere inasmuch as its interest is in people's souls, not wildlife.

The nests in such areas are quite close together so that an energetic pair of boys or girls can secure two or three hundred eggs in a day, or even more in a good season. The nesting birds are loath to leave the area and are also easily shot with the .22 rifle. In some places in Alaska the nesting and molting fowl are secured by netting them on the prairie. This has been true of the now rare emperor goose, a very beautiful bird which has been seen by but few white men in the world.

The white-fronted goose and the Canada goose nest near Beechey Point in areas regularly scavenged by the Eskimos; their eggs and the birds themselves are taken in great numbers each year. They are used for human food and dog food both. These birds aren't some vague, intangible creature unknown to the rest of us in civilization but are the same birds we had seen flying north over the United States; we know them well. They have returned to the North to breed. They are the hardiest of their kind, having survived the perils of two migrations. It seems a shame they should be molested and destroyed at the end of their journey. Then there arises the question of who is paying for this. The answer is simple: we of civilization are. Every time we buy a duck stamp, a box of shotgun shells, or any sporting goods we are taxed to pay the cost of protecting our continent's migratory wildfowl. This is a tax that sportsmen pay gladly. Yet today we keep a people living in primitive squalor upon what is actually the most expensive fare in the world—food so rare that we ourselves cannot afford to eat it.

After a week or two of hilarious song and courting antics the birds which had arrived north had settled right down to their nesting duties; they knew the summer was brief. The small rodents began to find shelter in the new grass. Now the Kuparuk River flooded the sea ice, as did the Colville, for miles about, and the white sheet of ice that lay before Beechey Point turned to water on top of the ice so that there appeared before us a false open sea.

We had wondered how the ocean would ever go about breaking up, and now we knew. First, as the snow melts hundreds of miles to the south it starts a stream of flood water coursing down a frozen river channel. Thus, the big rivers like the Colville in Alaska and the Mackenzie in Canada break first. Their comparatively warm water cuts away the ice and hurries north into the still frozen Arctic Ocean. While zero temperatures occur, and blizzards blow, the big rivers that head far south are busy breaking up.

It is these flooded rivers that the waterfowl follow north while all else is still frozen. When this flood water reaches the solidly frozen ocean ice it spreads out over the surface, forming an ocean of its own on top. The expanse of water from the rivers is often many miles across and extends twenty or more miles out to sea, usually being from two to five feet deep. The Kuparuk flood spread past our house at Beechey Point and kept spreading until it met the Colville flood, and thus we had what appeared to be open water all along our coast. For half a month this water covered the ice; then one morning early Connie happened to step outside and was attracted by a strange gurgling sound. Stepping down close beside the ocean she observed that through what had either been a tide crack in the ice or a seal breathing hole which had become enlarged by the floods the whole ocean was pouring as down through a water main: within a few hours the ocean before us was solid ice again, for the false ocean had drained off through holes that had finally melted through the ice. We stood on the beach and sighed.

While this had been going on, the melted snow had dissolved the prairie itself into vast sheets of water. It was June 21 and once more the land was flourishing with grass and mirrored ponds.

There would be a spell to wait even yet for the ocean ice to rot enough for an offshore wind to break it up and move it off its moorings.

Meanwhile Ook-sook and I took our last seal hunts on top of the ice, and Connie and I took our last caribou hunt in the arctic.

Dogs pull our canoe beyond the shorefast ice

The Beechey Point cargo boat

2

On July 18 all the village of Beechey Point turned out to push the thirty-eight-foot cargo boat into the first open water of the season. As one old man said to me, "All the women, lots of strong."

Yes, at last we were ready to go. Connie and I managed to pack our few things aboard; our new canoe, the Little Willow Two, was stowed in the empty whaleboat to be towed. We had carefully figured how much gasoline and oil we would need to get to Canada. It was midnight now, so we would all have a rest and start towards Barter Island when we awoke.

There is something so final about leaving a place where you have lived! You must be careful not to forget anything. The friends you have wish you luck and tell you to hurry back, but secretly you wonder if you will ever get back again, and perhaps they wonder, too.

Perhaps you are quickly balancing up all the good times and bad times you have had there, and suddenly, when it comes to parting, all the bad times are forgotten, and the good times are about all you can remember.

The people all stood along the sandy beach in their bright costumes, and the gentle waves lapping the shore gave an air of finality to all the proceedings that was almost unbearable. I looked at t little ground lark hopping about. His frail form looked strangely out of place in a severe land of ice cakes and brilliant light offset by barren gravel washed from the sea. Connie and I shook hands with each friend and wished him well. There were Ada's lovely girls, Jennie and Maria. And little crippled Martha in the middle of them. There was Nanny's broad honest face, and George Woods, his eyes troubled and his expression ludicrously grave. Even Little Jacob and Carrie, I suddenly realized, had come all the way here to Beechey Point to see us off. Looking at this sea of faces, we almost faltered.

It was, "Good-by George, maybe you write me letter?" "You come back. Soon we hope."

"Thanks for the sewing, Nanny."

"She always like you, this woman."

"You come back. Come back."

Ruth, crying openly, said, "No matter where you go, Connie, I will never forget you." Then she ran away behind the gaunt old trading post and hid, and we never saw her again.

When we hopped up on the bow of the boat with the crowd who were going part way to Canada in the big expedition to get wood which Abraham had negotiated for, George Woods still called, interpreting for the others, "You have friends among the Eskimos now. You come back, come back." From the height of the boat we could look down on the people as we backed slowly into the ocean. Connie looked at me as Beechey Point slid away into the vast distance and at last sank into the sea.

"Will we come back?" she asked.

"Why yes, since you ask me, I believe we might," I said. "But next time I don't think it will be by homemade canoe."

THE WIND HAD SLOWLY RISEN as we neared the Foggy Islands in the mouth of the Sagavanirktok River. As the fresh breeze blew the fog away we could see an old Eskimo igloo on the highest point of the main island. We ran into a channel between the islands to wait for calmer weather, for outside the shelter the ocean was quite rough.

Our party consisted of Abraham and Thelma, Ook-sook, Richard's older boy, Aivuk (Walrus), and a couple of other young men—Pete and Apiak, to be exact. Thelma had dressed as became her position in life, and she looked very well surrounded by these young men. Although Aivuk was supposed to be her boyfriend, the one everybody kidded her about, Connie said that she was really after Apiak.

After a few hours' sleep harbored between the islands, we awoke near 3 a.m. to find the sea calm; on the sky line seven caribou were silhouetted. Our party made no attempt to get them. We started for Pole Island, cooking and eating on the way.

The heavy ice a few miles out from shore had never broken up and there was much floating ice in the open water, held in by the solid pack ice on one side and the shore on the other. For hours we threaded our way through the ice cakes. Loons floated on the placid water while old squaw ducks dotted the ice cakes or swam about in between.

Near noon we anchored in a cove off Pole Island. A beautiful sun shone down while the surface of the ocean was now a mirror. The Eskimos all turned in to sleep but Connie and I had to explore the island.

We found Pole Island to be much like Cross Island. There was little vegetation except some banks of Iceland poppies on the high places; a tall driftwood pole marks this island from afar. Islands of this type are often the nesting places of many arctic birds, such as the eider ducks. Within a sheltered lagoon on one side of the barren island we saw what must have been a raft of 10,000 squaw ducks—that most numerous species of duck to be found in this ocean. Connie found some nests of down with green eggs in them lying on the bleak ground; the nests weren't hidden but were almost indiscernible until one was about to step on them—nests of the Pacific eider. Along one sandy stretch of beach were thousands of little piles of ground-up small clam shells. This was what thousands of eider ducks had eaten in times gone by. Little phalaropes were swimming in circles on a small pond as we waded out to the cargo boat. The crew stirred, and we soon were eating boiled caribou meat. The meat was furnished from a particularly fine bull caribou Connie had shot, but you wouldn't have recognized it now, for it was already full of sand. A bloody piece of meat on the prow of a power boat where people walk back and forth over it does not complete a romantic picture of Eskimo life, I thought. Eskimo life seems out of place on a power boat, but there you are: that's the way it is. We crawled into our sleeping bag and slept while the boat headed toward Brownlow Point.

When we awoke near Brownlow Point the next day we could hardly believe what we saw. Connie and I had become used to seeing only a flat expanse of prairie. The changed country took us by surprise, for here the Arctic Plateaus of North Alaska had given way to beautiful mountains rising abruptly back from the great plain over which we gazed. The whole was an unequaled stage for the few white tents and meat-drying racks of the people. The people stood like posts in a group around their tents as we drew near, while the deep blue of the ocean was set off by cakes of scalloped ice drifting and heaving.

We ran around the long sandspit and anchored behind it. The people all trooped down to the beach to meet us. Once again, we all shook hands and smiled. As Connie started walking toward the tents with a group of husky broad-cheeked women and I walked with another group of miscellaneous people, we heard separately but at the same time the story of a recent tragic happening which had occurred in this group.

A little boy named Jimmy we had met a year ago at Beechey Point, an orphan who had lived for a while in old Samuel's tent, had been out east here this year. He and Benjamin, Andrew the minister's youngest son, had had a hunting accident. The eleven-year-old boys had been hunting ducks with their .22 rifles. A bullet from Jimmy's gun had accidentally struck Benjamin just below the belt. After being shot the young boy lived twelve hours and then passed quietly away, and there was nothing that anyone could do for him. The people wanted to know what they should have done. But Connie and I were inclined to think it was hopeless from the start. If a radio call could have been sent out for help an airplane could have taken this boy to the hospital at Barrow or perhaps even to Fairbanks. But this was one part of United States territory in which neither airplane nor radio was available. Had there been available help the story might have ended differently, but there wasn't.[3]

Inside the tents we were served dried caribou meat, biscuits, tea, and back fat, by the solemn, sobered village, who had buried Andrew's

---

3   Since this narrative was written, much has changed along the north coast of Alaska with the opening of new camps and bases under the authorization of the U. S. Army and Navy. Some Eskimos are now even wage earners at these camps.

favorite small son not many hours since. Andrew was away and did not know the news; they dreaded to tell him.

These people had killed a hundred caribou during the first two weeks of July. They were prosperous and otherwise content. So many dogs were tied in the village that Connie, who made it her business to go with some of the women at dog feeding time, saw two whole caribou go just to feed the dogs for their rations each evening.

As the darkest part of night came on the inclination of everybody was towards some kind of celebration or entertainment for the visitors, and here Connie and I tried our luck with the others at the famous Eskimo jumping game.

Beside one of the tents the game had begun. We understand that originally a walrus hide was always used for the jumpers, but in this part of the ocean there are no walrus, and these people extemporized with a moose hide. The hide had a rope sewed around the edge for handholds. About fifteen people took hold of the skin, stretching it tight like a firemen's net. They chanted and jerked the skin taut and then slackened off in unison.

The dancer stood in the center of the skin and tried to hold his balance. If he succeeded he was shot higher and higher into the air. About the highest we saw dancers go on the hide was fifteen feet into the air. With a walrus skin and more hide holders the dancer can reach much greater heights. Many of our party had never tried this game before and one or two couldn't be induced to try.

The game looked easy, so upon being coaxed to join in, I gave it a try. At first, I tried to jump as the skin came taut, but the people explained that I had only to stand straight and land on my feet. The hide holders would always try to keep the dancer landing in the exact center of the skin and would run with the hide to catch him when he came down. I really didn't do so badly until I missed the skin and landed on my bottom while everyone roared with mirth.

About three in the morning we said good-by to our hosts and our party headed out for the boat. The people had all asked that we come back soon, and one old man, hearing how Connie and I liked to see wild animals, had even another plan.

He said, waving his hand to indicate the unknown mountains that rose from the plain, "Lots of sheep. You come back soon."

Connie and I certainly wished we did have a chance to see those bands of sheep and to explore these mountains, for although the mountains were named by the Sir John Franklin expedition back in the 1840's, as seen from their vessels on the Arctic Ocean, it seems very likely that no white man has ever set foot in that mountain range. Yet we must hurry on. We could not delay, for there were many ice jams yet ahead through which we must pass when we got the chance, if we were to get out of the Arctic Ocean and back to civilization this year.

Our cargo boat churned onward, ever towards the eastern ocean. Presently we came to Mr. Lynd's camp. How nice to see the Lynds again at their new home! The day was hot while the mosquitoes were very thick. The whole family greeted us: a few lone human beings on the longest unending gravel beach I have ever seen. They too had killed many caribou on the great plain from which the mountains rose, and people, dogs, and all, were fat and fine. We stopped only long enough to say hello and drop a sack of flour for them.

At Barter Island we met Charlie Gordon and his family. Charlie is the son of one of the best known of last generation's whalers who settled in the arctic, and as a boy he was educated in San Francisco. Connie, sitting in the Gordon tent, surrounded by many Eskimo faces, asked him how he liked it there.

"It's fine, I guess," he said in clear English, "but I didn't like it. I was always lonesome for the arctic."

I asked him then why he didn't like it there, or what he didn't like about big city life, and his answer was typical of many arctic people to whom we have talked, who have lived for a time Outside.

"It was too hot," he said. "I never did get used to that city meat. It hasn't any taste." And then he added, "It is dangerous there. Well, here we have good meat and it isn't so dangerous."

Barter Island, of which we had long heard, was one of the old trading centers of arctic waters. Here the ancient inland Eskimos met to trade with the coast dwellers long before the white man came. During the whaling days a trading post was maintained here by Charlie Gordon's father. Now all that remained was an old house and an old fallen-down warehouse, plus interesting memories of the visitors of bygone days.

Charlie and his Eskimo wife lived in a tent while the house nearby stood empty and deserted. The people here had been out of all food except their native fish and meat for many months. Connie brought in a little tea, some salt, and a loaf of bread from our own provisions, in which all of the guests as well must share. Then she brought in a can of something to be opened after we left: it was filled with hoarded cookies and sweets made especially for them.

After supper we said good-by to all and loaded up our boat and left. We ran down the island about three miles and anchored in a safe harbor. Charlie offered us all the fresh fish we wanted but Connie and I only took a half dozen. The weather had been so warm lately that we doubted if a great many fish would keep.

Now the familiar old cargo boat rode upon the still water and ice cakes drifted slowly by while the eiders dove for shrimps. This was as far as Abraham and Ook-sook and the gang in the cargo boat were going. From here on we would go in our canoe towards Canada.

We unloaded the canoe alongside the cargo boat and began carefully packing everything we needed inside. There were the camp stove, tent, a box of cooking gear—now much diminished, since we had sold many things or given them away—bedroll, gasoline, and little else except for a sack of bread. This sack of bread, our fish net, and one rifle were all we had when we made our way from Alaska to Canada. Of course, we have lived on fish for months at a time, and we consider a diet of fish alone an adequate one for the arctic: it should be what all travelers plan to live on in summer.

Midnight had passed in visiting with the Gordons and it was eight o'clock in the morning. We were tired from our previous travel, but we wanted to get started now and at least go a few miles before making our first camp alone. Everyone had helped us load and we now shook hands all around. I fastened the shiny kicker to the stern of the *Little Willow Two and* pulled the starter rope. A few minutes later there was only the broad Arctic Ocean once again, and Connie and I.

Our canoe weaves through broken ice

Connie's bull caribou will feed us on our journey to Canada

3

The arctic coast of North America is poorly mapped. Many of the bays aren't mapped at all, while those which we see on paper have merely been drawn in freehand. The charts Connie and I possessed were the best available, but they showed little detail that would be useful to us.

I have said that this ocean is very shallow near shore along the Alaskan coast. This makes it difficult to navigate, but the shallowness has the advantage of holding the heavy pack ice quite a few miles offshore in many places, while boats of shallow draught are permitted to travel along between the shore and the ice. Their chief trouble will be getting stuck on mud bars.

In mid-July, the earliest in the season that perhaps ever human being has run a boat in this ocean, we were traveling! Barter Island sank below the horizon behind us on an early morning glassy sea, while the low prairie shore line rose out of an ice-studded sea ahead. A band of caribou ran along a bay, splashing in the shallow water to rid themselves of mosquitoes. We couldn't have motored into that bay even had we wanted to! It was only four inches deep! The prairie plain rolled upward to glorious mountains. We relaxed in the sun within our furs and gazed on the scenes we loved.

It was warm, and the scent of millions of flowers drifted to us from offshore. Out to sea blinked the distant white ice pack, solid and unbroken. Now a breeze quickened the surface and soon little whitecaps began to roll. We were in the delta flats of some river and couldn't get in to shore because it was too shallow. For two anxious hours we tried to make shore, but each time we were turned back by breakers crashing as they broke upon the shallow mud bars while shore was still a mile away. Finally, a line through the breakers showed where deeper water ran. We headed in.

Those whitecaps had really got high and it was none too soon to find shelter from them. Our canoe trembled and sat poised as a big comber broke and we went flying over the bar onto the beach. Out we jumped while the big waves poured into our boots and filled half the boat with the next sweep. Taking just long enough to shed our fur parkas and throw them up on shore as far as we could get them, we hastily unloaded everything, pulled the boat up to safety, and then tied it down where it couldn't get away. After that we pitched our tent, hauled fresh water from a pond a few yards from the ocean's edge, baked a fish or two, and went to sleep for the rest of that day. We had a few pocket books to read, for we knew there would be many a windy day during which we would have to wait on some beach before we got to Canada. It is a good thing that human beings can't see too far into the future, for if we thought that landing was rough it was really easy compared with what was to come a few days later.

We awoke around midnight to find the sea calm. The sun blazed a path across its surface in which one of those great rafts of old squaw ducks floated. We breakfasted upon fish and bread; our boots were dried, and we were off again. The canoe sent ripples dancing towards the shore on one side and towards the distant ice on the other. It was like traveling along a large river except that we continually wove our way among large cakes of floating ice.

Abraham had said that we would be likely to meet much ice at Humphrey Point because deep water allows the ice to come in at this place. Here we would find living the last family we would see in Alaska—the family of Fred Gordon, brother to Charlie Gordon of Barter Island. We had a small package of tobacco for Fred from Charlie as the eastward brother had been out of it for a long time.

The hours from midnight to around 6 a.m. are particularly foggy, yet the advantage in traveling at this time lies in the fact that of all the twenty-four, these are the hours when the ocean is apt to be most calm. This is particularly applicable to those reaches of ocean we had to cross where we would not be protected by island chains. It was cold, foggy, and mysterious at three in the morning as we approached Humphrey Point. The ice grew thicker until we could see open lanes of water only for a few yards ahead. We wove in and out, and somehow the ice ahead parted when we reached it, and so we went on. Overhead in the early morning the male eiders were leaving for the south, although it was only July 23, while the females remained to rear the broods of young. Why, those birds had just got here!

Eiders fly in long lines just a few feet above the water. Often, they almost parted our hair as they bore down upon us. They would appear from the thick mist, weaving in and out among the ice cakes. These birds were going west along the continent in little groups. A line of the brightly colored, heavy-bodied birds would bear down on us, and just when it seemed we would crash they would pull up and flash by with but a few inches to spare.

Through the mist we saw two people standing on a cut bank a long way ahead of us. They vanished, and shortly a long plume of smoke arose from a spot below our vision. They were pouring the driftwood into the stove in anticipation of the arrival of travelers.

Within forty minutes we were inside dark-bearded Fred Gordon's roomy tent enjoying some very delicious alder- smoked fish and bread. We supplied the bread and they furnished the fish. Like many other people we had met, these people had money to buy food with but there was nothing to buy.

Fred lighted up his pipe and reclined on a bedroll. He told us about his own trip to Canada and of seeing Victoria Island. While the fire in the stove popped merrily we had a nice chat. But the information we gathered about Canada we found was of 1922 vintage. "I'm going to give them half our bread," said Connie to me, when we left. "They've been without it longer than we have and we're almost to Canada anyway." In return they gave us some smoked fish and caribou back fat which was of infinitely more value nutritionally.

From Fred Gordon we had learned definitely that there were no people between us and Herschel Island, a considerable number of miles into Canada. There might be an old man and his wife on the mainland near Herschel Island, he told us.

The ice slackened out for a ways past Humphrey Point and then set in again thicker than ever. We were approaching Icy Reef. Abraham had told us there was no use in the cargo boat's trying to make it clear to the Mackenzie River in Canada, for Icy Reef would stop it for sure; if it didn't, Demarcation Point with its ice farther on would keep a person sitting on the edge of the bank for most of the rest of the summer.

Following along inside the Beaufort Lagoon we counted the little sand islands flashing by; now it was time to cut out to sea. The next island we met would be Icy Reef, which is about fifteen or twenty miles long, and it would be necessary to travel on the outside of it probably, Fred Gordon had advised, because the lagoon within is too shallow to navigate. Icy Reef was easily identified when we got out there.

We found it to be an endlessly long gravel strip which rose but a few feet above the sea level, completely barren, and only a hundred yards wide. It paralleled the coast line of the continent about two miles offshore.

There is a good deal of driftwood on Icy Reef and on its western end stands a log cabin. The cabin is badly fallen down and no doubt dates back to whaling days. Probably someone tried trapping here. Right now, the yard before the old cabin was a riot of Iceland poppies and some tall blue flowers we couldn't identify; eider ducks had nested all about among the driftwood. On the tumble-down walls of the old drift log cabin were bright pictures cut from magazines, but we couldn't get any dates. About the floor lay the various discarded implements of the trapper: a rusted-out skillet, some broken traps, and an assortment of empty tobacco cans. A fancy kerosene lamp of long ago lay in one corner and Connie found a "Stone Age" mallet made of a rock bound to a wooden handle by thongs. She wanted to lug it along in the canoe! "No," I told her, "I've even seen the Eskimos use a mallet like that in the Beechey Point workshop. You see, it actually works better than our hammer for some things. I believe that's a modem Stone Age artifact."

We left the old cabin, canoeing onward with a feeling that we should meet some whaling ship of long ago coming down the line any minute. Such a ship could be hidden behind the big cakes of ice of the real polar pack which squeezed Icy Reef. As we progressed we found the ice lay tighter and tighter against the gravelly reef as we wove our way onward with dexterity. The water right off the reef a few feet was plenty deep.

We had made our way about halfway down Icy Reef when the ice ahead closed in so tight that at last there was scarcely an inch of water left; there was nothing to do but haul out on the beach—hence the advantage of the small canoe. Many an oceangoing vessel of past days will recall Icy Reef. It is seldom that any vessel can pass it until late August. This was July.

Here was wonderful traveling weather. There were clear skies overhead and not so much as a breeze; what a shame to waste a traveling day like this! A lot of these big ice cakes which were blocking our way were grounded ice; perhaps they would never move the rest of the summer. How could they?

Walking over the narrow strip of reef Connie and I looked toward the inward side to the lagoon which separated us from the mainland. There was not a speck of ice in the lagoon to be seen anywhere. Of course, Icy Reef held the pack standing outside. Now we didn't want to remain on Icy Reef indefinitely. If a violent storm should come it seemed an exposed position, too. "Connie," I said, "do you think we could portage our canoe and all our outfit across the reef to the open water on the landward side? How about trying the inside passage for a change?"

"O.K. Let's eat first."

We shan't forget the happy lunch we had in the warm sun that beautiful day on Icy Reef. The ice cakes were jammed so tightly against the shore that I was able to climb out on one and even secure fresh ice for our drinking water at this unlikely spot. The most plentiful piles of driftwood we had seen in a year furnished a fire for the little rusted stove set up on the beach, where we melted our water; the day was too hot for tea. We lounged in the sun in our parkas and ate bread and dried fish and raw dried caribou back fat sitting on a square-sawed log which had once been a railroad tie in some other part of the world! In the background across the silvery lagoon something which looked like the only arctic glacier we have ever seen came down to the sea in a three- mile belt from the mainland: it was merely overflow ice built up from a river in some way. We weren't able to get near it in our canoe because the water of the lagoon was too shallow to allow an approach to the mainland and the "glacier front."

The *Little Willow Two* was a heavy boat for Connie to try to lift; we would have to use our ingenuity to transport it over the reef. We selected round polished sticks of drift for rollers, and we rolled the canoe across the land in this way, using about eight rollers in all. Transport of the canoe was thus easily accomplished.

After we had eaten we were very lazy; actually it was time to rest again, even if we hated to take the time off from our interesting activity. It is best to be always in full strength in order to meet unexpected dangers ahead. So as soon as we had transported our canoe and duffel to the inward side of the reef, we decided to pitch camp and sleep a bit before going on.

On this ocean in summer it always seems the wind dies down near midnight when the sun is lowest and springs up after noon when it is highest. So, it was that we slept the rest of that day; at midnight we awoke to travel on. The temperature was freezing but the flowers didn't mind it.

Inside the lagoon the water was dead calm, and we made better speed than we had ever dared expect. Our kicker just cleared the ocean bottom by a few inches, but the bottom was so uniform that we never once struck it.

A few hours later we had passed Icy Reef and were out in the open ocean again, heading across Demarcation Bay. As we drew near what we knew must be Demarcation Point, which divides the two countries of Alaska and Canada, we saw on the horizon two old white man's houses similar to the trading post buildings at Beechey Point. Such houses are strange mixtures of prairie farm homes, whalers' ships, and Eskimo ways. These buildings were formerly erected by whaling companies as trading posts. When the trade in whalebone vanished in one year, the trading posts folded up. The people died out or moved away, and today only these musty ramshackle houses are left as relics of what has been. No one would try to live in them even if he wanted to stay here, for with driftwood scarce it would take all of his time to try to heat such a place.

As we drew up our boat beneath the cold somber skies and drizzling rain by which we conjure up our memories of Demarcation Point, we could see at once that this place was inhabited by no human beings, except perhaps their ghosts. The buildings looming up gaunt and vacant in the mist beckoned examination and yet repelled: we wouldn't even pitch our tent near them.

Caribou tracks were all over the place, hard by the very door of the old trading post. The grass grew tall in the near-by graveyard marked with many crosses. Inside the empty trading post the floor was littered with fox skulls and various other bones. There was a discarded dilapidated sewing machine; there were parts of old whaling ships, empty cartridge cases. Little snow buntings twittered outside around the eaves above the broken-out windows.

The wind had sprung up and it moaned through the loose boards. A trap door led into a dark attic. When we investigated it, a board fell down almost on our heads. I noted Connie stayed unusually close to me. Icy Reef was a good deal more cheerful than this!

We pitched our tent on the beach below the old trading post while the wind drove streamers of fog about us, and the white icebergs of the sea towered beside. Of course, it was warm inside our tent. While our last fish baked in the oven of the little stove, Connie read aloud from a child's book of verses we had found in the old house.

On July 25 we were determined to travel onward through ever-thickening ice cakes. At 10 a.m. we were weaving in and out among the big ice fields of the real polar pack. Because I had become used to judging ice I recognized most of it as grounded ice and hence harmless enough. The old vacant trading post at Demarcation Point seemed to follow us with eyes until we lost it in the mist; we were glad to be past this ice-jammed spot.

After a few hours the ice began to thin out. Directly alongshore the big cakes were jammed into a tight belt from fifty to one hundred yards wide, so that we were soon wondering how we could get ashore! Rather than go back, we continued onward, hoping for a break in the line. It did not seem a serious situation until an hour later the sea became open, and the waves became rougher and rougher!

The United States Army, in flying men over the North Atlantic near Iceland and over comparable northern seas, gives a man just a few minutes to live if he should be immersed in such waters of below-freezing temperatures; the human blood congeals, the heart stops. We had been in exposed positions a few times in our boat on the Arctic Ocean but had never given too much thought to just what capsizal would mean. Boating or canoeing was so natural that I guess we always figured that even in the event of some capsizal we could probably cling to our canoe until we were washed ashore. Here, any illusions about this were completely dispelled, as on and on the cruel ice barrier stretched as far as the eye could see, preventing any kind of landing.

Rolling waves coming from behind doused the little kicker. Soon we were running on but one cylinder. A big wave washed aboard. We were soaked and were suddenly thoroughly frightened. One or two waves like that and our buoyancy would be gone. Still we continued, for there was nothing else to do. Connie never stopped bailing with the tea bucket.

There was just one chance. Ahead loomed a great stranded mountain of ice. Rising forty feet above the water, it was large enough to furnish a windbreak from the open ocean.

"Connie, if we can just get to that big piece of ice, we can tie up behind it," I said. "We'll make it. Just hold tight."

As we pulled in behind this haven with seals rolling about us in the heaving seas, I took a glance at the ice-studded shore we wanted to reach, estimating our chances. This big ice monster was blowing before the wind, moving gradually. It was a temporary harbor at best. Our little motor was about to run dry of gas, for we had not been able to refill with the boat bobbing. Making a quick decision I headed the boat for the ice barrier along the near-by shore, against which the ocean broke as upon a wall of gleaming, jagged glass.

A small gap only about four feet wide showed in the ice barrier. Although a tongue of ice ran clear across its opening under the water, I figured we had a good chance of going over it on the swell. Spray shot high in the air as we drew up. Our canoe paused for an instant, while the little kicker churned on one cylinder; then over the ice tongue we shot through the passage.

Back behind the ice was a little quiet pond, just big enough to hold our canoe. Some loose floating ice blocked us; getting out on the grounded ice reef, I walked along, pulling Connie in the canoe, while we cleared a path as far toward shore as we could. From there we unloaded the canoe, pulled it out on the ice on its wooden runners which I had designed on its bottom, dumped out the water, and so dragged it and all our duffel ashore to safe land, where we were two of the most thankful people in all the world.

An hour later we were comfortably camped upon the shore as though nothing had happened. It was warm inside our tent while our things were neatly stacked under the sail. The boat lay on the beach and the ice pack was drifting by before the storm. Such was our first landing in Canada.

The storm continued to blow while the ice crowded in and by next day there was only a field of ice where those angry black waves had rolled. Where would Connie and I have been had we not made shore as we did? We would have been fish food, I suppose. We shuddered to think how narrow had been our escape. No person would ever have found us or our canoe, nor learned the story of our end.

Today we walked around the beach and went hunting inland. The fact that we had no food, but our bread did not even worry us; of course, we would get some food soon—that's a small matter. The only trouble was that we couldn't set our fish net on these days when the ice was in. We hadn't counted on that!

On a small lake a half mile from our tent two beautiful white swans rode. And we were getting hungry after a couple of days of it here.

"If we can't find something pretty quick I'll have to shoot a swan," I told Connie. What irony! To have to shoot the rarest wild bird in North America just to *eat* it? Those swans had a nest hidden somewhere near that lake. We were sorry these shallow lakes contained no fish.

"No telling how long we'll be here," I told Connie. "You know the natives kill swans all the time whenever they can get one."

Still the swans swam gracefully around the unnamed lake, keeping always on the opposite side from us, and placidly eying us. We studied their beautiful forms with the binoculars. I lay on my stomach, cocked the rifle, carefully adjusted the telescope sight—and just then Connie reached my side and stopped me. "Wait," she said. "We'll find something."

As we stood up the swans took off with a long taxiing run on the lake. They circled and flew by close to us. We walked a mile across the prairie in hopes of finding the usual parka squirrels or ptarmigan—but no luck. "There isn't a caribou in this part of the country either," I had told Connie a day ago. "And no sign of them."

At last we returned along the beach to camp. When we were nearly to our tent, I stopped suddenly and looked at the ground. "Look, Connie!"

What lay before us on the clean gravel was a large white- fish weighing about three pounds! It was so fresh the water had scarcely dried on it. A small trickle of blood ran from its gills, and its head had been pecked. No other part of the fish was touched.

A sea gull had caught this fish, or some similar bird, and had carried it over the land and dropped it here just for us! Did we accept it? I should say we did. That bird-caught fish was all we needed to tide us over a bad day until we could travel again.

Near noon on the third day the wind changed, and the ice slackened out, leaving a few open lanes for navigation. Our recent experience had taught us that the complete absence of ice is far from desirable; in fact, it had taught us that the ice can be a friend in its grim way. Therefore, we broke camp and soon were at our usual hobby of weaving in and out among the ice cakes. But this was polar ice, and it was very heavy. From the top of a tall cake I tried to see open lanes ahead but only succeeded in seeing more ice. Many of the ice fields seemed miles across. Even the binoculars caused all the ice in the distance to appear one solid mass. Only by actually approaching this ice could one find lanes through it close to the shore. We would have to go three miles to make one. The ice was moving slowly along with us in the direction we were going, however, and I trusted that this would help.

A dark spot in the sky ahead gave promise of Herschel Island, and soon we would be entering the influence of the Mackenzie River; after that, maybe we would not have any more ice at all. Now, if we could just make these last few miles!

Connie was timid, in view of our recent experience, as I boldly wove through the ice at sometimes a goodly distance from shore. But the ice was going our way! I always kept that in mind!

After a few more hours we had accomplished what would have appeared impossible—we had actually gone all along the coast through this ice; somehow at every blank wall there had been a way to go through it or around it, even though little water appeared in sight. Now the ice slackened as I had been sure it would, and we were in comparatively open ocean; the only kind of ice in sight now was merely light bay ice, and we had even grown to the point where we were contemptuous of that! The bold decision to travel on had been the wise one, else I think we might still be sitting on that bank near Demarcation Point to this very day.

Herschel Island, out in great Mackenzie Bay, effectively blocked the pack ice from coming in. The warm waters of the Mackenzie, spreading into the ocean for miles around, promised an ice-free voyage from here on. We didn't know it until later, but at that point we said good-by to the ice for good. If we had known, we were leaving the ice entirely we would have had cause for another kind of concern. The ice kept the big swells under control, it furnished us with fresh drinking water when we camped, its tall ridges made good lookout towers, and we had become so used to it, whether we knew it or not, that we regarded it as a forest dweller regards the trees—as a part of the scene.

We held a steady course towards the mouth of the Firth River, while Herschel Island, rising beside us out in the ocean, became a land of very visible cliffs and green verdant hills.

Herschel Island has figured prominently in the story of the American arctic. It came into prominence in the last century as an anchorage for old whaling ships. The harbor on the inside of Herschel Island offered a safe wintering quarters for the whalers where their ships were safe from the pressure of the pack all around. At one time quiet, a dispute arose as to whether Herschel Island lay in Canadian or Alaskan waters. This dispute led to what is known as the Boundary Survey, when the boundary between the two countries was laid out. But today we had found no marker to show where Alaska ends, and the Yukon Territory of Canada begins on this coast. All that is left of what was once the largest whaling center in the arctic is a few old buildings of the onetime city of Herschel, out on the island. No people, not even Eskimos, live on the island today, although there is some talk of a Royal Canadian Mounted Police outpost being reopened there. This was the year for the Canadian Police to visit it for a survey. A survey of all outposts is made by the Mounted Police once in every seven years. Thus, an official visit would be made to Herschel Island later this summer.

The evening was warm and the ocean placid as we left our   last ice near the mouth of the Firth River. As we took to our   paddles to pole across the shallow river mouth we noticed fish jumping. Presently we saw some dead salmon on a beach nearby; then we came upon the well-organized camp of the old Eskimo man and woman of whom Fred Gordon in Alaska had told us; their racks were loaded with salmon. Yes, salmon in the Arctic Ocean, running up the clear waters of the beautiful Firth River to spawn! But there are no salmon like this running up the Colville in Alaska or in fact any other rivers of the Arctic Ocean in Alaska. A few stray salmon are caught in nets at various places along the ocean between Point Barrow, Alaska, and Firth River, Canada, it is true, but they are rare. And these salmon were different again! The Eskimos told us these salmon do not die after spawning, as all western salmon do! These salmon, in short, may come from the Atlantic Ocean! They belong to the eastern part of the arctic world.

So, it was that we ate salmon with the Rolands, one of the nicest Eskimo couples I have ever known. One of the first questions Roland asked us was how Mr. Stefansson is. He had known the great explorer well, twenty-five years ago, and he supposed that probably all white people knew each other.

As we hadn't had a full meal in some time, we really enjoyed the meal the Rolands set before us. To make sure that our fish was as fresh as it was possible for it to be, Roland carefully pulled in the long fish net which he had pushed out from shore with a pole nearly seventy feet long; it was made by tying small poles together. About four dozen of the most beautiful silvery salmon I ever saw in my life came in with the net; studying the fish with a trained eye, Roland selected the very best one, gave it a blow on the head to stop its wiggling, and handed it to his wife. Soon his wife cooked it. She fried it to please us, we noticed, white man style. We were Eskimoized enough after a year to have preferred the fish boiled, however.

Roland carefully gave each live fish a blow on the head until he came to a large chee fish.

"Lots of this fellow, Akalavik," he informed me, smiling, and brought his executioner's club down on its skull with a thump. The nets were pulled in about every hour, we learned, with some forty fish for each haul. This single old man and woman, the industrious Rolands, did not even begin to touch the hordes of firm, pink-fleshed salmon which run up the Firth River of the arctic.

The Rolands were smoking the fish and drying them for human and dog food. Their camp was neat, and their dogs were fat. They had seen no one for several months and were eager for any news. We told them the news of their Eskimo relatives in Alaska, and they told us the news of Aklavik, which was several months old, and described conditions along the coast eastward, and we compared each other's parkas. It was interesting to Connie that Mrs. Roland's parka was made of muskrat skins. Caribou, it seemed, were scarce here. Mrs. Roland's parka must have taken forty or more muskrats, a clue that we were approaching an area where muskrats are not only available but abundant. We had already met a Canadian Eskimo hunter with the people at Brownlow Point whose parka was made of about forty wild mink. His parka was worth a thousand dollars easily, except of course that bellies of the animals were used in its construction as well as mink backs, and the skins were not as well matched as a New York wild mink coat would be.

"Come back soon," the Rolands told us as our motor caught and we drifted away. We had been very favorably impressed by our first Canadian Eskimos.

We headed for a low point on the horizon ahead; it was evening. The sun sank in the south; even now in midsummer the season was turning. Moreover, in coming eastward to Canada we had also followed the coast southward. We had entered a warmer climate. We were a hundred miles south of Beechey Point now! We had lost the midnight sun!

There is an awesome mystery about an arctic midnight when the sun dips briefly below the horizon. You seem to expect almost anything to happen. The waves grew rough and ominous. We put in to shore to make camp, thankful that no ice barrier barred us from land.

The next few days were a round of breaking and making camp. We would take down our tent and load our canoe the moment the wind dropped. But exposed to the open sea as we were now, the moments when we could travel became rare. No sooner did we start traveling than a wind would send whitecaps rolling over the ocean. There would be some anxious moments as we sought a landing along the base of high bluffs. Hardly would we have camp pitched again and our canoe pulled up beyond harm when abruptly the breeze would drop, and the ocean would calm. No longer did the friendly ice pack march on ahead to offer shelter from the big swells of the open ocean. We were at the mercy of miles of open water.

The whole family greets us

Children enjoy Connie's cookies

4

It was August fourth when we entered Canada's great Mackenzie River. Ours was the west channel—the waters of the Peel. Arctic Red. There are no signposts to direct one into this channel, up which the town of Aklavik lies. The delta of the Mackenzie is ninety miles broad.

We had traveled only a few miles inland when the brush grew high and we met our first spruce tree. We had never dreamed that the forest in the Mackenzie Valley comes to within eight or ten miles of the coast of the Arctic Ocean. Who would have imagined this? Seeing our first tree in over a year was such a great event that, the sun coming out brightly, we had to take a picture of it and carefully examine that tree all over. It was not a stunted tree but a full-sized specimen, about forty feet tall.

Soon the little groves of trees of this kind along the river- bank developed into a continuous forest as we proceeded. The entire Mackenzie River is heavily forested with spruce, willow, and cottonwood, going far into the arctic; Aklavik itself lies in the timber belt and divides the two lands from each other: the forested Canada of the Indian, who today is much mixed with the French blood of the ancient voyageurs, and the Barren Grounds of the broad-cheeked Eskimo to the eastward—a vast realm stretching out to Coronation Gulf, Victoria Island, Banks Land, the Prince William Land of

Kabloona, and many other lands of which white people on the whole have never known or heard. At one time we had thought to canoe onward east of the Mackenzie. But that would have taken a few more years.

We made good speed up the Mackenzie delta while flocks of pintail ducks eyed us from the shallows alongshore; we slipped from our hot parkas and basked in the sun, mosquito head nets on again. Occasionally we would see a hurried flash of white as swans beat a hasty retreat before us. There was no sign that human beings had ever been along here, but somehow the country had the look of being traveled by people; you could kind of sense it. Beaver cuttings now lay on the banks; the heat was oppressive. We stopped only long enough to make tea and eat the last big chee fish we had netted. The whitefish here looked nice, yet these warm-water fish were flabby and lacked something. We noted signs of rabbit, moose, and bear which we guessed was black bear, and there were blueberry bushes. It was thrilling to make all these discoveries as the country made itself quickly known to us.

I am sorry to say that the native people we now met impressed us very unfavorably. It is necessary to make this differentiation because the kind of northern Indians and Eskimos the reader will be apt to see in his travels will not be like the strong, broad-jawed people of Beechey Point—and how we missed our people here, by reason of contrast! Many of these people had come from Alaska, incidentally, but the "city life" offered by Aklavik had apparently attracted the very worst elements. These people had the vices of civilization; the camps in which they lived often spoke of squandered money and malnutrition all in one. Once more we heard the familiar cough of tuberculosis we had known formerly among Alaska's more civilized natives, and we saw skinny children with impetigo and skin sores. There was some drunkenness

(the natives secretly making their own home-brew in their camps); one fellow told us how much money he made and that he was rich. The funny part about it was that he was probably right; he made $30,000 in muskrats this year. Many of these families of muskrat trappers in the Mackenzie delta, we were to learn, make more money in a year than bank presidents normally do. At the same time, little is done to control the natives along lines of wildlife conservation. The idea in the Northwest Territories of Canada, even more than in Alaska, seems to be that the natives have a right to take whatever they want of the wildlife. We saw the feet and wings of both the rare swans and sandhill cranes scattered about native camps, for instance. Each native is given five dollars "treaty money" each year by the Canadian Government because of ancient pledges, in a land where romantic notions of treating them as "His Majesty's children" or "children of the great white father" still hold sway.

Mother and child

An Eskimo mother carries her baby in her parka

Girl with her dog

Mackenzie River Steamer

We arrive in Canada after 26 months

An ex-bomber carries us to Edmonton

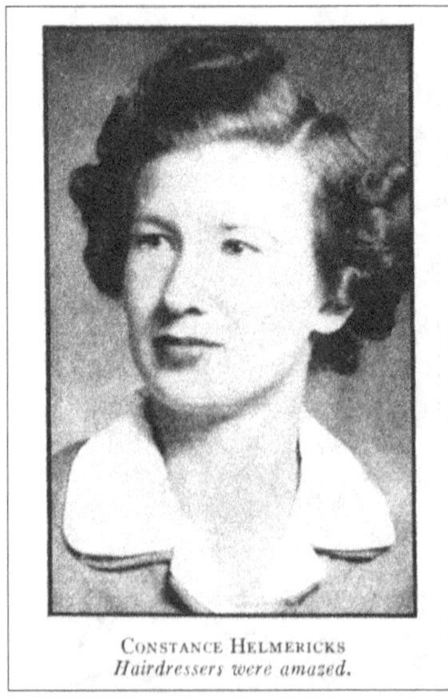

CONSTANCE HELMERICKS
Hairdressers were amazed.

Time magazine article focuses on Connie's hair

5

We found the town of Aklavik, Canada, Northwest Territories, to be as colorful as a Hollywood set. Here Mounted Police mingle with Anglican missionaries, forest Indians, and Barren Grounds Eskimos just in with their powered schooner from fabulous Banks Land, all in their various costumes; and traders, trappers, mining men, and oil scouts blend with writers of northern novels and movie photographers wandering about looking for material. Luckily getting a room at once at the Aklavik Hotel, which was crowded with hopeful businessmen and adventurers of one kind and another, Connie and I settled down to wait for a means of transportation Outside, now that we had got here. The first day we went shopping at the Hudson's Bay Company store and bought new clothes. Connie got herself some women's slacks. As the streets were knee-deep in mud, we continued to wear woodsman's boots for walking about. Soon we had visited with almost every white person in the small community and eaten cookies and tea at most of their homes.

The Royal Canadian Mounted Police were very kind to us. The first evening that we got into town, even before they found us a room in the hotel, a couple of them took us to their house and themselves cooked us a large supper. While we were eating we were questioned informally about our journey over from Alaska, but so tactfully that we hardly realized we were making an official report until we noted it was going down on paper in some detail.

In the meantime, we enjoyed asking our own questions about the private life of a Mounted Policeman. We learned that Mounties in the North, in this section at least, are not mounted and without their red uniforms look like other men. Rarely in the course of years do the Mounties actually wear the celebrated uniform except for some official visits to outlying tribes, in which case they may put the uniform on just before they arrive. This uniform has such a great tradition of authority about it that it is very impressive to the natives, who far outnumber the handful of white men who must police these vast tracts of land in the remote parts of the world.

For us, the junior Mounties with whom we most fraternized could be sized up as merely slender boys recruited from among thousands of worthy applicants who are the best of all Canada's young manhood in point of character and honor, and who are willing to work at a low salary with slow promotion for their country's good. Certainly, to all American people, to boys all over the world, and to those who have the so-called red blood of adventure in their veins, the Mounties are legendary. Actually, their lives are for the most part quiet. Furloughs to the outside world are few for these men in the remote outposts, their discipline is strict, and their behavior must remain at all times as pure as a nun's. Mounties may marry, and we even met some Mounties' wives stationed at Aklavik, but the men are not allowed to marry until a certain number of years have elapsed in service, and headquarters must give permission.

Quite a good deal of policing of large areas is done today by airplane, but there was no airplane belonging to the Mounted Police at Aklavik; it has been found that only the dog sled and power boat can actually enable the personal visiting in tents and camps that any close surveillance demands.

The existence of Canada's Mounted Police makes us wonder how Alaska's arctic gets along without a comparable force of officers to patrol it, but as a matter of fact Alaska seems to get along perfectly well. Of course, the arctic in Canada is a great deal more vast than anything the average citizen has any conception of. A good deal of even this is not at the present time seen by any white man, not even the Mounted Police. We had a good many constables ask us about the geography and conditions of the part of the arctic we had seen, and we told what we could. We do not pretend to know much about Canadian arctic problems, so we would not suggest that the Mounted Police are dated, yet one is constantly struck by the large part tradition and past history play in their ritual of life in view of the fast-moving needs of world development.

Connie and I wanted to get out to civilization; we turned our efforts without delay toward this. Transportation out of the arctic any place in Canada, we learned, means out by Edmonton. Edmonton is a flourishing city of around a quarter of a million in western Alberta, usually regarded as "the beginning of steel." Although it is true a branch line of the railroad runs north as far as Peace River Landing, everyone talks of going out by Edmonton. This lies some three thousand miles up the Mackenzie, the Athabasca, and the Slave Rivers by water passage if one does not go by air.

Why not ride the river steamboat all the way to the railway? It was a fine idea and one to which we prepared ourselves to devote the rest of the summer, but that was as far as it got. When the steamer came in a few days later, several people besides ourselves who were waiting at the inn were disappointed to learn that passengers would not be taken. The Hudson's Bay Company, which has owned almost everything in the outposts of Canada for almost three hundred years, answered the anxious queries of people about passage with leisurely indifference.

"Well, aren't there any other passenger boats running on the Mackenzie River?"

"No, ma'am," the steamboat official told Connie curtly. "No other company can operate passenger boats on this river." That was the first time Connie and I had ever heard anything quite like that, and we could at first hardly believe it. But that was that. Some tourists, who were traveling schoolteachers in riding breeches, had come down to Aklavik all the way on the steamer, but even they were put off and told they must take plane transportation back, which would be arranged for them, since hauling supplies in this part of the world and hauling out the furs trapped by the Indians are considered the only important business.

We went to the airlines representative then to see about air transportation out. This is the only other way to get out of the arctic, and of course it is the only way in winter. The agent was an old-timer; he wasn't particularly in sympathy with the conditions, but he explained patiently that only one airline, Canadian Pacific Airways, services Aklavik.

There is a very poor landing field at Aklavik; in fact, it seemed impossible to us, coming from an air-minded land like Alaska. Landings are made most often on the river by floats in summer and on the river ice by skis in winter. The landing field to which we have referred is really the baseball field and a waterpipe runs above the ground across a part of it which cannot easily be seen from the air. One of the first sights we noticed in Aklavik was a wrecked plane standing partially on end where it had crashed into the waterpipe. Some enterprising Alaskan pilot who had come over into Canada for business had seen his hopes crash with it just a few days before our arrival. There the wreck lay, unsalvaged, and the poor flier was probably broke.

Some of the people at Aklavik were in considerable agitation at the time we visited there over the general world conditions and they wanted a decent landing field. Then military protection might be brought in or at least a base of operations established in case it might ever be needed, inasmuch as valuable arctic oil fields lie all about. Yet the people of Aklavik, enterprising civilians with a pioneer spirit, have no means by which to build even so much as their own landing field for commercial use because they are not permitted to do so. Unlike our independent Alaskan traders, who often get out and clear their own landing strip for the sake of business, residents of the Northwest Territories in Canada are not allowed to build themselves an airport without practically an act of government.

Consequently, what with its atrocious landing facilities, Aklavik has few pilots who care to venture there, despite the fact that there are thousands of dollars' worth of business monthly left undone at that fast-growing place. Two flights a month to carry the mail are made by the airline which holds the franchise; passages by the white people are booked weeks in advance. As for the natives, they don't have a chance; the native people told us the company would hardly bother to take them.

The price quoted to us for this possible ride out to the railroad, 1500 miles straight south by air, made even our Alaskan-trained heads whirl. "Why, I could buy an airplane for that," I told the fellow truthfully. "Or I could fly all the way around the world on any other airline."

"I know," he had to agree, "but the company still claims to operate at a loss."

We had some film to send to the United States and as air mail was the only mail certain of getting out, I walked over to the post office with a small package. I thought I had heard wrong when the clerk quoted me $1.40 a pound! Yet gas is freighted easily down the Mackenzie River.

In general, food prices and clothing were as low as or lower than in a correspondingly northern community in Alaska, but one might expect that, due to the great advantage of having such a river as the Mackenzie convenient for transportation in the summertime, down river into the arctic all the way. The natives had been drawn to Aklavik even from the far comers of Alaska in many cases because of the availability of white man's food here, in contrast, say, to Barrow, and they were now regarded as Canadian subjects, since they lived here. On the streets of Aklavik we were constantly besieged by natives who regarded us as equals and friends since we knew their relatives in Alaska. From this standpoint they gave us many confidences.

We sold our canoe and all of our camping equipment and found ourselves taxed $85 on even our poor assortment of worn-out junk, for having brought it into the country; eager natives swarmed about to buy it, and we came out even on finances, at that, because they were used to paying even higher prices for tents and guns and motors! As for taxing us on our canoe, it looked for a while as though we would have to fork over a terrific tax for bringing a "boat" into Canada, according to government tariffs for the protection of their own boat-building industries. "Why, look here," we said. "You can't do that. This boat is tax exempt. As you can see it's just a few sticks and canvas. There isn't even two dollars' worth of paint on her. This boat was built in

Alaska out of your own Mackenzie driftwood which floated over to Alaska to us, and we've just brought your own wood back again."

This was true. The officials had to agree that the waters of the Mackenzie do carry the wood to Alaska, and besides, they hated the red tape as much as we did. Every item from pots and pans on has a different tariff rate in Canada; when the whole was figured out, we would have to pay a tax of one fourth the total estimate of what our possessions were worth. Resident Canadians suffer outrageous import taxes.

One could give a good many illustrations in everyday life of what's wrong with our arctic America to show why it has not developed. The obstacles lie largely in the realm of government interference and prohibition. It isn't because there is anything wrong with the country itself that it cannot go ahead. The Western Canadians are as far removed in outlook from the Montreal or Ottawa which most of us think of as "Canada" as is the Alaskan who lives in the brush from Washington or New York. Still farther detached are the people of the Northwest Territories from emotional alliance with England.

We had just about resigned ourselves to a few months' stay when a strange airplane circled over town. The pilot cautiously flew low over the unbelievable landing field and came in to a beautiful landing, braking the ship to a stop just in time to avoid the trees and the wreck which was already there, a gruesome reminder. Connie and I were the first ones on the field!

The pilot, co-pilot, and one passenger climbed out. The passenger was an Indian who had been to the United States on a charter trip, seeing the sights on his muskrat money.

Would the pilot take us to Edmonton?

He would love to. But we would have to pay a charter fee! How much would this cost? Connie and I looked nervously at one another, for the ship was a former Mosquito Bomber which had flown in the Battle of Britain, and it was a mighty impressive-looking job, as impressive as the young fellow, who was a flier just returned from the wars. The pilot and co-pilot consulted and finally they quoted us a price.

We almost fell over, for the price they gave was exactly half of what it would have cost us to ride on the regular airlines that claimed to be "losing money" on each passage. We could charter a seven-passenger twin-engined Mosquito Bomber for half regular fare!

We made a dash for the hotel to pick up our slim duffel sacks, and to have lunch with the pilots.

Was it possible? We would be in a great city within two days, stepping along the paved streets in Eskimo boots, hearing streetcars clang, walking into a big department store with only the clothes on our backs, fresh out of the North, but ready to dress from the skin out. We hadn't yet seen a bathtub, but that would come too. Edmonton sees many a person like us from out of the North. But none more happy and delighted, we suppose. How would it feel? It would certainly be a new adventure to us.

We hardly dared dream of the actual return. Even now we were afraid that airplane would get away, and that was why we never left the side of the pilots. We returned to look the Aklavik landing field over with them.

"Be sure your safety belts are tight," we were cautioned.

The plane bumped to the far end of the field and turned around into the wind. The trees at the end of the short field looked awfully close to me. Would we ever get off? The pilot released the brakes and the plane rushed at those trees like a lame duck. A sign above a handle at my right caught my eye. It read, "Open bomb bay doors before releasing bombs."

The trees were no longer at the end of the field; they were here. The plane gave a lurch and climbed steeply above the treetops; we circled Aklavik. It appeared as a tiny village swallowed up in a land of lakes. The steady drone of the engines came to us and the pilot looked back and smiled.

Constance Helmericks in 1956 when she published her 6th book

About the Author

I n 1942, at the age of twenty-four, Constance Helmericks and her husband, Bud Helmericks, paddled into the Alaskan wilds to live off the land. Over the next decade, Connie wrote five bestselling books on their adventures, and co-filmed and produced three documentaries with Bud. Their work was shown on national lecture tours, and was twice featured in LIFE magazine, including the cover. In her later books, Connie wrote of her wilderness journeys across Canada and around Australia with her young daughters, Jean and Ann Helmericks. She became an early environmental activist, walking much of the Pacific Crest trail alone while in her sixties. Connie was writing her ninth book about paddling Central American rivers when she died on Earth Day in 1987.